Joshua and Caleb

Journey to the Promised Land

JOHN
PAUL
DEWALT

I0778680

20 Twenty
Literary Group

ISBN
978-1-961250-97-0 (Paperback)
978-1-961250-98-7 (eBook)
978-1-961250-96-3 (Hardcover)

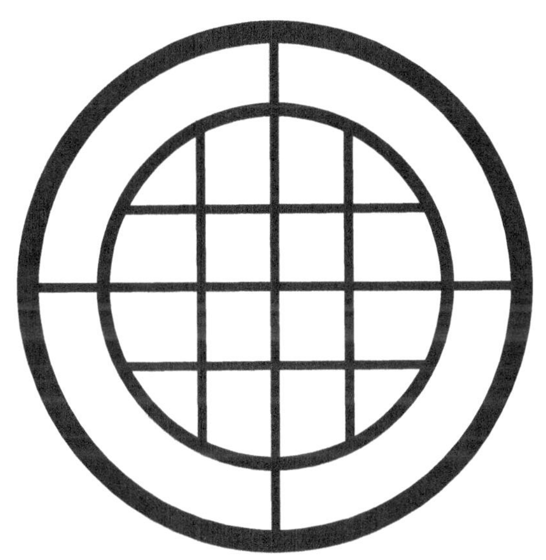

TABLE OF CONTENTS

FOREWORD

This story began in my mind when I imagined the cry of rage and frustration of Joshua toward the Israelites. They had disobeyed Yahweh's instruction to go up to take the land promised to them and their ancestors. They had listened to the fearful report of ten men sent to spy out the land and had spoken evil about Yahweh leading them into the land to get their families killed. Therefore, Yahweh sent that generation back into the wilderness to die.

One of only two spies to *encourage* Israel to go up, Joshua now faced forty years of wilderness wandering instead of driving out the Canaanites and beginning his life of freedom in the Promised Land. Therefore, his cry of anguish and rage.

This is not a nice, Christian romance novel with the adventure of escape from bondage and a jaunt through the desert. This story depicts the ugly nature of people when they fail to trust in God's provision and protection- when they exert rulership over other people, forcing them into vile acts. This novel is permeated with slavery, forced activities, idolatry, orgies, incest, stonings, and hard-heartedness in order to get things done.

This story also has moments of Yahweh's power at work in His people. There are healings, miraculous deliverances, empowerings to fight, songs of praise, and prophecies of hope.

PROLOGUE

"Mama! Abba!"

Tears streamed down the seven-year-old boy's dirty face as he ran into the weaving hut where his parents labored to make the fine cloth their master sold. He flung dirty arms around his mother's waist and laid his bloodied, filthy face on the length of fabric she was inspecting for flaws.

"Hoshea, no!" Simichek shoved him away and brushed at the smear left on the linen. "Nun, come get your son!"

The boy's father grabbed Hoshea by the neck of his dirty tunic and shook him. "This is why you're not allowed in here! You've ruined half a day's work!"

Hoshea clenched his fists in outrage and pointed out toward the neighbor's backyard. "Abba! Some boys were going to open Father Joseph's tomb to look at the bones! I had to stop them!"

His father went to the open doorway and looked out. "They're not there." He turned and jabbed a finger in the boy's direction. "If they come back, don't you start throwing stones at them. Fighting isn't allowed and those stones could hurt someone."

"Now scoot!" He turned his son around and swatted him toward the doorway.

Hoshea sobbed as he gathered rocks into a defensive position in front of their forefather's tomb. Now that his grandfather was dead, no one would help him. No one cared about what worried him. He would have to do everything for himself…by himself.

⚬⚬⚬⚬⚬⚬⚬⚬⚬⚬⚬⚬⚬⚬

Born in the land promised to his great-grandfather Abraham, Joseph ben Jacob had been sold by his brothers into slavery in Egypt. There he had risen to rule, first over the household of the captain of Pharaoh's guard, then over the prison into which he had been unjustly thrown, and finally over the whole land of Egypt. As Pharaoh's viceroy, Joseph had saved the Egyptians then his own family from starvation during seven years of famine.

Jacob, by then called Israel, had brought his whole household to Egypt where Pharaoh, through Joseph, had given them the land of Goshen to occupy. At his own death, Joseph had foretold the return of Israel's people to the land God promised them. He made his sons, Manasseh and Ephraim, vow to take his bones with them. Now entombed in a small pyramid in the backyard of one of Ephraim's descendants, Joseph's bones waited for the day God would deliver His people from slavery in Egypt.

⚬⚬⚬⚬⚬⚬⚬⚬⚬⚬⚬⚬⚬⚬

Meanwhile, Hoshea gathered rocks with which to threaten anyone else who came to desecrate the tomb.

He sorted the rocks again into piles by size and thought about other uses for each size. The smaller stones would fit into a sling that he'd seen an older boy twirling above his head. The slabs the size of his head he set upright to form a wall around his position. He looked at the middle pile and shook his head. He had no idea what to do with those yet.

He didn't see his father's master, an Egyptian general, study him from the front of his house.

Part 1

Bondage in Egypt

CHAPTER 1

Suzerainty Treaty with Egypt

Nineteen-year-old Hoshea ben Nun of the tribe of Ephraim looked from behind the shoulder of Bomani, his master, at the mix of officials and military officers gathered from various countries for this audience with Pharaoh. He saw their tension as they murmured to one another, shuffled their feet, and watched the Nubian embassage.

The Nubians were a proud people and only the might of Pharaoh's father had conquered the dead king. No one could predict which way the southerner would turn.

Would the new king from the country south of Egypt renew the treaty Pharaoh had held with his recently-deceased father or would he rebel and insult the lord of the Nile to his face? The delegates from Libya on the left scowled at the black men. So long was their submission to the throne of Egypt that they considered any rebellion a criminal act. Next to them, the Hittites hoped to ally themselves with a country that could distract Pharaoh from their own plotting in the North.

The Nubians stood stiffly in the middle. Their king was a young man with dark brown skin, a smooth face, and full lips. A tall headdress of peacock feathers fanned up from the top of his head. A robe of lion skin covered his black body, the lion's mane circling the back of his neck and flowing over his shoulders. The hair under his headdress was tightly curled into a springy mass. He stood serene at the front of his entourage, a mix of young, middle-aged, and elderly men. All wore soft skins of various animals– some of them predators. Hoshea had heard that these were deemed more ceremonial than their usual woven-fiber robes so he sought to quell a sneer of disdain. His admiration of their orderly ranks helped this effort.

The men and women of the Egyptian court lounged to the Nubians' right. Softened by decades of prosperity and arrogant from their hold over their Hebrew slaves, the Egyptians wanted nothing to do with war. They shuffled their feet or spoke with exaggerated levity to the Canaanites on the far right.

Bomani's troops stiffened as the ruler of Egypt strode in, leading his court officials and carrying his scepter with a lion's tail tied to it. Hoshea immediately dropped to his knees and tapped his head against the floor as the rest bowed in respect.

Pharaoh stepped up on the raised platform that held his throne. He sat and everyone in the throne room stood upright.

An official at Pharaoh's left spoke. "Your majesty, the new king of the Nubians begs you to hear his words."

Pharaoh stared at the black men then nodded.

The southern king approached the dais. He removed his headdress and placed it before the dais then knelt and lowered his head three times to the floor. Straightening to face Pharaoh, he spread his hands apart, palms up.

"Hail, great Pharaoh! King of all Egypt! Lord of the Nile! You are the embodiment of Ra who has overcome the gods of our country and defeated our armies. We come to you seeking peace.

"O great Pharaoh, renew with us the treaty that you held with our old king so we might come under your protection and be your people. We will worship Ra as well as our own gods and pay tribute to you as his representative in the land."

The Nubian king stood, picked up the headdress and tucked it under his arm. He looked up and waited.

The Egyptians relaxed while the Libyans looked pleased and the Hittites scowled in their places. Several of the Canaanites shook their heads.

Pharaoh said, "I have heard you, O Nubia, and will make a treaty with you to be your lord and protector. Hear again the words of the treaty which I made with your father and would renew with you." He motioned to a priest holding a papyrus scroll.

The priest opened the scroll and read, "These are the provisions of the covenant: I am Ramses, son of Seti who made a treaty with you and your people before his death. As you served him, so shall you serve me. You shall have no other ruler over you."

There followed a long recitation of the history between the two countries, including Nubia's failed attempt to win its freedom. Then the priest of Ra read a longer list of stipulations required of the vassal Nubians.

Hoshea shifted his weight from one foot to the other as he waited behind his master, General Bomani of Pharaoh's local army division. This reading of the treaty was taking long. Rather than give in to wishing his enslaved people had a similar vassal status under the Egyptians, the Hebrew took note of a huge, young soldier among the Canaanites. He had a rather disturbing aura that made Hoshea's skin crawl.

After a short statement of disposition– the treaty scroll would be housed in the temple of Ra– the priest read a rather short, vague list of blessings on the Nubians for obeying the terms of the treaty and an explicit list of curses for disobedience. Hoshea watched the Canaanite soldier stoop to murmur to the man next to him. They shared a chuckle.

Hoshea hoped the ceremony would finish soon. He still had much to oversee in preparation for the dinner his master would be giving for visiting military leaders that evening. The general relied more and more on the Hebrew's organizational skills in running his household as well as in obtaining supplies for Pharaoh's army and the garrison in Memphis. Seeing the youth's intelligence and how he prepared stones for the defense of a backyard tomb, he had brought Hoshea into his home as a personal aide.

Hoshea had not wept or even looked back as he marched away. The indifference of Nun and Simichek in raising him had made him callous to others, intent only on getting tasks organized and completed.

CHAPTER 2

The General's Feast

Overseeing preparations for that evening's feast, Hoshea barked at the other slaves as they scurried to position couches outside the tables and add place settings just so as he directed. He growled when a pretty, young woman carried in a small basket of flowers.

"Adah! Put that down and get back to the kitchen!"

The young woman's eyes widened at the sharpness of his tone and she nearly dropped the basket. The young overseer marched after her as she turned and fled.

In the kitchen, Hoshea grabbed her arm. "You stay in here, wife! I don't want to see you out there again. Do you hear?"

Adah pouted. "I was just trying to help out." She winced at his grip on her arm.

"Never mind helping out." Hoshea released her arm and pointed toward a washtub piled with dirty pots and pans. "You clean those and stay out of harm's way."

He turned toward the busy cook and didn't see her tongue stuck out at him.

Later, Hoshea impatiently tapped his overseer's cane against his leg as he closely watched for blunders among the slaves who served heaping dishes and goblets of wine to the reclining guests. The servers, especially the women, tried to avoid the large, young Canaanite soldier he'd watched earlier, a general or some high-ranking officer.

That guest's eyes followed the pretty females, dressed as they were in filmy robes that barely hid their nakedness. He hardly glanced at the acrobats who tumbled around inside the open space created by the tables.

"Ahiman, my friend, you're not enjoying the entertainment I've provided." Bomani gestured toward the acrobats.

The Canaanite shrugged. "I prefer other amusements."

"I noticed you were amused at one point during the reading of the treaty this afternoon."

Ahiman smirked. "Yes. I couldn't help but wonder how your army managed to force Pharaoh's will on the Nubians and compel a suzerainty treaty with them. How do you plan to enforce the curses listed in the document?"

Bomani bristled. "You speak as though you think Pharaoh's army isn't capable."

"Not from what I've seen."

Hoshea's master narrowed his eyes. "You think we can't fight to hold what we have won through negotiation?"

The giant shrugged. "Not really."

The general of Pharaoh's army rose to his more than average height and strode between the tables, curtly waving away the servers and acrobats. He drew his bronze knife. "Maybe you would like to prove your point."

Ahiman rolled to his feet and towered over his host. He did not draw the large blade in his own belt. Bomani faked a slash with his weapon, his thumb on the blade to reinforce it. The Canaanite didn't move.

The Egyptian stepped forward to slash across the guest's belly. Ahiman jumped back and pushed the arm past him, twirling his host away.

Bomani whirled back, slashing across the other way. The Canaanite merely jumped back again.

Now really angry, Pharaoh's general thrust forward. Ahiman stepped aside, grabbed the general's wrist, and twisted it behind the Egyptian's back. He snatched the knife and tossed it away then bent the man across a table and pressed his huge body against him.

"If I were like my brother, I could sodomize you right here. What I'd rather do is hear you admit you can't enforce your will on anyone."

Bomani grunted in pain but shook his head. Ahiman drew his iron knife and laid it where the Egyptian could see it. "Come now. Surely you don't want me to use that."

The general widened his eyes at the scarce metal of the blade and its honed sharpness. He sighed and nodded. When the huge soldier didn't release his arm, he grunted, "I admit I couldn't enforce my will on anyone."

Ahiman released the man's wrist and patted his back. Resuming his place, he quipped, "Now, that's what I call entertainment."

The other guests goggled and leaned away from him.

Hoshea watched in stunned outrage as his master stumbled back to the head couch, rubbing his shoulder. The squat overseer curtly motioned for a serving girl to offer him wine. The general gave her a small smile and a pat on the rump as she moved away.

The girl shot a glare in Hoshea's direction. He merely shrugged and turned his attention to the other guests. They were finishing their drinks and calling for cloaks, having decided that the party was over.

Slaves began scurrying about, fetching cloaks and clearing the tables. Hoshea called the serving girl over. He murmured to her. "I want you to help the master to his rooms and offer him comfort if he wants it."

"What! No! How dare you!"

The overseer grabbed her bare shoulder and glared at her. "I realize this isn't something you want to do but there are always things we must do anyway. We exist to do what the master wants. Now go!" He shoved her toward Bomani. *Did she not realize their master's manly pride had been damaged tonight?*

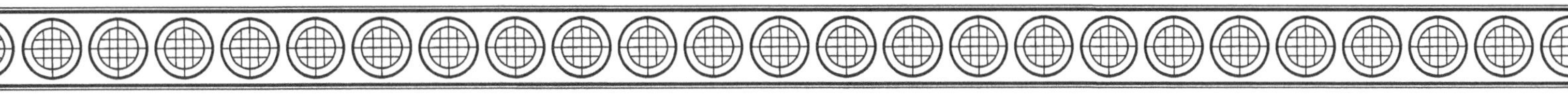

Hoshea and His Wife

As Hoshea followed the slaves with the last of the party cleanup, he heard piteous crying coming from the kitchen. He wrapped his fist around the butt of his overseer's wand and gritted his teeth.

The moment he stepped into the kitchen, the overseer saw his young bride huddled in a corner. She wailed as she rocked back and forth. He stood in front of her, his fists on his hips. Adah looked up and with a glad cry launched herself into his arms.

"Hoshea, save me! That beast has threatened to beat me. He says he's only waiting for your permission."

The young man glowered. Taking hold of her skinny arms, he set her aside and stared at the cook.

That man looked back warily then straightened his back and held out his hand for Hoshea's rod. Adah cringed behind her husband.

Hoshea folded his arms and moved to protect his wife. "What was her crime?"

The cook grunted, "I caught her stealing a melon slice from a tray bound for the party."

"I was hungry," the young woman protested. She wheedled, "And it looked so good!"

Hoshea turned on her. "Adah, you know you're not supposed to take food from the master's tray or any of the guest trays!"

She pouted. "But I was hungry!" She rubbed a delicate hand across her small belly.

Her husband sighed with exasperation and turned to the cook. "I will deal with her."

"She needs a beating," the man persisted.

Hoshea glowered. "If she needs a beating, I will give her one." He waved the man away and turned back to Adah.

He crossed his arms. "Show me the pots you were supposed to clean."

She hung her head and lifted a trembling hand toward the washtub in the corner. Bronze pots and shallow cooking pans sat in a pile next to buckets of water and sand and the skeletons of sponges from the Great Sea.

Hoshea scowled. "Why aren't these done?"

"The sand and water make my hands hurt. They end up all raw and bleeding." Adah turned on him, her fists at her sides. "I asked to serve with the other slaves. I wanted to see the guests in their fine clothing, watch the tumblers, hear the music. That beast refused to let me go."

Hoshea grabbed her arms and shook her. "I told 'that beast' to keep you in here where you'd be safe. You would have seen other slave women taken away to the bedrooms for special entertainment. As beautiful and delicate as you are, you would have been one of the first and I couldn't have done anything to stop it." He closed his eyes and murmured, "The Canaanite would have hurt you… and laughed about it."

Adah's eyes widened in fear and realization. "You protected me."

Her husband nodded. "And now I must beat you."

The young woman backed away. "No, please!"

"Adah, you broke the rules by eating from the guest tray. You didn't clean the pots as you were told. You must be punished for your disobedience."

Hoshea seized a wrist and forced her to kneel with her back exposed to his rod. The first blow brought a shriek of pain; two more returned her to piteous wailing.

Adah and her husband walked in sullen silence back to their hovel behind the master's house. Hoshea had started her cleaning the pots then asked another slave to help out and lent a hand himself until the cook was satisfied with the results.

In the hovel, Hoshea spread out the package of food brought from the kitchen. Adah made a face at the barley loaves, leeks and onions, and jug of beer. She brought out their crude clay cups and poured their beer. She sat and nibbled at the food while Hoshea ate voraciously.

He said, "I thought you were hungry."

"What I wanted was melons from the party."

He wiped his hands on his Egyptian skirt. "Those are not for such as us. If you don't eat, you'll get sick and die." He scowled. "I would not like that."

Adah raised her head with a small smile then winced. With a pout she said, "My back hurts."

Her husband grunted and began to clear away the food. "You finished?" At her nod, he wrapped the food and took it to their storage area. Without turning as he rummaged through the stores, Hoshea said, "Take off your tunic and kneel on the bed."

"Aw, Hoshea," she responded. "Not tonight! And certainly not like that!"

The young man turned to see his wife backed into a corner, her hands behind her back. With a scowl, he held out the small pot of ointment he'd found. "All I want is to rub this on your back."

"Oh." Adah moved to obey and soon pulled her tunic back on. She lay near the wall, facing it.

Hoshea disrobed and lay with his back to her. He remembered the trouble his parents had given him over choosing to marry Adah.

A few days after being put in charge of the general's household, Hoshea toured the kitchen and came upon the cook berating a pretty, young woman for her clumsiness. She cowered, her arms covering her head, over the smashed pieces of a jar and pool of cooking oil.

Hoshea's heart went out to the woman and he stuck his overseer's wand between her and the cook's angry face. "Instead of brow-beating her, why don't you just tell her to pick up the pieces and clean up the oil?" He raised an eyebrow and the cook harrumphed and turned away.

The young man knelt beside the cowering woman and began to pick the pottery pieces out of the oil. "Where's a rag or bucket of sand for soaking up this oil?"

He looked up into her adoring face and frowned. "Don't just stand there. Pick up these pieces and show me where you dump such trash."

She grabbed several large pieces and scurried off to the corner midden while Hoshea kept people from sliding in the oil. The young woman returned lugging a bucket of scrubbing sand, which she scattered over the puddle.

While they disposed of the mess, Hoshea learned her name was Adah and she lived with her parents on another part of the estate.

"She's such a child," his mother had later exclaimed. "She always complains about the work to be done in the kitchen."

His father had added, "She is a pretty thing but she's so childish."

Hoshea's temper had flared. "I'm not asking your permission. I'm telling you what I want." His grip on the wand tightened and its tip rose slightly. "The people of this family have been intent on keeping me from having what I want. Now that I'm the overseer, things will be different. As for Adah being childish, she'll just have to grow up."

Months later, they were married, though Hoshea learned the wisdom of his parents' objections. However, he could not bring himself to regret the decision.

As soon as he heard her quiet snores, he rolled over and placed an arm around her waist. He kissed the back of her head and, in an endearing tone he could not express in his wakened state, he whispered, "I love you."

CHAPTER 4

Unfriendliness and Failure

Hoshea elbowed his way roughly through the people crowding the marketplace of Memphis in Egypt. He hated the task given him by his master. He'd been sent to order a number of new tents to replace those ruined in the latest of military exercises led by his master.

Hoshea especially hated the delays caused by these people as they stood in his way and bargained with tradesmen and shopkeepers. The general had interrupted important work to send him on this errand.

He hurried past a team of slaves hauling a cart full of bricks to a nearby building. He winced at the snap of a leather whip against a bare back.

"Step together, there." The overseer cracked the whip in the air. "One, two, three, four."

Hoshea watched another group pass, going the other direction. Their overseer marched along beside them, head up and shoulders back. He swung his folded whip back and forth in time with his steps. He occasionally stopped to watch the Hebrews shuffle quickly past.

Their heads hung, their shoulders slumped, as each followed the man before him. Hoshea saw the stripes of previous whippings on many backs. He hunched his own shoulders against the memory of whippings he'd received.

He finally came to the tentmaker's doorway and happily found the shop relatively empty. The short, robust, young man entered and approached the Israelite slave bent over a length of heavy cloth. He noted the look of concentration on the man's face. The slave glanced up and smiled past the thread clenched in his teeth.

"I am looking for Jibadé, the tentmaker," Hoshea said, fists on his hips.

The Israelite mumbled something and returned to his work.

Hoshea grabbed the man by his shoulders and shook him, causing the work to unravel and fall to the floor. The Israelite jumped to his feet and raised clenched fists. Before Hoshea could respond, he felt a stinging blow across his back. He turned to face an older man brandishing a short whip.

"I am Jibadé, the tentmaker. I'll thank you not to disturb my helper while he's working."

The Israelite cringed before the raised whip and lifted his hands both in entreaty and to ward off further blows. "Forgive me, master. I did not know. He didn't give me any answer to my entreaties."

"He did. You just didn't wait to hear. Whose slave are you, Hebrew?"

Hoshea told the tentmaker his mission. The Egyptian shook his head and pointed the whip toward the doorway. "Get out. You'll get nothing here with your attitude."

"Please, master. My master, the general, will beat me if I return without the tents."

"I care not about your problems," the Egyptian stated. "You've created problems for me."

Hoshea trembled as he pushed his way back through the marketplace crowd. What was he to do? The master would be enraged at his failure.

Bomani looked up from plans he was reviewing. "When will we receive the tents I ordered?"

Hoshea fell to his knees and clasped his hands. "Forgive me, master. I told the tentmaker what you wanted but he refused me."

The general eyed him with suspicion. "How did you offend him? Surely you did something to make him angry."

The slave explained what happened then pressed his head against the ground at his master's feet.

Bomani grabbed up the overseer's cane and delivered several blows onto Hoshea's exposed back. Tossing the rod to the ground, he sat on his chair.

"So, you were frustrated by my interruption of your work plus the crowds in the market plus the refusal of the man in the tentmaker's shop to attend to you right away."

Hoshea nodded, tapping his forehead against the floor at his master's feet.

The general continued, "So frustrated were you that you nearly assaulted an Egyptian and failed to do what I had sent you to do."

The slave tapped his head against the floor again.

"I hope you realize the man's kindness in not turning you over to the authorities. Then you would have been severely beaten."

Hoshea noted the master's emphasis on "severely".

The general spoke softly. "Get up, Hoshea, and pick up your cane."

The overseer grasped his instrument of authority and rose to his feet. He rolled his shoulders, trying to ease the pain in his back.

His master said, "You mustn't let your reactions to other people's actions get in the way of completing your mission. People will always cause you problems. Deal with them or ignore them but get on with the mission."

Hoshea nodded. "Yes, master. Now what should I do about the tents?"

"We'll send someone to Jibadé who hasn't offended him and repeat the request."

"Yes, master."

As Hoshea turned away to fetch another slave, Bomani spoke more kindly. "How's that pretty wife of yours? What was her name again?"

Hoshea's face lit up as he turned back. "Adah is wonderful. Thank you for asking."

The general looked at him. "If you were friendly toward people, asked about what they loved, you would go far with them."

Hoshea looked skeptical. He had always had to take care of himself...get things done by himself. Other people usually just got in the way.

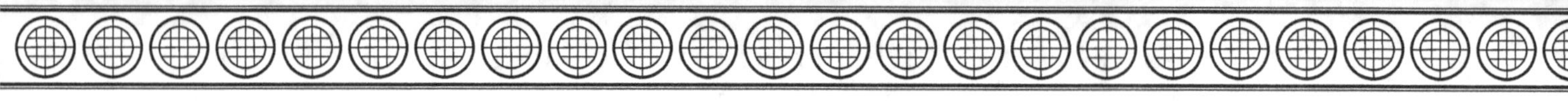

Musician in Bondage

A formless tunic covered the twisted, slender frame of Caleb ben Jephunneh as he sang. The hunch of his back caused him to bend over the lyre he strummed.

El Shaddai is my hiding place

El Alyon is the stronghold of my heart

He keeps me safe, come what may

Oh, how I love Elohim, my God!

A shadow fell across Caleb's closed eyelids and he opened them. His master stood over him with fists on his hips. Benipé scowled.

"Is that a new song?"

"Master?" The middle-aged man didn't scramble to his feet, as other slaves were required. Benipé understood how difficult it was with his twisted right arm and leg. Instead he watched Caleb sweep long, graying, red hair away from blue eyes and turn his head to look up.

"Did you just create that song?"

"No, master." The musician had created it days before when crying out to the Lord about Sarah's plight and their bondage to this man.

"You say you cannot create new songs for festivals and parties where we entertain but you sing something to your foreign god that I've never heard."

Caleb shrugged. "How many songs to El Shaddai do you know?"

"Very few." Benipé crossed his arms. "I still think you could create songs for us if you wanted."

Caleb lowered his eyes and head. "As you say, master."

The troupe leader nudged a pillow in front of Caleb and sat on it. "Tell you what: You create a new song for the festival of Tekh next week and I'll grant you some small wish."

The musician grinned. "Meaning you wouldn't set me free."

"Correct. An extra day of rest, some meat for your supper."

Caleb looked directly at his master. "Don't let some man take Sarah off for personal attention."

Benipé lurched back. He started to reach for the switch he used on his slaves but Caleb's steady look stayed his hand. He rose to his feet.

"That's no small wish. All my customers get what they request."

"While your slaves get only heartache."

Benipé said, "Be glad I don't beat you for your insolence." Then he walked away.

Late that afternoon, Caleb hobbled his way to the hovel where he lived with Sarah. In a sack, strapped like a pouch over his shoulder, he carried the week's ration of millet from the master's storehouse.

Once inside the makeshift door, he laid aside his walking stick, hoisted the sack onto the bare wood table, and hung his lyre on its peg on the wall. A look toward the curtained-off bedchamber told him Sarah was at the baths. She would be getting cleaned for that night's party. Caleb shook his head to dispel the image of her dancing naked for the client's guests. He sniffed an armpit and decided he should wash as well.

The crippled man pulled off his tunic.

He struggled to lift a stone jar full of water to the table with his good left arm. Then he carefully poured some water into the washbasin.

He cleaned himself as well as he could despite his curled right hand. He was glad his movements were limited more in his fingers than in his shoulder and elbow.

Finished, he carried the basin outside and tossed the water. He returned to dress in a freshly washed linen tunic.

∞∞∞∞∞∞∞∞∞∞∞∞∞∞

Caleb moved his legs quickly, struggling to keep up with Benipe's troupe of musicians and dancers as they stepped through the streets of Heliopolis. With his crippled hand, he cradled his lyre and stool against his curved torso as his left hand supported him on the walking staff.

Beside him, Sarah walked as upright as a statue, her pace slowed to match her husband's. A traveling cloak hid her small, statuesque body but passers-by stopped to admire the beauty of her face and dark hair.

At the client's home, Caleb set the stool in a corner out of the way of slaves hurrying with preparations for the party. He groaned as he collapsed on the stool and sat panting with the lyre in his lap. Only then did he turn his head to look up at the arrangements.

Several couches and low tables formed three sides of a rectangle. The open end faced the doorway through which early guests began to arrive. Sarah and the other dancers sat in another room, readying their costumes and waiting their turns to perform.

Lamp stands stood in front of richly colored cloths that draped the walls. His breathing eased, Caleb looked to the corner in which the musicians sat tuning their instruments. The harpist heaved to his feet and carried his stool and instrument over to join them.

Benipé finished conferring with his client, the host of the party, and came over to speak to the musicians. "Nothing special is desired for this evening. We'll start with the usual songs of thanksgiving to the gods for their blessings and go on from there."

The troupe leader looked at the nodding heads topped with aromatic cones already lit. He raised his staff and beat the tempo for the first of the songs.

Later, Caleb strummed the last chord on his harp and watched the bevy of young, female dancers scurry away to the applause of the party guests. Benipé glanced at the harpist over the heads of the other musicians and murmured the name of the next song.

Caleb shifted around on his stool so he could still watch the master but avoid seeing his wife in the open area between the tables. Having witnessed one of Sarah's performances and its effects on male guests, he didn't want to see it again.

In the waiting room, the dancer raised her arms over her head, her hands crossed at the wrists so her palms met. Lifting one knee and pointing her toes, she slowly extended and straightened the leg to place her foot flat on floor. Repeating with the other foot and rolling her hips, Sarah strode out to stand between the tables. A long, orange veil covered her long, dark hair and wrapped her small body to the ankles.

Benipé thumped four measured beats on the floor with his staff and the musicians began to play. Sarah spread her arms and waved them to the beat of the music while slowly unwrapping the veil from her undulating body. Beneath, she wore nothing but a sheer linen skirt that hardly hid her nakedness.

Dropping the veil, Sarah danced between the tables, thrusting and rotating her hips and upper torso, crooning the words to a bawdy song. At times, she danced to a guest, caressing his face in smiling invitation. As the music swirled toward completion, she danced behind the honored man and caressed his hair, his face, his chest, all the while singing about the pleasures of love. Without missing a beat, Sarah took his hands, pulled him to his feet, and danced out of the room with him.

⚬⚬⚬⚬⚬⚬⚬⚬⚬⚬⚬⚬⚬⚬

Caleb stumbled tiredly through the entrance to his home. His sour mood was not helped by the sight of his wife's brother seated on a stool at the table.

"Where is she?" Perez ben Yakov demanded. He didn't rise to lean over the stooped musician. He didn't have to.

Caleb turned his head to look on the same level with his seated brother-in-law. "She is continuing to entertain one of the master's clients tonight."

Perez snorted. "Only one of them?"

Caleb turned away and hung his lyre on its peg then limped over to the cupboard for a drink of beer. He didn't offer any to the other man.

When he turned back, Perez still glowered at him. Caleb asked, "What do you want me to do? Refuse her to the master and his guests? How long do you think I'd live after that?"

"Coward!" Perez rose and stepped toward the doorway.

The stooped man mumbled, "Just because you can't have her tonight…"

Perez stuck his head back in through the doorway. "What did you say?"

Caleb turned and looked up at the larger man. "I just said you're welcome to go rescue her as you always do."

Perez scowled and disappeared. The musician smirked at the jab he'd given his brother-in-law. Perez had been unable to protect his sister from the Egyptian rapists who had also injured her husband. Blows to the head had crippled Caleb's right side. His fingers had curled into a claw and his leg and back had turned so he hobbled stiffly.

Taking back a husband's care for his sister, Perez had returned to taking a husband's favors. Caleb had objected to his master but Benipé had merely shrugged.

"This is Egypt. Brothers often marry their sisters, especially among the exalted ones."

Sarah had tried to soothe him. "Please, Caleb, don't make trouble with my brother. You know how aggressive he can be when thwarted. I don't want him to cause you more harm."

Caleb had given her a pained look and turned away.

Much later, Sarah skulked back into the hovel. She immediately pulled the loose robe off her small body, poured water into the washbasin, and rapidly washed all over. Finished, she picked up the basin and turned to see Caleb watching her. Blank-faced, she carried the basin outside and returned. Her back to the bed, Sarah pulled on a clean tunic over her dark head. Then she lay on the bed apart from Caleb.

He reached to put his good arm around her for comfort. She stiffened and he withdrew.

"I love you, Sarah."

She snorted quietly. "I wish you could show it by keeping the master's clients away from me."

"As my Creator lives, so do I," he sighed. "It hurts me to hear you say that. It hurts worse that you need to."

Sarah sat up and held her knees to her chest. She rocked back and forth.

After a while, she wiped her hands across her eyes. "I know I should be grateful that you gave of your health to defend me. It just angers me that it wasn't enough…that it's not enough now."

Caleb turned onto his hunched back and cradled the claw of his right hand with his supple left one. He massaged the tight muscles in his forearm in an attempt to relax their pull on his fingers. Inwardly, he thanked God Most High he could use them still to pluck the strings of a harp or lyre.

He looked at his wife. "I wish you would let my good arm comfort you. I have the need to hold you as much as you need to be held."

Sarah paused in her rocking. "If only it would help. Only if it stops will things be better." She resumed rocking.

"And I would give my good arm and leg for that to happen!"

Sarah sighed and lay down again. This time she scooted back against him and reached to pull his good arm around her. "Why, Caleb? Why must I go through this? Why must you go through seeing me go off with other men?"

His arm tightened. "I don't know, Princess. I wish I did. All I know is someday soon, El Shaddai will remember His promise to Abraham and rescue us from slavery in Egypt."

Some time later, Caleb sighed as he lay on the floor of his hovel. He gently beat his head against his sound left hand and the claw of his right.

"How long, O Lord, will You keep Your people in bondage to their oppressors? How long will You continue to allow these Egyptians to mistreat Your chosen ones? How long must Sarah and I endure abuse at the hands of wicked men?

"El Shaddai," he groaned, "Your promise to Abraham goes unfulfilled. Because it does, Your people suffer from the cruelty these Egyptians inflict upon them. Because of that, my wife is forced into wickedness and pain. How long, Elohim, must we go on?"

Caleb remembered a storyteller speaking of El Shaddai's promise to the patriarch. God himself had passed between the halves of a heifer, a female goat, a ram, and two birds. The Creator declared,

> **Know this: your descendants will live as outsiders**
> **in a land not theirs;**
> **they'll be enslaved and beaten down**
> **for four hundred years.**
> **Then I will punish their slave masters;**
> **your offspring will march out of there loaded with plunder.**

Caleb remembered the storyteller's astonishing words. "Abraham believed the Lord and it was credited to him as righteousness." The musician clenched his left hand into a fist.

"Help me, O Lord, to have the faith of Abraham. Help me to believe You will deliver us as You promised."

He waited for a time, listening to the silence in the hovel, hearing only the beating of his heart. Finally, he rose, lay on his bed, and cuddled his trembling wife.

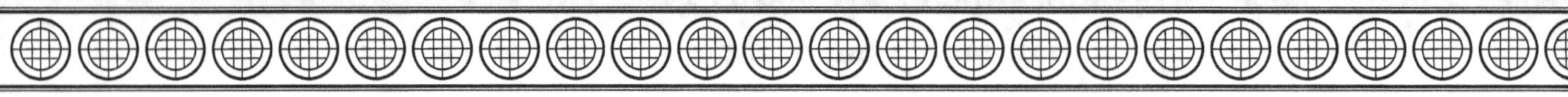

CHAPTER 6

Moses and the Promise of Freedom

General Bomani threw his *khopesh* against the wall inside his house. As it clattered to the floor, he turned to his overseer who widened his eyes at the display of outrage.

"Hoshea, you won't believe it! I wouldn't myself if I hadn't been there!"

"Master?" The young Hebrew scurried to pick up the sickle-sword and examine it for damage.

The Egyptian threw himself onto a padded seat and shook his head. "His majesty held audience today as I stood by. First, Pharaoh called for the priests of Ra and told them of dreams he had during the night. Pharaoh said in his first dream he saw the shadowy figure of a lion come from the East and maul the people of Egypt. The Nile ran red with blood, followed by various other catastrophes. In a second dream, Pharaoh said he saw a young sheep travel from house to house of the Hebrews, marking each one with its blood. Then it led a multitude of slaves out of Egypt and into the Wilderness.

"Pharaoh snorted and held up his scepter which, you know, has a lion's tail tied to it. He said, 'I have hunted lions in the Wilderness and as for sheep…' He waved his hand in scorn.

"As the priests discussed what these dreams could mean, in walk these two old men through the assembled finery of the foreign emissaries. One is clad in the robes of a Midianite shepherd. The other is a Hebrew. The shepherd hands his staff to the other who steps forward and stabs its end against the floor."

The general jumped up and struck a commanding pose. "The Hebrew pointed at Pharaoh and said, 'Hear the word of Yahweh, the God of Abraham, Isaac, and Jacob. He desires His people to go out into the Wilderness and there to make sacrifices to Him. You will let His people go.' Then he stepped back beside the Midianite."

Bomani relaxed. "We were all shocked, of course. His Majesty looked around at the assembly then at his advisors. Then he burst out laughing. We all laughed at the absurdity of allowing many thousands of slaves to leave their masters."

Bomani sat down again, his face serious. "Then His Majesty slammed the forked end of his scepter against the arm of his throne. He said, 'Who is this Yahweh that I should listen to him? I am the embodiment of Ra, who rules this land. You Hebrews have become lazy if you can find time to invent a story like that.'

"He turned to the chief supplier of straw. 'You will no longer provide straw to the Hebrews for the bricks they are making. Let them find their own straw.' And His Majesty dismissed the two men with a wave.

"The shepherd, a man named Moses, nudged his companion who tossed the staff on the floor at Pharaoh's feet. The staff turned into a viper, which hissed at His Majesty. His Majesty called for his sorcerers who tossed their staffs on the floor. These, too, became vipers but the shepherd's staff swallowed up the sorcerers' staffs. Then the Hebrew picked up the staff, returned it to the shepherd, and they left."

Overjoyed and hopeful at the news that El Shaddai had sent someone to deliver His people, Hoshea sought out where Moses was staying. He listened as the prophet told the tribal elders of meeting Yahweh in a burning bush and of the promises He made. One night, he approached the prophet, whose long and lean body rested against pillows in his brother's hovel, his hands quiet in his lap. His white hair and desert-weathered face made him look seventy or eighty years old.

Hoshea explained his position as the general's overseer. He asked, "Do you have any idea how many thousands of people you plan to lead out of Egypt? How do you plan to organize us for the trip to Canaan? How will we obtain food and water? How will we defend ourselves against wild animals, marauders, or even the Egyptians if they come after us?"

Moses nodded, staring intently at the young man. "You ask good questions. Are you saying you have the skills needed to come up with good answers?"

Hoshea merely held out his hands, palms up, in offering.

Moses clasped both of them. "I accept. Thank you. Can you come tomorrow and tell the elders how you organize for the needs of Pharaoh's troop?"

Hoshea thought a moment then nodded. He raised his hand to stop Moses from turning away. "Do we pack up and leave, herding our animals to the Wilderness as I remember we used to years ago or do we go in formations? We'll have better control over the people if we don't see ourselves as run-away slaves."

Moses dropped a hand on the young man's shoulder. "Well said! We go out as a conquering army…in ranks as soldiers."

⚬⚬⚬⚬⚬⚬⚬⚬⚬⚬⚬⚬⚬

"Sarah! Sarah! Come quick!"

"Caleb?" A pang of concern rushed through the woman. Her husband hadn't sounded this excited since Seraiah had been born to his brother, Kenaz.

Sarah hurried to the door of their hovel and watched the musician limp quickly toward her. "What is it, husband?"

Caleb grabbed her arm with his sound hand and waved his stiffly-curled one back toward the elder's home. "El Shaddai has heard our cries and sent someone to deliver us from slavery! Nahshon says that a man named Moses has come to demand of Pharaoh that we be released. Moses says that the God of our fathers will take us back to the land He promised them."

Sarah marveled to see her reserved husband joyously stumbling around despite his twisted right leg. "Caleb! Please! Come inside and sit before you hurt yourself!"

The tall, middle-aged man returned to clutch her shoulder. "Sarah! You don't understand! We're going to be free! We're going to have our own land! Moses says it flows with milk and honey!"

"Caleb," she pleaded, "what can you do with a piece of land? How will you farm it?"

"Sarah, please!" He drew himself up as far as he could. "I don't know right now! Seraiah can work it for us." He waved away the unknowns with his good hand. "We'll figure that out when it's within reach. The important thing is we're leaving Egypt! We're going home to the land of our fathers!" He looked wistful. "We can return to my family's farm near Hebron! El Shaddai will make it happen for us!"

He reached out a tentative hand. "Will you not rejoice with me, beloved?"

His wife merely shook her head and turned toward the hovel.

As Adah moved about the small room, setting dishes and preparing onions, leeks, meat scraps, and bread to eat, Hoshea reached into the pockets of his robe and withdrew fragments of papyrus and parchment. He sat at the table and sorted then read through them.

"What are those, husband?" Adah set a flat bowl down beside the scraps.

He looked up at her before reaching for bread. "Moses says Yahweh wishes the tribes to march out of Egypt in ordered divisions– not like a mob of escaped slaves." He indicated the fragments of writing. "I'm working out how to organize them."

Adah's mouth curved in amusement. "And just how do you plan to get weapons for these divisions?"

Hoshea shrugged. "I don't know yet. I do know that El Shaddai promised to Abraham that his descendants would be enslaved and that they would leave that country with great riches. I imagine weapons will be part of the loot we take with us."

Hoshea glanced up at Adah and gripped the sides of the small table in their hovel. "I'm going to another meeting with Moses."

His wife looked up from her bowl, her eyes wide. "Hoshea, no! I don't want you to go!"

The young man fought to keep a scowl off his face. "These meetings are important."

"But I get lonely when you go out after supper. Noises outside scare me and I can't get the sleep I need for the next day."

Hoshea scowled. "Come on. There's nothing to be afraid of." He swung a hand toward the outside. "My parents are right next door. You can call out to them."

Adah crossed her arms and looked away. "Your parents treat me like a child."

Hoshea stood and collected his papers. He muttered, "I wonder why."

She leapt up and put her arms around his neck, batting her eyes at him. "Wouldn't you rather spend your nights with me than a bunch of old men?"

Hoshea frowned and pushed her gently away. "Moses said he needs my ability to organize. There's so much that needs to be planned before we leave for Canaan."

Adah crossed her arms and turned away. "So, you *would* rather be with them!"

"It's not that. We're preparing for Yahweh to free us from the Egyptians."

She spun back. "And going out into the Wilderness will be better than what we have here? We know what to expect here." She flicked dismissive fingers. "Out there are all kinds of unknown dangers!"

Hoshea scowled. "Here in Egypt is a life of misery and bondage! Out there is freedom to make it on our own as God intended! Yes, there will be dangers–dangers we can overcome and that will strengthen us. When we prevail over them, we will build our faith in Yahweh and in ourselves."

The young bride clutched at his sleeve, her face white. "Hoshea, please! Don't leave me!" Tears rolled down her cheeks.

Her husband thinned his lips together and wrenched his arm away. "Adah, grow up! You won't get hurt while I'm away." He stomped out the door.

At the meeting, one of the elders raised a hand to be heard. Moses finished muttering to Aaron and called on the elder to speak.

"My lord, Moses, we are meeting openly here in the sight of Pharaoh and all of his officials. They know we talk of leaving and returning to Canaan. I can't help wondering why they have not come to kill us."

The men sitting around nodded their heads and muttered. Hoshea shook his head at their lack of nerve. He stood and cleared his throat.

The prophet and his brother scowled at his rudeness. Moses asked, "What is it, Hoshea?"

The young man scowled at the men around him. "My master, the general of Pharaoh's troops, asked me why we were talking instead of sleeping so late at night. I told him of Yahweh's promised deliverance.

"He laughed. He said Pharaoh merely shakes his head at reports he hears of Moses's words to us.

Hoshea clenched his fists at the arrogance. "He said, 'Our gods have held you here these hundreds of years. What makes you think they will let you just walk away?' And he waved a dismissive hand."

With a hand toward Moses, he continued, "Yahweh has promised to deliver us. There is no need for fear."

∞∞∞∞∞∞∞∞∞∞∞∞∞∞∞∞∞

Upon his return, Hoshea closed the hovel door quietly and carefully crossed the only room by the light of the single lamp. He shed his clothes and slowly lay down next to his wife.

He sighed when he heard her soft sniffling. He rolled to put an arm around her waist and draw her into his embrace.

"Come on, Adah. You don't have to cry like this. I wasn't gone all night."

She lay without responding so the young man rolled over and settled to sleep.

CHAPTER 7

Plagues and Preparations

Time after time, Moses and Aaron went to Pharaoh. They demanded, in the name of Yahweh, that he release the Israelites to go into the Wilderness and offer sacrifices. Pharaoh refused.

First Aaron used Moses' staff to turn the waters of the Nile into blood. Everyone in Egypt, including the Israelite settlements of Goshen, suffered from thirst.

Pharaoh refused again and frogs swarmed out of the Nile and into ovens, kneading troughs, and onto beds. Pharaoh's sorcerers duplicated these plagues, so he hardened his heart again.

Aaron smote the dust on the ground with the staff and the dust became swarms of lice. The sorcerers tried but were unable to do the same.

Still Pharaoh refused to let the people go so Moses called for flies to cover the land.

However, in Goshen where most of the Israelites lived, no flies came at all. When a plague killed all of the Egyptians' livestock, no one Israelite animal died. When Aaron threw soot into the air, boils covered the Egyptians while the Israelites remained untouched.

Pharaoh sought to negotiate. First, he said the men may go but women and children were to be left behind. Then he said all the people may go but their livestock must stay. Finally, he said they might all go but not so far as the Wilderness.

Yahweh caused hail to destroy the nation's flax and barley. Then He sent locusts to consume what little was left. Finally, thick darkness covered all the land. Only in the houses of the Israelites was there light to see.

Meanwhile, overseers spoke to the gatherings of Israelites. "We warn you. You will die in the Wilderness. There will be no food, no water. Marauders and wild animals will attack you and your children. Moses came from the desert. Ask him if this is not true."

The prophet raised his hands to calm the people's murmuring. "What these men are saying is true. There are dangers in the Wilderness. However, Yahweh has promised to lead you out of bondage here in Egypt. He has said He will take you into the land He promised your ancestors. Believe in His care for you."

⚬⚬⚬⚬⚬⚬⚬⚬⚬⚬⚬⚬⚬⚬⚬⚬

After nine of the plagues, Moses told the tribal elders to prepare for a celebration feast and their flight from Egypt. The people were instructed to go to their Egyptian masters and ask for gold, silver, clothing, tools of trades. The cowed Egyptians were glad to load up their former slaves with the wealth of their households.

Hoshea's parents dismantled and packed for travel the loom they had slaved on along with bundles of thread and already-woven cloth. Their son asked the prophet if he should go to the general and ask for war materiel: tents, weapons, supplies, and such.

Moses pondered a bit. He nodded his head. "Yes, do that, Hoshea. It would be best to ask your general for authorization to take from the arms depot whatever we want. I'll have the elders send carts to haul the weapons and other supplies."

The young man said, "If you'll send just animals, the depot has carts."

The next day, Hoshea went to the room where the general planned campaigns and wrote orders. He explained his mission in the name of Moses and Yahweh.

The general sat back in his chair and studied the slave who stood before him.

"So, you're one of those rebellious Hebrews that wants to go into the Wilderness."

"Yes, master, I am. For many years I have wished for my own plot of land. I believe the promises Yahweh has spoken through Moses.

"More than that, though, I have been sent by Moses to make this request. Again, I believe he speaks for Yahweh."

The general slowly twirled a writing stylus between his fingers as he continued to watch the waiting slave. "So, I'm not to merely grant you your freedom and lose the services of an excellent organizer, I'm also to allow you and your people to make off with valuable war materiel."

Hoshea spread his hands with a shrug and waited.

The general tossed the stylus on his desk and leaned forward to reach for a clean section of papyrus. He picked up the stylus again, dipped it into ink, and wrote.

> **Be it known that Hoshea ben Nun, bearer of this order, has been sent by highest authority to receive weapons and supplies for an extended trip into the Wilderness of Shur. You are to provide carts loaded with whatever weapons, equipment, and supplies he requests.**
>
> **By my order, Bomani, General of His Majesty's troops in Memphis.**

As he waited for the ink to dry, Bomani looked up. "You seem to have had some good out of the beating I gave you. Your god has given you Hebrews the upper hand over us. We dare not refuse your demands for gold and supplies."

He rolled the order and tied it loosely with string then handed it to Hoshea. "I don't even dare offend your Yahweh by withholding our war materiel.

"Now, you could have come in here and demanded this order as you did with Jibadé, the tentmaker, but you haven't. You made the request in the name of your god and his prophet then waited for my compliance. You've learned."

Hoshea bowed at the compliment, raised the scroll in salute, then turned and walked out. It never occurred to him to thank the general for being a kind master.

He made his way to the weapons depot where he presented the scroll to the officer in charge. The man frowned as he read the order. When he saw the signature at the bottom, he shrugged. The officer turned to servants waiting for instructions. "All right, let's get moving! We need all the empty carts taken throughout the stores and loaded with weapons, bivouac equipment, and supplies."

Hoshea and the officer strolled behind the carts and watched the servants scurry in and out of storehouses with their arms loaded down. In some carts, they carefully stacked *khopeshes*, the Egyptian sickle-swords. Into others went shields for infantry. Spears and light javelins were stacked in more carts. In another, bundles of straps of leather twice as long as a man's arm were held down by shoulder bags of lead shot.

Hoshea stepped to this cart and pulled free a strap. He examined the leather and pulled to test its strength. With a nod of approval, he folded sling and tucked it into his belt. He stuffed a pouch of shot into his waistband then waved the driver on.

More carts were filled with bows and quivers of arrows. Some carts pulled up to storage rooms for weapons components and were loaded with wood shafts, fletching feathers, and tips for spears and arrows. Bundles of gut for bowstrings were stuffed into other carts.

After Hoshea started the carts rolling toward Ra'amses for the gathering of the tribes, he took the scroll to Jibadé. The tent maker clasped his hands together and begged, "Please, your lordship, do not punish me for my ill treatment of you before."

Hoshea replied, "Your judgment of my attitude and behavior was right. When I returned empty-handed to my master, I received the beating I deserved. I have learned my lesson."

He held out the scroll. "Now I have another order from Bomani."

The tentmaker read the order and looked at Hoshea with anxiety. "How many tents will you require?"

"Thousands. We need to outfit as many tribes as possible."

Jibadé dropped the scroll and lifted his arms to cover his face and head. "Please, my lord, have mercy! You'll beggar me!"

Hoshea crossed his arms and scowled. "Given your people's enslavement and oppression of my people, I can't say I really care. There is the order." He nudged it with his toe. "I'm waiting for you to fill it."

Moments later, he walked away with the promise of compliance clamoring in his ears.

Hoshea went with the carts and wagons full of equipment to the large open country near Ra'amses. The elders of Reuben sent out men to help the young organizer.

He set men to staking out and stretching ropes for boundaries. They gathered the equipment in the middle of the camp and had the ropes radiating out to mark the boundaries of tribal areas. They laid out tents at spaced intervals for families to put up themselves. Some men he set to digging latrines at points around the outside of the area.

He decided to leave the equipment under the protection of Yahweh so the men could return to have the celebration meal with their families.

Then he returned to Moses' dwelling and told him of his successes.

"Yahweh be praised," the prophet exclaimed. "We'll be able to shelter our people against the elements and arm them against enemy attack. Now, will they be able to defend themselves?"

"My lord," the young man replied, "I have spent the better part of my life as the slave of Bomani, the general of Pharaoh's troops. I have watched him train with his men. I believe I can put together a defense among those willing and able to fight."

Moses stroked his beard and nodded. "Yes. I see great potential in you for leadership."

<hr>

Caleb stumbled into the clan leader's house, jostled by other men entering with him. He took a seat against one wall and looked around. Thirty or so household leaders of his clan sat crowded into the open space before the clan leader, who perched on a bench along the back wall.

The leader clapped his hands together and everyone turned his attention that way.

"Brothers, have you all selected male sheep or goats for the celebration feast Moses declared and taken them into your homes? Have your women prepared bread without yeast and purged all yeast from your houses?"

Nods and murmurs announced their compliance with Moses' instructions. A couple young men raised their hands to say their households were too small for such quantities of food. The leader gestured to some of the men with slightly larger households.

"Can you men add these smaller families to your households for the meals?"

Those heads of households nodded and said whom they would take in.

"Good," the clan leader smiled. "Be sure when you slaughter your animals that you catch blood and use hyssop to splash it on the top and sides of your doorways. Then Yahweh's Destroyer will pass over your homes and spare your sons. Moses says Yahweh will move that night and kill all the firstborn of Egypt."

The men seated around the room recoiled and cried out in horror. The leader let them argue with one another for a moment then he held up his hands until they quieted.

"Our God is doing what He will and we must not object.

"Now, once we are released, we will travel to Ra'amses where all the tribes are gathering. We will set up tents in our part of Judah's area.

"When Moses tells us to march, we must pack our tents and draw weapons from the supply piles then gather into formation by tribe and clan." He looked at Caleb.

"You, of course, will never be able wield a sword or spear. Do you think you could draw a bowstring?"

The musician pushed his left palm against his clawed fingers, which he tried to stiffen against the push. He shook his head.

"They're good enough for strumming a harp but could not take a bowstring."

The leader nodded and Caleb continued with a grimace.

"It's just as well. I wouldn't want to handle weapons anyway."

CHAPTER 8

Passover

"Hoshea! Get that smelly thing away from my clothes!" Adah waved her hands to shoo away the year-old goat that had wandered into the hovel from their neighbor's home.

Hoshea grabbed up the animal and carried it next door. He returned to his weeping wife and stood before her as she sat on the bed. "Come on, Adah, there's no reason to cry. He didn't do that much damage."

The young woman flared. "Not that much damage! That, that…thing… chewed holes in the best garments the master's wife gave us! They were so pretty! I looked forward to wearing them! And now they're ruined!" She dropped her face into the gown she held.

"Listen, Adah, you mustn't take things so hard. Besides, we're going to be traveling. You need to get this finery packed."

A wail was smothered as the woman dropped further onto the bed. Hoshea turned away and continued wrapping the bags of his master's gold coins and jewels into larger parcels. He judged there was enough silver to handle expenses on their weeks-long journey.

Hoshea looked back at his wife and shook his head. If she didn't get it together, she'd never get her things packed in time. However, he could never harass her as he had seen officers do to their men.

Though he had seen her often enough in the master's kitchen, preparing foods, she had been nearly a stranger on their wedding night. Since then, Hoshea had discovered a growing tenderness toward this waif who had entered his lonely home.

He passed a gentle hand over Adah's shoulder. "I'm going to see how things are going next door. Why don't you get those packed away and get the bread started."

She sniffled and nodded.

He stood then looked at her. "Remember, no yeast. Yahweh has said to get all the yeast out of the house."

His wife nodded again and pushed herself upright. "I don't understand it but if you say so…"

He frowned, thinking about the instructions for the night's meal. "Not me. I like your leavened bread. It was Moses who said 'No yeast'."

Hoshea left his hovel, calling out to his parents who were them for the night. Upon his return, he helped his wife finish her packing.

Because his parents lived by themselves, Hoshea had arranged for Adah and himself to join them for the celebration feast Moses had ordered. As Nun's and Simichek's only son, he was determined not to venture out that night.

Late in the afternoon, the general's two children ran up as Hoshea helped his father slaughter the goat. He held the animal's head while its blood pumped into the basin Nun held.

As the boy innocently inquired what they were up to, Hoshea glanced up and scowled. He looked at the older man and shook his head. He knew what was coming and pitied the boy.

Nun rose stiffly to his feet and said, "We were told to slaughter a goat one year old and catch its blood in a basin. Now watch what I do with it." He applied the blood to the doorway top and sides with a leafy hyssop branch, taking care to not splatter onto his clothing or graying hair.

Hoshea nudged the eight-year-old girl aside as he pulled out a dagger to skin the animal.

"That's my papa's knife!" the child exclaimed, reaching. "Give it back!"

"Careful, little one." He pulled it out of reach. "Your father gave this to me along with other things."

He cut down the front of the goat and pulled off the skin. This he folded around the inedible parts. He cut the rest into manageable sections and took these to his mother, who seasoned them and placed them onto the roasting spit.

Back outside, the boy asked about all the preparations. "Why are you doing all this?"

Nun sat on a bench against the wall warmed by the sun. He beckoned the boy over to sit down beside him.

"Many years ago, our ancestors came from the land of Canaan. It was a time of great famine but El Shaddai had sent His servant Joseph ahead to gain favor with the Pharaoh of that time.

"Since they were great fighting men as well as herders and of other trades, Pharaoh sent them to live here in Goshen to help defend the roadways to Canaan. They would herd their flocks into the Wilderness of Shur for the months of the Nile's great flooding every year. Then they would return to farm the rich soil left behind.

"Life was good for us Hebrews until the first Seti took the throne and forced us into hard civic labor. Instead of using us to fight alongside the men of other peoples, we were put to making bricks and building temples, government buildings– even the new city of Ra'amses. No longer were we allowed to take our flocks to the Wilderness."

Nun leaned down toward his listener. "Do you know what happened next?"

The boy shook his head.

"El Shaddai sent a Hebrew baby to live in the palace of the Pharaoh. He grew up to become a prince and a great general."

The older man paused with a frowning look then shook his head. "For some reason, Moses just disappeared. Some say he killed an Egyptian and fled for his life. Others say he got tired of seeing his people oppressed by Pharaoh and his overseers and simply left.

"The next thing we hear, Moses has returned and gone to the Pharaoh. 'Let my people, the Hebrews, go into the desert to worship Yahweh. He has chosen them to be His people,' he said."

Nun looked at the boy. "Have you been aware of the plagues in other parts of Egypt?"

The boy nodded. "Some. Why?"

"Moses kept going to Pharaoh, telling him to let us go into the desert. Pharaoh kept saying 'No'. Yahweh kept sending plagues. But He didn't send the plagues here to Goshen. He made a distinction between you Egyptians and us here.

"When your cattle got sick, ours didn't. When your people got boils on their skins, we didn't."

The boy rubbed the bare skin of his leg where a scar marked the recently healed site of a boil.

The old man patted his hand and continued. "When there was deep darkness all over Egypt, we enjoyed light in our homes. There were so many signs of Yahweh's power and of His love for us who are His people.

"Now Moses has said to make ready for one more plague. Every family is to sacrifice a year-old male goat and sprinkle his blood on the doorway of their home. Then we are to eat its meat roasted and burn all the rest in the fire. We are to eat bitter herbs and bread without yeast. We are to wear traveling clothes and be ready to leave Egypt immediately."

He refrained from speaking about the Destroyer who was expected to skip over their blood-covered house but attack the houses of the Egyptians.

⌁⌁⌁⌁⌁⌁⌁⌁⌁⌁⌁⌁⌁⌁

The little girl watched as Adah chopped herbs and horseradish. "What are these for?"

The young woman slapped at a grasping hand but the girl managed to get a taste to her mouth. The youngster immediately spit it out. "Eww! Nasty!"

Simichek handed her a cloth. "That's right, dearie. With the roasted goat tonight, we're serving bitter herbs and unleavened bread."

The girl wiped her mouth and dropped the cloth on the floor. The old woman looked at her and pointed to the bits of greens. "Now, wipe up your mess on the floor."

The youngster lifted her chin. "Wipe it up yourself! I'm not a slave to be doing your bidding."

Adah rounded on her, her knuckles white on the chopping knife. "And tomorrow, we won't be slaves to be doing yours!"

Simichek grabbed the knife wrist. "Easy, dear."

Adah set aside the knife and glanced around the hovel. "Tomorrow, we're leaving this pigsty and no one's going to stop us!"

"Leaving?" The girl's eyes went wide. "You can't leave! Who will make date cookies for us?"

The young woman put her hands on her hips and glowered. "I'd like to know who you're going to play with after your brother dies tonight."

The little girl shrieked and ran for the door, leaving Simichek scolding her daughter-in-law.

Later that evening, Caleb helped his brother, Kenaz, lift the roasted goat out of the fire pit and onto the table. Sarah cut the meat off the bones and served it into various eating bowls. Their sister-in-law broke off large pieces of unleavened bread and placed these into the bowls while her daughter served out the bitter herbs.

Finally the whole family sat at the table and after a prayer of thanks to the Creator, they began to eat. They also talked about the coming trip into the Wilderness to sacrifice to Yahweh.

At one point, Caleb's nephew spoke to his father. "Abba, why is this night different from other nights? We have all this meat to eat like it's some Egyptian holiday but we're dressed for travel?"

Kenaz looked at his brother. "Caleb?"

The older man leaned back against gaudy pillows taken from some rich Egyptian's house and looked at the strip of meat in his hand then at Seraiah. "You know Moses told us we'll be leaving Egypt tomorrow."

The youth nodded and Caleb continued. "He said we should be ready to leave at a moment's notice. That's why all our belongings are packed and ready to go onto the cart and the donkey's back. That's why our walking staffs are by the door and sandals are on our feet." He lifted the meat he held. "We're to burn whatever we don't eat before we leave.

"Yahweh also told us to choose a male, yearling goat and keep it for fourteen days. He said we were to slaughter it and collect its blood then sprinkle the blood on the doorposts– on the top and both sides."

The middle-aged man paused and frowned thoughtfully. "I'm sure there's some symbolic reason Yahweh had for that particular instruction. I wish I knew what it is." His face cleared as he looked up again.

"Anyway, Yahweh said He would kill every firstborn male throughout Egypt tonight– both people and cattle. He said the Destroyer would pass over only those houses with blood on them. Because you, Seraiah, are Kenaz's firstborn, your father put the blood on our doorway."

Caleb shook his head sadly. "I pity the Egyptians. The Destroyer will wreak a terrible judgment against them tonight."

The youth picked up a heavy chunk of bread. "Why did Aunt Sarah make the bread without yeast? Usually she makes it light and fluffy. This is so so…" He grimaced.

His uncle nodded. "Again, we have to be ready to leave quickly. There's no time to let the bread rise with yeast. And again, because Yahweh gave us this instruction, I suspect there is some special significance." He shrugged at his ignorance.

The boy nodded thoughtfully. "So, why these bitter herbs?" He picked up a sprig of parsley and set it down with a scowl.

"These herbs are meant to remind us of all the bitter years of slavery here in Egypt. You know how hard your abba had to work to make bricks. And he got very little to live on for his efforts. It's been particularly hard since Pharaoh refused to supply the straw. Those days are ending– as I said– but we must remember the bitter bondage from which Yahweh is delivering us."

"Uncle, one more question. Normally, we eat sitting up but tonight everyone is lying down. Why, on this of all nights?"

Caleb struggled to sit upright. Finally, he grasped the hand of his brother and wrapped his left leg under himself. "Slaves, by necessity, sit upright to eat because at any moment the master may send word and the slave would have to jump up to perform the required service. Only free men may recline when eating at table. Note also, we were told to eat the meat roasted. Only the rich eat it thus.

"Tonight, Yahweh will do a powerful thing for us who are His people. Tonight we become free men and eat lying down. With the plunder we have taken from the Egyptians, He has also made us rich."

Suddenly, Caleb's nephew shuddered violently. The youth and various women cried out as a deep darkness passed by the window. In a few moments, their master's voice rose in anguish.

"My son! Someone help my son!"

Kenaz jumped up and started for the door but Caleb grabbed his arm. "No! Don't go out there!"

The younger man blinked and shook his head violently. "Sorry, habit."

"Yes, I know. We were well trained. Come back to the table. We must learn how to live as free men." Caleb tore a piece of the bread and had it passed around the table. Before he took a bite, he said, "Let us forget the evil in the land for the moment and rejoice in what Yahweh is doing for us this night."

The head of the family poured wine into a cup and motioned for it to be passed to everyone. "Let us rejoice in Yahweh's great love for us."

As he drank, an unnatural warmth pressed gently on his head, his back, and his crippled arm and leg. The warmth in his head grew into a hot ache and Caleb suddenly pressed both his palms against the sides of his head.

Surprised he was able to fully open his right hand, he bolted upright, standing straight on both feet. The middle-aged man turned his hand back and forth, opening and closing his fingers. He turned his head and looked *down* at his wife who hurried from her end of the table to him.

Caleb looked at his leg– straight and sturdy. He looked up at the ceiling and flinched at its closeness.

Sarah grabbed his arm. "Caleb, what has happened?"

"I…I don't know, wife. Suddenly, I felt a burning in my head where I was injured and now I can move my fingers. I can stand firm on both feet and I feel like I'm going to bump my head on the ceiling."

He moved away from Sarah's grasp and waved his arms, hopping from one foot to the other. "It is just as Moses said! Yahweh has made a way for me to go into the Wilderness with ease! I feel as though I could go outside and run all the way to Ra'amses!"

"Uncle," his nephew protested, "you wouldn't let me go out!"

Caleb clasped the youth in his arms. "Seraiah, I don't have to worry. My brother, Esau, was born before I was. He died many years ago." Releasing the boy, he clapped his hands together.

"Now, let us return to this meal Yahweh has provided for us and rejoice in the freedom He is winning for us."

He sat and handed the cup to Kenaz. The younger man drank and passed the cup to Seraiah. Then Kenaz began to sing a spontaneous song of praise to Yahweh. The boy beside him passed the cup to his aunt and clapped his hands in time to the music.

Caleb jumped up and lifted his harp from its place among the packs. At first he only plucked slowly in tune with the song as he had done for the past few years. Soon, he was picking lyrically and with speed. His face shone with the joy of using all his fingers to make the music.

Meanwhile, Sarah drank from the cup. She gasped as she handed it on to her brother-in-law's wife and nearly dropped it. At first, she shook her head as if to clear it. Then she lowered her head to her fists on the table. Finally, she wailed and beat at her breast.

"Oh, God, be merciful! I have sinned greatly in Your eyes! I have been unfaithful to my husband!"

"Sarah?" Caleb strode to his wife and caught her in an embrace. "What ails you?"

The beautiful woman clung to his chest, sobbing. "Caleb, please forgive me for all the times I went off with other men. Many times I had no choice but I was still guilty of being unfaithful."

She wailed about all the evil she and Caleb had endured at the hands of the Egyptians. The newly-healed man stood tall and patted his wife's back. "Sarah, I always forgave you when you were forced to go away with other men. There may be more to all of this but we will speak of that later. Tonight, Yahweh is doing a great work, destroying the firstborn of Egypt but passing over ours, bringing healing to my limbs and a spontaneous song from my unmusical brother and forgiveness of your sins.

"Tomorrow we leave this place of bondage and follow Yahweh into a new life. Let us rejoice in His love for us and the great things He plans for our future."

Caleb and his wife returned to their seats at the table and all turned their attention to eating the roasted goat, the unleavened bread, and the bitter herbs.

Before they could finish eating, a loud knocking on the door interrupted them. A harsh voice called, "By the command of Pharaoh, open this door!"

Kenaz hustled to open up, his brother right behind him. The light of the rising sun shone past the bulk of a burly soldier, lighting the inside of the hovel. The soldier stepped in, his face grim with grief and impotent fury.

"By the order of Pharaoh, all occupants of homes with blood on their doorposts are cast out of Egypt. Take your cattle and your herds, take the gold and silver which you have looted from your masters, take your weapons and supplies, and go, serve Yahweh, as He has said!" The soldier turned to stomp off to the home next door.

Caleb turned, his arms and his mouth spread wide. "Free at last! Free at last! Thank God Almighty, we're free at last!

"Sarah, gather all the bread into a basket. What's not baked we'll cook along the way. Kenaz, gather all the uneaten parts of the goat and burn them in the fire. Seraiah, help me with these packs."

Caleb stooped to gather up their belongings and carry them to the cart. He marveled that he could easily carry as much with his right hand as with his left. With the boy's help, he tossed the bundles into the cart, placing his harp in a protected place near the front. He released their new ox from its pen and yoked it to the cart.

Back in the hovel, he saw that the remnants of the goat were sizzling and smoking in the fire pit. Kenaz had smashed the crude chairs and placed the sticks in the fire to keep it going. Caleb could see that if they left the fire unwatched, it would consume the hovel.

He laughed. Good riddance! He never wanted to come back to this place.

The musician walked to the members of his family, embracing each one. At the ox's head, he half turned and waved everyone forward.

"Come, my loved ones. Let's go up to the land Yahweh has promised us."

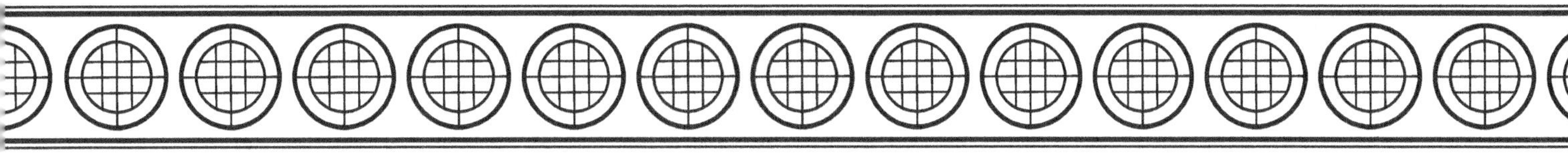

Part 2

Journey to Sinai

CHAPTER 9

Military Matters

All the tribes of Israel came to the great gathering at Ra'amses:

Reuben, led by Elizur son of Shedeur, their troops numbering 46,500.
Simeon's troops, following Shelumiel son of Zurishaddai, numbered 59,300.
Judah, led by Nahshon son of Amminadab, had 74,600 troops.
Zebulun's troops, following Eliab son of Helon, numbered 57,400.
Issachar, behind Nethanel son of Zuar, their troops numbering 54,400.
Dan, led by Ahiezer son of Ammishaddai, had 62,700 troops.
Gad's troops, following Eliasaph son of Deuel, numbered 45,650.
Asher, behind Pagiel son of Ocran, their troops numbering 41,500.
Naphtali, led by Ahira son of Enan, had 53,400.
Manasseh's troops, following Gamaliel son of Pedahzur, numbered 32,200 troops.
Ephraim, with Elishama son of Ammihud, their troops numbering 40,500 and Benjamin, in the train of Abidan son of Gideoni, had 35,400 troops.

Levi, in the train of Aaron son of Amram, were not numbered as troops but were counted at 22,000 males. These were taken into the service of Yahweh in place of the firstborn of all Israel.

In all, 603,550 troops, the 22,000 males of Levi, and all their women and children gathered together. In addition, Moses took the bones of Joseph out of his tomb and placed them into a box for carrying. Joseph had made his sons swear to do it because he believed God would one day lead them to the land of promise.

(Manasseh and Ephraim were the sons of Joseph to whom Jacob gave the double-portion of his inheritance. That inheritance of having their own tribes was passed to Joseph's sons.)

For two days the tribes gathered and filled their food baskets and their water skins. Hoshea directed each tribal elder to his tribe's place on the gathering field around the depot of military supplies and instructed him to pitch the tents placed within the boundary ropes that marked out its area.

Caleb and Sarah were tired and footsore when they reached the area reserved for Judah at the end of the day. They helped Kenaz and his wife set up both their tents while Seraiah sought out the location of weapons among the equipment in the middle of the camp.

The next day, the Israelites rested while Nahshon, the elder of Judah, sent men from one gathering of families to another.

"Listen to me, people of Judah! With so many descendants of Jacob on the march and many other people joining us in leaving Egypt, we must be organized and follow the instructions of our leaders. Moses, the prophet of Yahweh, will be leading us along the path Yahweh wants us to follow. Hoshea ben Nun has made plans for setting up each night's bivouac. Nahshon will place the standard of Judah in the area marked off for our tribe. We must set up our tents within that area." The men gave further instructions for finding water and food and other needs.

The men collected weapons from the carts of military supplies. Moses instructed the elders to form their men of military age into divisions according to their tribes and to drill them in marching.

That first morning, Hoshea changed his Egyptian skirt for Hebrew clothing. He tied on a clean linen loincloth and pulled a fresh cotton tunic over his head. A worn robe came next then a head covering. At his waist, he tied a wool girdle into which he thrust his *khopesh*, a sickle-sword.

Later, Hoshea stumbled when the man behind him trod on his heels. The young man almost toppled the man before him but managed to fall sideways onto his shield and out of the formation. Cursing, he pushed himself erect with his heavy spear and watched the ranks of men lurch past.

He shook his head at the mishmash of weapons and disordered steps. One small man in the second row lugged a heavy infantry spear but a light infantry shield. Nearly dragging the butt of the spear on the ground behind him, the man almost jabbed its point into the back of the man in front. Behind him, a large man with a slinger's pouch tied to his waist skipped and hopped to avoid the lurching spear butt.

Hoshea shook his head and strode forward to speak to his clan leader. The leader stepped aside and watched his men march past. He nodded.

When the tribe stopped for a midday meal, the clan leader took Hoshea to see Elishama, Ephraim's elder. "We have got to get the formations better organized. This jumble of weapons and stumbling steps would get us killed against any army."

Elishama looked at Hoshea. "What would you have us do?"

Hoshea squatted and pulled his knife to draw boxes and symbols in the dust. "The tribe needs to put light infantry weapons in front and at the rear. If they meet heavy opposition, heavy infantry, marching closer to the middle can move to support them. Archers and slingers can send their missiles over the heads of the infantry. And, being in the middle, they're protected by the infantry."

The young man stood and looked at the elder. "Each man must march in step, an arm's length from the man in front of him. That way, they're not stumbling over each other."

The elder nodded and tilted a water skin to his mouth. Wiping his face with his sleeve, he offered the skin to Hoshea, who accepted it. "How do we get them organized by weapons?"

Hoshea sighed. "Get everyone to turn in his weapons now and learn to march in ranks without them until this evening. Tomorrow, give them a choice of which weapon or which men with whom to march. Then put the formations in order as I showed you."

Elishama said, "I'll speak to Moses about this."

Hoshea lifted a hand. "Please, tell him this was my idea."

"You want glory from this?"

"No. He chose me to organize things. He'll accept the idea from me."

Once the Ephraimites had eaten and refilled their water skins, they reassembled into the morning's ragged formations. Elishama faced them and called Hoshea to join him. Weaponless, the young man marched forward and turned to speak to the men.

"Your way of marching this morning was horrible! I saw one man nearly skewer another with a spear. I myself fell out of formation when the man behind me trod on my heels."

When the men began to mutter in protest, Hoshea raised his voice. "I was slave to the general of the Egyptian army. I saw how they marched toward battles like professionals and you aren't that! If you want to be any good against the Canaanites, you'll need to learn how!"

Hoshea shook his head in dismay at the silence and the nervous looks the men gave each other. The idea of actually conquering the Canaanites overwhelmed them.

He huffed. First things first. "Return your weapons to their carts. You won't need them for the rest of the day."

When the men began to argue among themselves and protest, he roared, "You need to learn to follow orders! Now, get those weapons back to their carts!"

Elishama laid a hand on his arm. "Hoshea, please. Let me." The elder raised his voice to be heard over the men's protests.

"Brothers, please listen to what Hoshea has told you. He knows of what he speaks. Put you weapons back on their carts and return here to form into ranks."

The men's reluctance showed in their slowness and muttering as they complied. When they returned, Hoshea showed them how to dress their ranks and keep in step.

∞∞∞∞∞∞∞∞∞∞∞∞

The next day, the men chose their weapons or their companions and were ordered into formation accordingly. Hoshea liked how much better the Ephraimites marched and was gratified to see Moses and various tribal elders observing them. Over the next couple days, six hundred thousand men learned to march in formations. Many others were put in charge of herding the cattle and flocks. All their families and carts mixed in between the formations.

∞∞∞∞∞∞∞∞∞∞∞∞

The day before departure, his clan leader stopped by Caleb's tent at the gathering. The healed man looked up from picking at the strings of his harp, joyous wonder on his face. He stopped the song of praise he sang and scrambled to his feet. He grabbed the leader's hands in both of his own.

"Did you see that? I no longer have to struggle to rise when visitors stop by."

He gestured the leader to sit and turned to call out.

"Sarah, we have a visitor. Would you bring him a drink?"

The woman emerged from the tent with a silver cup brimming with water. This she offered to the visitor who sipped carefully then drank more deeply. He raised the cup to her in thanks.

When she stepped behind her husband, the leader looked at Caleb. "I heard the wonderful news you were healed. Could you now wield a sword?"

The older man grimaced and struck a sour chord on the harp. "Watching Kenaz and his son swinging their swords around, I thought about it. Even if I could, I would not. I'm a musician, not a warrior. I'm too old to learn to fight."

The clan leader nodded slowly. "We planned the formation without you so you won't be missed. However, Moses has called for all able-bodied men to join the formations." He grinned. "I am glad to see you now have become such."

Caleb shook his head. "We have gained our freedom as individuals as well as a people. I'd rather not get drawn into combat."

The clan leader slapped his thighs and rose. "That settles that."

He bowed to Sarah. "Thank you for the drink."

On the third day, the tribes rose early, folded their tents, and completed the packing of their carts and wagons. The men formed into divisions according to their tribes and all set out for the Way to the Desert of Shur.

When the tribe of Reuben set out toward the road to Shur, a huge pillar of smoke appeared and went before them. It looked to be about twelve paces wide and so long its top disappeared into the sky. It was made mostly of dark smoke but bright fire shone from its depths.

Moses called out, "See the presence of our God! He will lead us in the way we should go. Follow Him!"

Caleb pulled out his harp and with Sarah sang songs of praise and love to Yahweh. Caleb sang a new song of El Shaddai, who gave healing and strength to crippled limbs and victory over the enemies of His people. Hearing the music of others, they left their wagon in Kenaz's charge and gathered with a company of musicians. These sang a song of praise to Yahweh.

> **Praise be to Yahweh, the God of Israel!**
> **He has come to be with His people**
> **and to deliver them from slavery!**
> **Yahweh has remembered His covenant with Abraham**
> **He has extended His promises to Abraham's descendants**
> **He has rescued us from those who enslaved us**
> **so we might serve Him fearlessly in holiness and righteousness.**

Two days after the exodus, Hoshea noticed that most of the men trudged with their families and carts instead of in formations. Scowling, he strode up to a clan leader he recognized, his fist clenched on the hilt of his *khopesh*.

"Why aren't your men in formation? And why do so few of them carry weapons?"

The leader returned the young man's scowl. "What more do we need of formations? And why do we need to carry weapons? We're out of Egypt. We don't need to impress our former masters nor ourselves now that we are no longer their slaves."

Hoshea grunted, not sure whether to agree. "But the weapons." He gestured to the man's empty girdle. "Even you are without one."

The clan leader took in the sword handle Hoshea was clenching in annoyance. "I suppose you never go out and leave your sword behind."

"Never. I know something of the dangers the Wilderness holds. I never want to be unable to defend my wife or myself."

The leader crossed his arms. "What dangers are those?"

"There are various vipers and cobras, scorpions, desert foxes, and leopards. Midianite traders cross the desert and would think nothing of robbing and killing. Amalekite marauders often attack."

Hoshea gestured with impatience. "Ask Moses. He knows."

He turned and stalked away.

<hr>

Hoshea kept an eye out for men around him wearing swords or carrying spears or other weapons. These he called to his tent during the midday rest.

"Men of Ephraim, when we come to the land Yahweh has promised to us, we will have to fight to drive out the people who live there. What's more, on the road there are wild animals and other dangers. We who carry weapons have shown ourselves ready to deal with those dangers.

"I would like us to organize into patrols to travel up and down the sides of the company of tribes. I would also like to set over-night sentries to circle the camp and guard us against raiders– whether men or beasts."

A large, good-looking man, wearing the colors of the tribe of Judah and carrying a spear, stood to speak. "I am Perez ben Yakov. I don't know you or your abilities. Who has appointed you as general over us?"

Hoshea took an immediate dislike to the man's haughty expression and words. He leapt to his feet. "I'm not trying to set myself up as general over you, fool. I'm merely trying to point out a need I see to men able to meet that need."

Before the two men could advance on each other with sword and spear, others leapt up to intervene. One said, "Brothers, let us not fight on this day of going forth in freedom. Hoshea, your thoughts have merit and your ideas should be implemented among all our tribes. However, you should not seem to be imposing your will on us. We are free men now."

The younger man replied hotly, "Do what you will. I'm only trying to show the need and suggest a solution. We must have men conditioned and ready to fight when we get to the land of promise." He sat again.

The man turned to the spear wielder. "Perez, we are, as I said, free men now and must not let another gain mastery over us. On the other hand, Hoshea ben Nun speaks well from his time of service to the general of the troops at Memphis. We will do well to listen to his ideas."

The large man nodded his head and hefted his spear back to the rear of the assembly. The speaker sat and addressed Hoshea. "Do you have other ideas for us?"

"No, I have not fully thought things out. I would welcome other ideas."

Another man, who had a bow and quiver at his side, spoke up. "Someone should speak to the elders and carriers of weapons of the other tribes about these ideas."

"Good thought," Hoshea said. "Would you be willing to do that?"

The man looked abashed. "I only wished to give the idea."

Perez raised his hand in the back. "I'll do it."

Hoshea responded, "I thank you," but he didn't like the smirk he saw on the man's face.

The next time Hoshea met with Moses to discuss plans for feeding and bivouacking so many people, the prophet turned to him. "It was good to see the men of Israel march out of Egypt in formations. We need to continue the formations as much as possible."

Moses stroked his beard. "Someone said he had the idea that we keep men in battle dress along the sides of the route to guard against wild animals and other dangers…What's wrong?"

Hoshea's face had darkened. "Was this someone a large man with a spear?"

When the prophet nodded, Hoshea continued, "Another man suggested this at a meeting of armed men. Perez ben Yakov of the tribe of Judah said he would relay the idea to tribal leaders. He didn't say he would claim the idea as his own."

As they marched along the Road to Shur, the tribes approached a *migdol*, a fortified tower that stood as a guard post for Pharaoh's army. That night, the pillar of Yahweh burned like fire over the camp to light it. Perez strode through the camp toward Moses' tent. He entered and stood outside the seated tribal leaders, leaning on his spear.

Moses paused in addressing the men seated before him and looked up. "What shall I do for you?"

Perez pushed his way to the front of the listeners and thrust the bronze head of his spear into the ground. "I wish to lead a troop of men against the *migdol* ahead. I have two thousand men ready to go with me to capture the tower. Two of my men spied out the situation. They say the tower is lightly manned and could easily be captured."

The pleasant look left the prophet's face and his aide scowled. Moses asked, "Why would we want to capture one of Pharaoh's *migdols*?"

Perez said, "We could put men in the tower ourselves and guard the road until the tribes are well beyond the border of Canaan."

Moses shook his head. "No. For one thing, we don't know how close behind Pharaoh is with his chariots. We'd be caught between two trained forces. For another, we're turning south to go deep into the desert."

Everyone present murmured and looked intently at the old man. Hoshea spoke up.

"My lord, the Road to Shur is the shortest route to the promised land. Why are we turning away?"

The prophet waved his hand toward the walls of the tent. "Are these former slaves ready to take on the armies of Canaan? Are they ready to defend themselves against Pharaoh's army, which is surely coming after us?"

Several of the men sitting about cried out in fear.

Onlookers voiced objections. Perez jerked his spear out of the ground and held it at ready position.

"My men will defend us."

Hoshea eyed the spearman. "What training have your men had in fighting battles?"

Perez sneered, "I have drilled them in how I handle my weapon of choice."

Hoshea asked, "What about shields? How will you defend against archers' arrows and slugs from slings?"

The big man blinked then gritted his teeth. "Get them close to my spearmen and we'll deal with them."

Hoshea shook his head. "They would stay at a distance and slaughter you."

Moses raised his hand to interrupt.

"Yahweh doesn't want us to merely march into Canaan to bring judgment on the people there. He wants to make of our tribes a nation under His rule, His own people under suzerainty treaty with Him. When He knows we will follow His laws, then He will drive out the Canaanites before us and give us the land He promised to our ancestors."

Perez again jabbed the point of his spear onto the ground. "So, we're just going to turn away and wander into the desert? That's absurd!"

Moses straightened in his seated position. "Yahweh has ordered it."

Perez jerked up his weapon, turned, and stalked out of the tent.

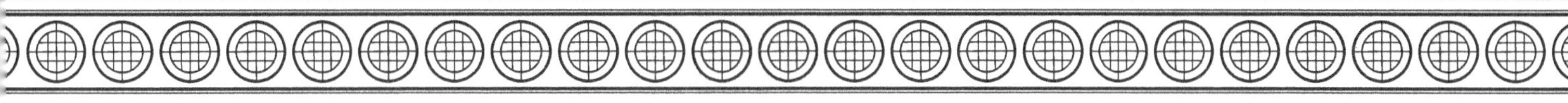

CHAPTER 10

Crossing The Sea of Reeds

Thus, the tribes traveled from Succoth to Etham to Pi Hahiroth, but turned off the Road to Shur, the direct route to Canaan. Instead they followed a road from the small fortress to the Sea of Reeds. As they traveled, the huge pillar of smoke led them along the route. During the day the people could see mostly dark smoke but at night bright fire shone from its depths to light the whole camp.

Armed men patrolled the sides of the main company, keeping a lookout for wild animals and other dangers. The tribe of Rueben sent scouts ahead to clear the way of hazards and to find watering holes and level places to camp overnight. Benjamin set a rear-guard against the possibility Pharaoh would send an army to recapture the fleeing Hebrews. Finally they came to the shore of the Sea of Reeds.

⸎

"Enter, my lord Moses," Adah welcomed the prophet at the entrance of Hoshea's tent. "My husband is within, changing as befits this occasion."

The young woman was dressed in linen and other finery from Egypt. She bade the old man to sit on a fine rug with pillows placed about for reclining. She offered him water in a silver cup– one she had loathed cleaning until it was taken from her master's kitchen.

Hoshea came out from behind the inner curtain of the tent, dressed in new finery. A wide, purple cloth girdled his waist and held a light blue robe closed over a cleanly bright, knee-length tunic. A white head cloth covered his long, dark hair.

He bowed to his guest and smiled as he sat next to the prophet. "I am honored, my lord, that you accepted my invitation to dine with us this evening." He turned to his wife. "Adah, you may serve the meal."

The young woman ducked behind the curtain and returned with a large, shallow cooking pot containing a lamb stew. This she set between the bent knees of the two men. She went back inside and returned with a second pot piled with rounds of flat bread. This she set in front of her husband.

Hoshea took up a loaf, tore it in half, and handed a piece to his guest. Moses accepted it, scooped up a bit of stew, and took a bite. He crooned, "Wonderful!"

Adah beamed and sat to eat with the men.

Her husband said, "I heard a wondrous sight was part of Yahweh's call on you as our deliverer." He waited with an expectant look at their guest.

The prophet set his bowl aside with a bit of a frown and folded his hands in his lap. "The wonder is that Yahweh chose me in the first place."

He studied his listeners. "Have you heard why I came to know the Wilderness and herded flocks around Mt. Sinai? No?"

His face took on a grim look. "When I was half my age now, I was a prince in the court of Pharaoh. I had been raised by His Majesty's daughter though I had been born a Hebrew.

"Certain Egyptians learned of my low birth and never let me forget it. Despite my high station. One day I saw one of them beating another Hebrew and I killed him. Rumors flew through the court and I fled for my life.

"I joined Jethro the Midianite, married one of his daughters, and became a shepherd. It was while tending the flock on Sinai that I saw a bush on fire that was not burning up. When I climbed up to examine it, Yahweh called me, a murderer, to this mission." He shook his head in wonder.

Hoshea gaped at him, his food forgotten in his lap. That his hero had done such an evil astounded him.

The prophet gave him a bemused look and picked up his bowl. "It's obvious Yahweh has forgiven me. He called me to this great work despite what I did."

Hoshea took a deep breath and nodded, returning to his meal. "Does bringing us out of Egypt complete your mission?"

"Certainly not! Yahweh wants to turn Israel from a family of tribes into a kingdom under His rule. Then He will lead us into Canaan and give us that land as He promised our ancestors. We are to be His special people before the whole world."

The evening darkened and the pillar of cloud gradually glowed with fire. This illuminated the whole camp except under the dark goat hair tents and awnings.

Adah lit a couple lamps to brighten where they sat under their awning then frowned when a youth ran up.

"Moses," he gasped out, his hands on his knees.

"Go away," the young woman commanded with a scowl.

"Adah!" her husband admonished, "it's got to be important."

The prophet gestured the boy to take his time. "Take deep breaths then speak your news."

The boy drew heavily on the muggy air off the Sea of Reeds. Finally, he stood and pointed toward Egypt.

"Chariots of Pharaoh's army have been seen approaching. My leader says they look to be bedding down for the night but will surely be upon us in the morning."

Hosea quickly handed Moses a linen cloth with which to wipe his beard and hands then helped the old man to his feet. The younger man hustled into the tent.

Moses turned to Adah who had risen to her feet. "Thank you, my dear, for an enjoyable meal. The food was delicious and the conversation pleasant."

"I only wish," she replied, "my lord could have finished the evening with us."

Hoshea returned with his *khopesh* stuck into his belt. He hustled past his wife after the retreating prophet. They hurried to Benjamin's area. In the distance, they could see a wall of shields stuck into the ground. Beyond the wall shone the light of hundreds of fires.

Hoshea snapped his fingers. "A shield wall. I knew I was forgetting something."

Moses looked at him. "Yahweh is a shield wall around His people to protect them from their enemies."

A large group of men with various weapons gathered around them to look at the Egyptian camp. Hoshea raised his voice. "Who is the leader here?"

A middle-aged man stepped in front of him and the prophet, carrying a sword. "I am Nagid ben Chazaiah of the tribe of Benjamin. We stand ready, my lord Moses, to defend against the Egyptians attacking us from behind."

Hoshea looked at the scrawny group of men and their haphazard arrangement and mix of weapons and shook his head. "Nagid, you may be willing but you don't look ready to fight. Why don't you form your men into a fighting unit?"

The middle-aged man sputtered, "How dare you? The elders of Benjamin have entrusted me with the leadership of the rearguard. We have practiced with our weapons every day since leaving Succoth."

"Fine," Hoshea said, meaning it wasn't. "What do you know of the enemy forces? How many are there? How are they positioned? How do you intend to attack them?"

Before the leader could respond, Moses laid a hand on his aide's shoulder. "There will be no need to gather that information or attack the Egyptians. Stand and see how Yahweh fights for you."

As the prophet turned away, Nagid pointed with a gasp. Moses and Hoshea looked up to see the bottom of the pillar of fire rising high over the camp. All those around them turned their heads and bodies as the pillar passed slowly overhead. It settled between the two camps. Light continued to illuminate the Israelite side but the Egyptian campfires could still be seen in darkness.

Moses said, "We might as well get some sleep. Nothing will be happening tonight." He turned away and headed in the direction of Levi's camp.

Hoshea scurried to join him. "My lord, wouldn't it be prudent to set a guard to keep an eye on our enemies?"

The prophet stopped and pondered. "My heart says there is no need with Yahweh standing between our camps. However, it is always prudent to be alert to guard the flock against the predations of wild beasts." Then he strode off again.

Hoshea returned back to the Benjaminites. "Moses has agreed you should set sentries to guard against the enemy. Please inform me if anything unusual happens during the night." With that, he turned and ran after the prophet.

In the morning, Hoshea rose early, dressed, and took up his sword. He left the tent to perform his ablutions then headed for the Benjaminite camp. It was still dark enough for the pillar of fire to light the way.

When he arrived at the first post, he found the sentry huddled on the ground, sleeping. The young Ephraimite drew his sword, raised it, then kicked the sentry in the side.

As the young man scrambled to his feet, Hoshea roared, "You fool, if I were an Egyptian, your head would be on the ground instead of your shoulders and your wife would be under my body! How dare you sleep on sentry duty?"

The man dropped to his knees and clasped his hands together. "Forgive me, master. I am a dog and do not deserve to live but I ask mercy for my sin."

Hoshea lowered his sword. "I am not your master but go to your leader while I take over your post. Tell him what you have done then tell him I wish to speak with him here."

The man rose quickly and scurried off. Meanwhile, Hoshea turned to examine the Egyptian camp in the growing daylight. In the distance, he could see men moving or sitting about their fires. In the center area, a knot of men stood by a large, splendid tent, looking his way.

Some time later when the sun was fully up, Hoshea turned at the approach of Nagid and the man who had been on sentry duty. The middle-aged leader strode right up to the shorter man and leaned over him.

"Who are you, Ephraimite, that you threaten my son with death and his wife with rape?"

Hoshea pushed him away and pointed at the miscreant. "I care not whether he is your son. I found him here on the ground, fast asleep. I didn't threaten him. I pointed out that an Egyptian would have killed him then taken his wife.

"Now, why are you so slow to observe the enemy this morning? Pharaoh's men are already at breakfast and making ready to recapture us. What have you done this morning to prevent that?"

Before the leader could reply, pandemonium began back at camp. "Egyptians! They've come to kill us!" The noise of panic grew as people came from the camp to look across at the Egyptians.

Moses strode into their midst, his hands and staff raised for attention. "People of Israel, do not fear!"

But the people cried out, "Weren't the cemeteries large enough in Egypt so that you had to take us out here in the Wilderness to die? What have you done to us, taking us out of Egypt? Back in Egypt didn't we tell you this would happen? Didn't we tell you, 'Leave us alone here in Egypt— we're better off as slaves in Egypt than as corpses in the Wilderness'?"

Moses spoke to the people: "Don't be afraid. Keep your mouths shut! Stand firm and watch Yahweh do his work of salvation for you today. Take a good look at the Egyptians today for you are never going to see them again. Yahweh will fight the battle for you.

"Now, go pack your things, fold your tents, and be ready to move out. Yahweh, your God, will show His power over the Egyptians one more time. Then you will be utterly free of their slavery." Then the prophet turned and strode through the camp toward the Sea of Reeds.

Hoshea hurried to his tent to help Adah with packing their things. He found her huddled on the ground, wailing piteously.

"Why, O God, have You brought me out into this Wilderness to die? I was happy to live in the house of my master, eating scraps returned to the kitchen from the meals the family ate. I could look happily on the fine clothes the master's wife and daughter wore."

Adah looked up and spied her husband coming toward her. She held out her hands to him. "Hoshea, save me! I don't want to die!"

Her husband lifted her up and shook her lightly. "Stop this noise, woman. We are not going to die. Moses has said Yahweh will fight the Egyptians for us. Now, go pack our things and fold the tent. We must make ready to move on."

"Move on where," the young woman wailed. "If the Egyptians don't kill us, we'll drown in the Sea of Reeds."

"I don't know what Yahweh has in mind but we have been given instructions. We must do those things and wait to see what the Lord will do."

He turned her around and pushed her toward the tent.

Moses strode through the fearful shouting of the crowd to a rocky outcropping that protruded into the water. Climbing to the top, he lifted up his staff and held it over the water. Softly, a flow of air pushed against his back. Slowly it increased, becoming a gentle breeze. This grew into a wind that blew the prophet's beard and hair out before him and stirred the water below into chop. The wind became a mighty gale, pushing against the leaning figure of Moses and the water at his feet.

Slowly, the water level lowered before the prophet and rose high up on each side across the width of the Israelite camp. When he saw the seabed pale from the drying of the wind, Moses lowered his staff and turned to call to the people. "See the salvation of Yahweh! Go forth into the Sea of Reeds and cross to the other side! Your old life of slavery is over. Your new life as the people of Yahweh begins today!"

Hundreds of people stood, openmouthed, along the marshy edge of the sea. Seeing the prophet striding toward his tent, they all hurried off to pack.

Elizur son of Shedeur, elder of Reuben, led his tribe to the water's edge. He waved his hand forward and stepped out between the walls of water. All through the morning and into the afternoon, the people of Israel moved tribe-by-tribe into the path between the waters of the Sea of Reeds and climbed out again on the other side.

As they waited their turn with the tribe of Judah, Sarah sang a song of deliverance while Caleb played on his harp. They stopped to move out into the Sea of Reeds while other musicians continued to praise. The middle-aged couple began again as they walked across on the dry seabed.

When Adah saw the multitude of Israelites escaping across on dry land, she was overjoyed with relief. She left the wagon in Kenaz's care and joined a large group of children who raced back and forth from side to side. She plunged her hands deep into the walls of water and twirled around, flinging moisture about.

Fear and wonder filled the faces of the Israelites as they looked up and up the shimmering walls. Some of the elders held their tribes back until most of the path before them had cleared. Then they urged their people to hurry across. The people flung wide-eyed glimpses over their shoulders as they harried their flocks to scamper along.

Meanwhile, Pharaoh and his troops were thrown into confusion. No matter how they tried to approach the runaways, a towering darkness clouded their way. Again and again, Pharaoh urged his chariots forward. Always they were blocked and forced back. The water from the Sea of Reeds blew up and showered the ground, turning it into mud that mired the chariots wheels.

Suddenly, the darkness lifted and the Egyptians gaped in amazement. The last of the run-away slaves were climbing the bank out of the far end of a passageway between walls of water.

Bomani took one look and drove his chariot beside Pharaoh's. "Your Majesty," he begged, "do not pursue these people. Their god is mighty on their behalf. I fear disaster if you pursue them."

Hatred blazed from the relentless eyes of Pharaoh. "Speak not to me of fear, General. You are relieved of your command. Go you into the ranks and pursue those slaves!"

The general threw down his rod of authority. "Gladly will I go with my men to whatever fate befalls them. I require only that Your Majesty lead the way."

So saying, he thrust his spear into the driver of Pharaoh's chariot and killed him. Then he smote his spear across the horse's rump. As the chariot sprang forward with Pharaoh swinging his spear wildly, the general roared, "Forward after those slaves!"

Every chariot of the Egyptians plunged madly down between the piled up waters of the Sea of Reeds. On the other side, the rearguard of Benjamin, followed by Moses, climbed out of the seabed and turned to look back. They saw the whole body of Egyptian chariots on the dry seabed, charging full-speed after them.

Moses stretched out his staff and the whistling wind suddenly stilled. Starting on the far side, the walls of water roared together and onto the Egyptians. Braced against a final whoosh of wind, the Israelites watched in horror as broken pieces of chariots and the bodies of horses and Egyptians swirled within the maelstrom.

Then the eighty-year-old prophet of Yahweh turned with a mighty shout and began to dance around and chant.

> **I sing to Yahweh because He has gotten a great victory!**
> **He threw the chariot and its rider into the Sea of Reeds!**
> **Yahweh is my strength; He is the reason I sing**
> **Yahweh is the One who saved my life**
> **He is my God and I will praise Him**
> **He was my father's God and I will extol Him**
> **El Shaddai is a warrior; Yahweh is His name**
>
> **The chariots and Pharaoh's army Yahweh has hurled into the sea**
> **The best of Pharaoh's officers are drowned in the Sea of Reeds**
> **The deep waters have covered them**
> **In their armor, they sank like stones**
> **Your right hand, Yahweh, was awesome in its power**
> **Your right hand, O Lord, destroyed the enemy**
> **In the greatness of your majesty**
> **You threw down those who opposed you**
> **You unleashed your burning anger; it ate them up like straw**
> **By the blast of your nostrils the waters piled up**
> **The surging waters stood firm like a wall**
> **the deep waters congealed in the heart of the sea**

Then Miriam, the sister of Moses and Aaron, picked up a tambourine. She gathered other women about her– Sarah among them– and began to dance and sing.

> **I sing to Yahweh because He has gotten a great victory!**
> **He threw the chariot and its rider into the Sea of Reeds!**

Hunger, Thirst, and Amalekites

Israel marched in triumph from the Sea of Reeds south along the western horn of the Red Sea. At first, they followed the pasture lands where their ancestors used to graze their flocks during the Nile's flood season. These soon gave way to rocky hills and desert mountains.

Meanwhile, the supplies of unleavened bread gave out. The closer the Israelites came to the Wilderness of Sin, the scarcer became game to hunt and the people began to worry.

Adah whined as she plunked a bowl of unleavened bread scraps in front of Hoshea. He had returned from hunting empty-handed and grim.

She said, "That's the last of it. It won't feed the both of us."

Hoshea looked at her and chose the largest piece then slid the bowl toward her. "Here, you take the rest."

His wife grabbed up the bowl and devoured the remains. She rubbed her belly. "I'm still hungry. Why can't we kill a goat or something?"

Hoshea shook his head. "Those we have are to start our flocks when we get to the land promised to us. Besides, Moses hasn't said what we are to use to sacrifice to Yahweh."

He held out a hand to reassure her. "Yahweh will provide. You'll see."

Adah frowned and rubbed her stomach.

∞∞∞∞∞∞∞∞∞∞∞∞∞∞∞∞∞

A mob of people gathered in front of the tent of Moses, generally muttering and sometimes yelling.

The prophet came out and spoke mildly, "What can I do for you?"

The people were offended by his unruffled attitude. "We have no food and our children are hungry! Did you bring us out to this desert to starve us? We were content in Egypt with our pots of meat and leeks."

Moses gaped at them. "Why are you complaining? Yahweh knows what you need. Ask Him for your food." He grew stern. "Where is your trust in Him?"

The people merely scowled and muttered.

Again, Hoshea was astonished at the people's complaints. They had just witnessed God's destruction of their enemies- the Egyptian army of chariots. Why were they complaining?

Meanwhile, Moses lowered his head in prayer. Yahweh answered,

I will rain down bread from Heaven for you. The people are to go out each day and gather enough for that day. In this way I will test them and see whether they will follow my instructions. On the sixth day they are to prepare what they bring in, and that is to be twice as much as they gather on the other days.

So Moses and Aaron said to all the Israelites, "In the evening you will know that it was Yahweh who brought you out of Egypt, and in the morning you will see the glory of Yahweh, because He has heard your grumbling against

Him. You will know that it was Yahweh when He gives you meat to eat in the evening and all the bread you want in the morning, because He has heard your grumbling against Him."

That evening, quail were blown in by a strong wind to carpet the ground. The Israelites scooped them up, wrung their necks, and prepared to feast. The next morning, white flakes covered the ground like frost. The people examined handfuls of it, perplexed.

"What is it?"

Moses said, "This is the bread of Heaven. Get baskets and gather as much as you can eat. Take only enough for today. Bake what you want or boil what you will. Do not save any for tomorrow."

Adah gleefully pulled out a large basket and gathered double-handfuls of the manna. She laughed as she watched it flow between her hands into the basket.

After lugging the heavy load back to their tent, she filled the pot half full of manna and filled the rest with water. This she set on the cooking fire to boil.

The young woman sat with the basket beside her and began to press the flakes together then flatten them into thick slabs like dough. These she laid on the cooking bowl and browned them on both sides.

Adah checked the boiling pot and found it about two-thirds full of a thin gruel. She decided to let it cook.

Before returning to making more baked bread, she hesitated then sought out a smaller basket with a snug lid. She filled this with some of the flakes and stored it away.

When Hoshea returned with his sling but no game, she showed him the baked bread and the manna she had boiled as thick as oatmeal.

He sat and said, "I hear we have Yahweh to thank for this big meal."

Adah frowned. She'd worked hard at preparing it.

Hoshea took a bite of bread and closed his eyes. He chewed slowly and swallowed then smiled. "Adah, this is wonderful!"

He picked up his bowl of pottage and took a bite. Again, he chewed with pleasure. "Adah, this is wonderful! This is the best I've ever eaten!"

She smiled at that. Between them they cleaned out the pot and ate all the cakes.

Hoshea looked around. "Is that all? I could eat more."

His wife widened her eyes at him. "You want more? But you ate so much!"

"It was delicious!" he patted his belly. "And I'm not full yet. Is there more?"

Adah thought of the manna she'd stored away but shook her head. "That's it." She hid her face by bending to pick up the eating bowls.

∞∞∞∞∞∞∞∞∞∞∞∞

Thinking of Caleb's slender build and her own petite frame, Sarah took a smaller basket to gather manna. She studied its sticky texture. It was white like coriander seed. She put a pinch of it in her mouth. It tasted like wafers made with honey.

Back in the tent, she decided to simply boil it in water and see what happened. When Caleb returned, she set two large cups between them. Each was full of a thick, hot gruel that smelled delicious.

Caleb picked up his and examined the contents. "Interesting." He looked around. "Is this all you gathered?"

Sarah shrugged. "This is what it boiled down to."

They drank and licked their lips. Caleb said, "I saw some women patting the stuff into flat rounds for baking. Maybe you could try that tomorrow."

Sarah looked surprised. "You think we'll get more of this tomorrow?"

"Yes. Moses said to gather it six days but not on the seventh. What you gather on the sixth day will last over the day of rest."

Sarah nodded and finished her drink. She watched Caleb drain his and set his cup down. "Did you have enough?"

Her husband gave a delicate burp. "I did. Thank you." Sarah nodded, pleased. "Tomorrow I'll try making breads of various thicknesses to see how they turn out."

Early the next morning, Hoshea got up to use the latrine. It puzzled him to pass several tents from which came a foul stench. He returned to his own tent to find his wife wailing beside a basket full of a slimy, smelly mess. Maggots crawled over its surface.

"Adah, what is this?" Then he knew. "Adah, you saved some manna from yesterday, didn't you?"

His harsh tone made her look up and scurry away from the anger in his face. He grabbed her shoulders, lifted, and shook her.

"You saved some yesterday, didn't you? Why?"

"I remembered how hungry I was the day before. I wanted to make sure we'd have some for today."

He let her crumble to the floor of the tent. "You disobeyed the instruction to not save any! On top of that, you lied to me! I should beat you for that!"

Hoshea wrinkled his nose. "Instead, I'm just going to make you carry this… stuff…to the latrine. And I will go after today's portion."

"It'll drip all over my clothes!" Adah gagged at the idea.

"That's your punishment. Now, get that stuff out of here!" He picked up the large basket from the day before and left.

When he returned and set the day's manna to boiling, the wonderful smell overcame the stench of the leftover mess. Adah came in wearing different clothes.

Hoshea said, "Where are your soiled clothes?"

She scowled and gestured. "I left them outside to air."

He said, "Let's try something. Spread them out in here."

"They'll stink up the place again!"

He asked, "What do you smell now?"

Adah sniffed and smiled. "It smells good!"

Hoshea grinned. "I put today's manna on to boil and the smell banished the stench of yesterday's mess. Let's see what it does for your clothes."

Adah hurried outside.

Three days later, the clan leaders went among the manna gatherers. They said, "Today is the sixth day. Remember to gather more manna today and store half of it for tomorrow. Do not go out looking tomorrow; it is the rest day."

Someone called out, "What if it goes bad again?"

"Moses says it won't. Don't go out tomorrow."

When the people complained they had only manna to eat, Yahweh sent a glut of quail and they became sick from overeating. From that day, except on the Sabbath, the manna did not fail to cover the ground and the quail did not stop falling into the camp until the tribes finally entered the land of Canaan.

After several weeks, the tribes turned east and came to Rephidim in a broad valley between high walls of rock. In the middle of Hoshea's discussions with the prophet, he and Moses heard growing murmurs, shouts, and outcries. The younger man went out of the tent to investigate.

Men from various tribes stood outside the tent, their hands clenched and anger in their eyes.

Hoshea planted himself in front of the opening to the tent and folded his arms across his chest. "What do you want? You're disturbing the prophet's work."

"Step aside, Hoshi," an older man ordered, "we want to talk to Moses."

The prophet stepped out of the tent and laid a hand on his aide's shoulder. "It's alright, Hoshea." He knew how much the younger man hated the child's form of his name.

Moses lifted his staff to advance on the crowd. When they stepped back, he halted and leaned on his rod of authority. "How can I help you?"

The gentleness of his voice startled those who had heard the stories of his confrontations with Pharaoh. They also remembered the prophet's powerful call for deliverance on one side of the Sea of Reeds and his shouts of triumph on the other side.

The spokesman lifted his shoulders and hitched up his broad leather belt. "You have dragged us out into this desert where there is no water and now our families and livestock are dying of thirst. It would have been better to leave us in Egypt." Murmurs of assent supported his words.

Moses bowed his head against his staff and closed his eyes. At first, the crowd waited in quiet then, as the prophet continued his contemplation, they began to murmur again. Cries of "What's he waiting for?" and "Make him hurry; we're dying here!" caused Hoshea to retreat to the tent for his *khopesh*.

When he reappeared, Moses was calling for various leaders of the people. After they had assembled, Moses strode forth and led them to a huge boulder partially embedded in the mountain.

The prophet turned to face the leaders and the rest of the crowd. "Behold, Yahweh has heard your cries against Him in this place of quarreling and testing of His care for you and He is gracious to provide." He turned, raised his staff, and struck the boulder. Out of a crack, a trickle then a stream gushed forth. The water ran through the middle of camp and people hurried out with leather buckets and bowls to capture the flood.

Animals rushed toward the stream until Hoshea forced their owners to water them downstream from the camp. He also demanded the owners clean up the animals' droppings and carry them beyond the camp boundaries.

∽∽∽∽∽∽∽∽∽∽∽∽∽∽∽∽

Soon afterwards, the descendants of Amelak attacked the outskirts of the camp, shooting arrows from astride the backs of camels. Perez ben Yakov lifted a heavy spear over his head and cried, "To me, men of Judah! To me! Let us go fight these accursed marauders!" He turned and led a group of men with spears and swords toward the place of attack. The large man stood in the way of the camels and swung his lance back and forth against the enemy.

Meanwhile, Hoshea grabbed his sword and shield off their place inside his tent and ran up the side of a nearby hill. He watched the men in flowing headdresses and white robes ride their camels, shooting arrows at knots of men with heavy lances. When the Israelites ran in panic, the Amalekites picked them off individually.

Looking back toward camp, he saw groups of men milling around, undirected. He flew down the hill, calling out to them. "I need men with shields! Come with me!"

Glad of instructions, a bunch of Israelites lifted their shields and followed at a trot. Near the front, Hoshea gestured right and left. "Spread out before the spear men and protect them from the arrows."

The shields became a wall of wood and leather between the Israelites and their opponents. Perez knocked aside the man who tried to protect him and continued to use his lance against any Amalekite whose camel came within reach. Then an arrow pierced his arm and he could no longer hold the heavy spear. The large man scurried for the shelter of the shields.

By this time, dusk had arrived and the camel warriors retreated. Soon the Israelites saw campfires spring up in the distance. As he watched, men and some womenfolk sorted the wounded from the dead of the thirty or so bodies strewn across the ground. Hoshea spotted Moses also watching and strode over to salute in the manner of Pharaoh's guards.

"My lord, they'll be back tomorrow."

The prophet peered at him. "Yes, they will. You did well, calling those shield men to cover the others."

The young man snorted. "They were stupid, going up against archers like that without protection. I also noticed that those who stood firm together survived better than those who ran as individuals."

Moses nodded, watching the younger man. "And what would you have done differently?"

Hoshea told him.

The prophet nodded again. "Tonight I want you to organize the fighting men as you have said." He gestured to the hill that held the huge boulder. A stream of water continued to flow through the middle of camp.

"Tomorrow I will stand on yonder hill and raise my staff to Yahweh as you fight the Amalekites."

The young man saluted again and hurried away.

Early the next morning, Hoshea stood before the assembled men. He explained the plan for battle then looked at them proudly. "Some of you will die today. Be encouraged. You will die fighting Yahweh's battle. You will die fighting for your families and friends.

"You have shields in front of you. You may not die as long as you face the enemy. You will be exposed to death if you turn and run.

"Remember, Moses is on the hill, supporting us before Yahweh. Trust in Yahweh and in His might. Stand your ground and you will win. Advance when ordered and you will win. Retreat in good order to regroup only when ordered and you will win."

Hoshea raised his sword. "Men of Israel, are we Yahweh's chosen?"

A roar of assent filled the air.

"Then we will win, by God!"

The former slaves turned and moved toward their positions. The archers and slingers stepped out in front and prepared their missiles. Across the field they saw the Amalekites, seated on their camels, bows and arrows ready. They looked to the hill and saw Moses, his staff raised high in the air.

"Archers! Slingers! Get ready!" Hoshea's order rang clearly through the air. Archers nocked their arrows while slingers dropped stones into the pouches of their slings.

The Amalekites charged forward on their camels. When Hoshea estimated they were close enough, he called, "Loose your missiles!"

Arrows and stones flew through the air and dropped targets among the enemy. More volleys dropped more Amalekites until the camels were almost among the archers and slingers. The unprotected men fled back toward those Israelites who had shields.

Hoshea grimaced at his mistake. "Israel! Protect those men!" He glanced toward Moses' hill and saw him standing with his arms hanging tiredly, Aaron and Hur at his side.

The Amalekites regrouped and charged again. The man on the hill had lowered his arms and this time the shield wall wavered and broke. Then the camel riders picked off individuals as they fled. Again the warriors retreated to regroup.

On the hill Moses tightened his hands around his staff and thrust it skyward. The Israelites rallied and renewed their efforts against the enemy.

Again and again, the Amalekites assaulted the Israelites and were met with slugs, arrows, and shields. Whenever the man on the hill held up his staff, they could not prevail. When he lowered it from fatigue, they gained the upper hand.

Israelites with spears pushed forward among the white robes of the Amalekites, slashing wildly. Soon they were surrounded and driven under the camel hooves.

Hoshea screamed at their rash action. The warlord roared along the battle line. "Israel, retreat!" He fell back slowly with the men around him until the Amalekites let them go. He looked and saw the prophet again tiredly dangling his arms. "Come on, Moses," he muttered. "We need your help here."

On the hill, Aaron and Hur hurried toward a large rock and levered it out of the ground. They rolled it toward their brother. They seated him and held his arms up with the staff.

At the rally point, Hoshea gathered the company leaders together.

"We have got to work together in this fight. Put the swords in front with shields and tell them to keep in line. Put the spears right behind them so they can thrust over the swordsmen's shoulders. Get any archers and slingers that are left to stand behind the lines and loose their missiles over the men's heads."

Perez of Judah lifted his hand. "Hoshea, someone should stay behind the lines and coordinate the battle."

The warlord caught his breath. He saw the wisdom of the idea but didn't want to step back from leading his men forward.

Perez went on, "I'm volunteering to coordinate."

Hoshea shook his head at that. A glance at the hill showed Moses seated on a large rock and his companions holding up his arms.

"No," the younger man sighed. "I must lead from behind. I'll have someone take my place at Ephraim's front."

Perez scowled and stalked away, jabbing his spear into the ground with each step.

Israel again spread out along the battlefield. When the camels came this time, the arrows and stones flew from behind the front line and felled many of the enemy. When the two lines met, swords slashed as one while spears jabbed from behind.

Slowly the Israelites pressed the enemy back. Hoshea turned and saw Aaron and Hur holding up the arms of Moses. Fear overcame the Amalekites. By this time, most of their camels were dead so they broke formation and ran.

Seeing this, Hoshea let out a cry. "Yahweh be praised! The day is ours! After them, Israel! Destroy the enemies of Yahweh!"

The Israelites cast aside their cumbersome shields, lifted their sickle-swords, or hefted their spears. They leapt forward and surged after the Amalekites. By the time night fell, the enemy was completely overwhelmed and defeated.

The next morning, Moses built an altar on the hill overlooking the battle and sacrificed a thank offering. He turned to the people and cried out, "Let this altar be known as Yahweh Our Banner, for hands were lifted up to the throne of Yahweh."

Like most of the Israelite men, Caleb had not contributed to the battle, content to let those fight who were willing. He did, however, join in the roar of praise from the throats of the Israelites surrounding him. "Praise be to Yahweh our Helper!" He marveled at the ebb and flow of the battle as Moses raised and lowered his hands.

After worshiping Yahweh, the prophet said to Hoshea, "Now, take up your pen and write down the story. Yahweh wants an account for the people of Israel to remember because He is determined to completely wipe the very memory of Amalek off the face of the Earth."

Part 3

Establishing a Nation

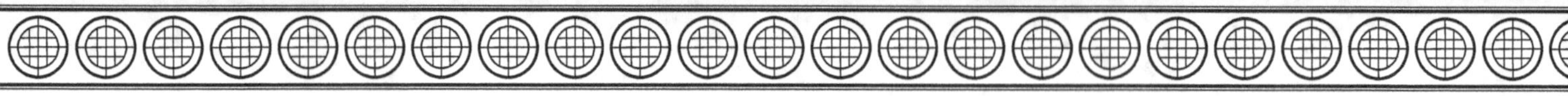

CHAPTER 12

The Character of Hoshea and Caleb

From Rephidim, the pillar of smoke and fire led the Israelites through valleys and mountain passes to the Desert of Sinai.

Hoshea awoke in the dark to the sound of Adah vomiting outside the tent. He listened as she plodded back inside and poured water into a cup. In a few minutes, she slipped behind the curtain and lowered herself slowly to the sleeping rug.

The young man reached around her waist to draw her close. "Are you well, wife?"

She groaned and shook her head. Hoshea squeezed with his arm to comfort her and kissed her neck. At the touch of his morning stiffness, Adah pulled away.

"Please. Not this morning, Hoshea. I feel awful."

Feeling misunderstood and rebuffed, her husband rolled away and began to dress.

Adah pleaded, "Hoshea, please don't be angry at me."

He looked at her with a scowl. He didn't understand why she pulled away from his comforting.

The military leader shook his head and pulled on his sandals. "I'm going around the edge of the camp to check on the guards. I'll want to eat when I return."

With that, he stepped outside the curtain and picked up his small water skin. He adjusted his sword in his girdle and jogged to Ephraim's latrine area. There he performed his ablutions, including rinsing his hands from the water skin.

The rugged hills to the east were gray from the shadow of the sun behind them. The clear sky darkened from blue above the hills through shades of gray to the western horizon. The morning star glowed bright high in the east while the red wandering star shone in the west.

The dim light revealed dusty earth and rock hills, mostly barren of shrubs. There were no trees. High overhead, a vulture circled the camp, looking for scorpions or rodents as they scuttled across the young man's path.

Hoshea saw none of it. His head down, he scowled in thought. *Why did she push me away? All I wanted to do was comfort her– not have my way with her. Didn't she realize I wouldn't bother her when she felt so ill?*

So childish! Running from one side to the other, sticking her hand into the wall of water. Crying when she doesn't get something pretty and frivolous.

Yahweh God! She even wanted to go back to the bondage of Egypt!

As he approached the edge of the camp, Hoshea looked up and saw the lit faces and still-dark backs of men clustered around a campfire. His jaw set, he changed direction. Moments later, he pushed his way among them.

"Why are you men gathered around this fire? You're supposed to be spread out along the edge of the camp! Some dangerous animal– even an enemy– could sneak in, kill you all, and attack people you're supposed to protect!"

Some of them dropped their heads. Others glared at the young man and gripped their spears. One man spoke in anger. "We been watching!"

He pointed over the fire toward the next sentry fire in the distance. "I been watching that way."

He indicated the men across the fire and tossed a thumb over his shoulder. "They been watching behind me."

"Is that so?" Hoshea crossed his arms over his barrel chest. "Then how is it I just walked out between here and that fire…" He pointed over the man's shoulder. "…and in again on that side…" He tossed a thumb behind himself. "…and no one challenged me?"

He drew his sword. "I could have killed several of you before you noticed."

He thrust the weapon back inside his waistband and waved his hands to both sides. "Now get out there and do your jobs!"

The men muttered obscenities but dispersed. The young man just shook his head at their obstinacy.

Hoshea returned to the tent where Adah dragged about tearing bits of meat from the previous night's quail. These she heated and seasoned in her curved cooking pan. Soon, she lifted the pan from the fire and placed it on the ground next to a small stack of manna bread baked on the curved surface of another pan inverted over the fire.

The young man sat cross-legged before the pan of meat and motioned his wife to sit and eat with him. Together they gathered the meat with folds of the bread and stuffed them into their mouths.

Throughout the meal, Adah remained silent. Hoshea eyed her then shrugged. He decided to not berate her for her sullenness. Instead he thought through training plans for the day.

〜〜〜〜〜〜〜〜〜〜〜〜〜

Caleb shook his head as he watched men with spears, sickle-swords, and shields practice against each other. He had no desire to learn combat. His desire was to sing songs to Yahweh and to learn His ways. He took up his harp and went to the tent of Moses.

The prophet looked up from talking with the elders seated before him. "What can I do for you?"

"My lord, Moses, I am Caleb ben Jephunneh the Kenizzite. I travel with the tribe of Judah. I have been faithful to El Shaddai since my childhood in Canaan. I was sold into slavery in Egypt and have now joined your great exodus to return to my family's lands.

"I wish to learn the ways of Yahweh. I would also like to offer my music training to lead the worship of Yahweh."

The prophet studied the middle-aged man and his red-gray hair. He had heard Caleb singing and playing his harp for Judah during the marching. He knew the man was good. He glanced at Aaron who sat nearby then shook his head.

"The Lord has appointed the Levites to provide for His worship. There are plenty of them who can sing and play."

Caleb lowered his eyes and thinned his lips. He raised his eyes again. "Might I at least offer to teach what I've learned about music? Please do not try to prevent me from making music to Yahweh. I could not bear that."

"Well said!" Moses laughed as he clapped his hands together. He turned to his brother. "Aaron, I'm sure you can find a place among your musicians for one who cannot keep from worshiping the Lord."

The prophet's brother smiled and nodded his head. "I hear you have created some songs of your own."

"Yes, my lord," Caleb sighed his relief. He looked at Moses again. "My lord, Moses, how can I learn from you more about Yahweh?"

The prophet thoughtfully scratched at his neck through his white beard. "Well, I don't know. I want to gather all the stories of our ancestors and how Elohim made all things, about the flood that covered the whole land, and such things. I will write them down and talk with Aaron and his sons and grandsons about what they reveal about Yahweh."

He looked at Caleb. "Maybe you could join our discussions. We will talk about how He wants us to live. Then I will write the laws of Yahweh for our people."

Caleb grinned. "I would love that! I know many songs my people sing about El Shaddai. I would offer these."

Moses said, "That would be good."

So Caleb joined in the discussions with the descendants of Levi, his graying red hair nodding among their darker heads. He shared stories of his ancestors among the Midianites and songs they sang and songs he himself created.

Caleb and Sarah also became popular entertainers among the families of his clan. He occasionally told of his injuries and the effects on his life in Egypt and how Yahweh healed him during the Passover meal.

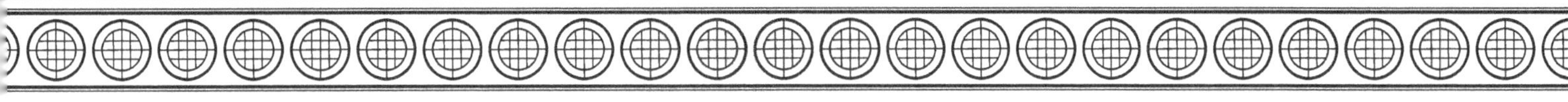

CHAPTER 13

Epiphany on Sinai

Three months after leaving Egypt, Moses sent the scouts of Reuben ahead the short distance to Mt. Sinai. He instructed them to string extra boundary ropes across the base of the mountain.

He said, "Yahweh commands,

Be careful that you do not approach the mountain or touch the foot of it. Whoever touches the mountain is to be put to death.'

Soon after their arrival at Sinai, Moses said to the elders, "Yahweh has called me to go up the mountain to hear His word. He has brought your tribes out of bondage in Egypt. Now, He wants to make you into a nation under His rule. Prepare yourselves and your people to make a suzerainty treaty with Yahweh."

The elders nodded and rose to talk with the people. At the appointed time, all the men of Israel gathered at the foot of Sinai. Moses lifted his hands and called out, "Men of Israel, listen to what Yahweh, your God, has declared."

You have seen what I did to Egypt and how I carried you on eagles' wings and brought you to Me. If you will listen

obediently to what I say and keep My covenant, out of all peoples you'll be My special treasure. The whole Earth is Mine to choose from, but you are special: a kingdom of priests, a holy nation.

As the prophet spoke, a wave of apprehension passed through the people. It seemed to them as though the mountain behind Moses loomed over them and a powerful presence looked down upon them. The Israelites all responded together, "We will do everything Yahweh has said."

Moses said, "So be it. Return to your tents."

As he walked back toward his own tent, the prophet said to Hoshea, "Prepare yourself tonight. In the morning, you will be with me when I go up the mountain to Yahweh."

"My lord?" A big smile lit the young man's face. Then he went pale. "Me? Why do you want me?"

"You're my aide. I may need you. If I am overcome by Yahweh's presence, I will need you to get me away." The prophet peered at Hoshea. "You must keep watch in case I die."

The young man stumbled a moment. "My lord!"

Moses clapped him on the shoulder. "You'll do fine. Now, go. Do not lie with your wife and do not eat in the morning. Before dawn, wash yourself completely and put on your finest clothes. Then return here, ready to go up with me."

Hoshea saluted and left for his tent. In the early morning, he returned dressed in a fresh loincloth, his finest tunic, and a brightly colored robe, belted with a white sash. He wore a white cloth on his head, held by glossy, black ropes.

Moses wore a dark robe over his white tunic. His white hair shone from a fresh washing. He handed Hoshea a large scroll and writing tools. Then he picked up his staff and led the way to the boundary of the mountain.

The two men climbed up the mountainside and disappeared into a heavy mist. When Hoshea put his hand to the prophet's back to support him, the older man merely looked back and grinned then pulled ahead.

Late in the afternoon, they neared the summit, pushed through a narrow defile to the mouth of a cave. Inside they found large rocks suitable for seats and working surfaces. Both men pushed the rocks into a semblance of a workspace and sat to catch their breaths.

After a time, Hoshea opened the blank scroll at its beginning and set out the writing tools. He looked at Moses who sat with his eyes closed and lips moving without sound.

The young man yawned and shook his head to clear it of a wave of sleepiness. He closed his eyes and nearly drifted off. Then he remembered Moses' words about staying alert to watch over the prophet. Hoshea jerked himself awake, still heavy with fatigue.

His mentor had moved to stand at the opening of the cave. A bright light silhouetted the prophet. As Hoshea watched, the older man lowered himself to lie on the floor. The aide quickly followed his action.

Again, he struggled with sleepiness. Excited over this trip, he hadn't slept much the night before. Now, drowsiness tempted him to close his eyes again for a nap. Hoshea balled his fists and beat the dust of the cave floor.

No! I will not sleep! In his mind, he cried out, *Lord, help me!*

A figure stepped out of the brightness outside and over the prone figure of Moses. It motioned for Hoshea to rise, which he did. He flinched when he saw his body still lying on the floor.

He looked at the figure, which wore a white robe trimmed and girded with gold. A white turban crowned its head. Bright light shone from a face framed by white hair and beard. One hand held a bright sickle-sword, which the figure raised in salute then set aside.

Hoshea gave his own salute. "My Lord?"

"Be at peace, my son. I have chosen you to lead these people into the land I promised them. And I will bring you into all that you desire."

"All, my Lord?" He thought of the many things he wished were true. That his wife cared for him more than for all the silly things she wanted from him. That people gave more heed to his suggestions and instructions. That they were already in the land of promise.

The figure spread his hands. "What do you want more than anything?"

Hoshea's mind raced through the whole of his present life and the people he knew. "My Lord, I wish more than anything to be loved."

"My son, to be loved by flesh and blood, one must first love and sacrifice for them." The figure opened his arms. "To be loved by Me, one need do nothing." He smiled. "Come to Me and it will be easier to see how very much I love you."

Hoshea stepped toward the figure and felt himself enfolded in a powerful sense of love and joy. He reveled in the feeling until a hand shook his shoulder. He opened his eyes and rolled over to see Moses kneeling over him.

The prophet smiled. "I perceive that you, too, have encountered Yahweh. Tell me about it." He helped his aide up and onto a rock seat.

After Hoshea's tale, Moses stroked his beard. "Interesting. Most people would say you are highly favored by such an encounter but the Lord wishes all to so encounter Him.

"Now," he said, turning to the workspace. "Write as I speak the laws of Yahweh for His people."

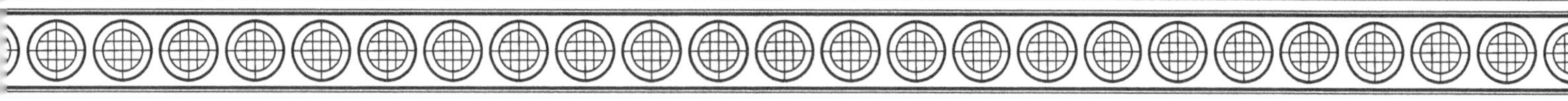

CHAPTER 14

The Golden Calf

Moses stayed on the mountain with Yahweh for forty days though Hoshea went up and down several times. The young man stayed with the prophet through the final several days of fasting.

Meanwhile, the people grumbled. "Where is Moses? He said he would lead us to Canaan. Where is Yahweh that we might worship Him?"

Calling for gifts of gold to sculpt, Aaron made the image of a calf for the people to worship according to the prevailing culture. He said, "Rise up, O Israel! Here is Yahweh who brought you out of Egypt!"

Men ran throughout the camp with news of the image. Sarah had readied herself for a special welcome to bed for Caleb. Dressed in the filmy scarves in which she used to dance, her hair flowing freely down her back, the still-beautiful woman grabbed up her tambourine and hastened to the middle of the camp. She joined other women in dancing around the statue and letting men grab scarves from her outfit.

Caleb, waiting at the foot of the mountain for word of Moses, heard the sound of the revelry. He hurried back, arriving in time to see people coupling on the ground and a man wrest the last, transparent scarf from over Sarah's breasts. Caleb pounded his fist into the man's face, grabbed his wife, and hustled her toward the tents of Judah.

"Caleb! You're hurting me!" Sarah pulled against his grip on her arm.

The middle-aged man turned and yanked her to him. "I haven't even begun to hurt you," he hissed. "Do you have any idea what you've done?"

Sarah's eyes went wide at a rage she had never seen before in her quiet husband. She stumbled behind him to her brother's tent.

"Perez! Perez, are you in there?"

The door flap moved aside and the big man stepped outside. His eyes narrowed at the sight of Sarah's clothing and Caleb's face. "What's happened?"

Caleb told him then said, "Will you keep her safe here? I don't want anyone coming to look for her."

Sarah's brother nodded and gestured his sister inside. He called out as Caleb strode off, "What will you do?"

The musician turned back, ready for a fight. "I don't know yet. Something must be done!" He resumed his march back toward the idol.

Carrying the large scroll and writing tools, Hoshea helped a famished Moses stumble down the mountain path, two small tablets of lapis lazuli in the prophet's hands. They held the suzerainty treaty between Yahweh and the Israelites.

The aide looked up. "I hear the sound of distress in the camp— maybe of combat."

Moses shook his head. "No. What you hear is the noise of revelry."

They came in sight of the camp and saw at its center the gold-covered statue of a calf. As Aaron stood before an altar at the calf's feet, his hands raised in worship, adults of all ages danced around the idol. Most were half-naked. Many others could be seen coupling on the ground.

Moses pointed toward some musicians who were playing before the idol. "Get me a trumpet."

Hoshea ran, grabbed an instrument away from its player, and raced back to the prophet who stood upon a boulder. Moses put the ram's horn to his lips and loosed a mighty blast. Heads jerked around, bodies stopped whirling, bare torsos leaned up from the ground.

Moses handed the trumpet to Hoshea and held aloft the two stone tablets. He roared, "You said you would do all that Yahweh commanded you! Yet when I come with the treaty the Lord would make with you His people, you have already broken the first two stipulations! This covenant is broken!"

He smashed the tablets against the boulder then raised his voice again. "Who is for Yahweh? Who will fight His battles? Come over to me!"

Several hundred men in the colors of the tribe of Levi stepped before Moses' rock. He looked at them. "All of you go through the camp and slay all those worshiping this…this idol." His derision shone. "Kill those openly engaging in…lewd behavior. Put to death all who are drunk. Go now!"

The Levites hurried to their tents and returned with swords and spears. They began to slit throats and open the bellies of dazed Israelites who huddled around the golden calf.

Several turned to advance on Aaron, who knelt before Moses, his arms wrapped protectively over his head.

The prophet stepped between his brother and their clansmen. He spread his arms to stop their advance.

"Not him. Yahweh has called him for a special purpose. He must live."

A man in front protested. "He led the idolatry. How could he be chosen by Yahweh?"

Moses raised his out-stretched arms in a shrug. "I understand your zeal. Aaron should die with those he led. However, Yahweh has chosen him."

The prophet paused and glowered at them. "You are my kinsmen, born of my tribe. I know you. You are not without guilt before Yahweh."

He waited while their protests died away. "Yahweh has chosen you, as well, for a special purpose. Now, go throughout the camp and kill those who joined in this revelry."

The Levites closed their gaping mouths, nodded, and glowered at Aaron. Lifting their *khopeshes* and spears, they trotted away. Some of them looked rather eager. Before they finished three thousand lay dead.

Moses turned to his brother. "What do you say for yourself?"

Aaron raised his hands, beseeching. "My lord, the people threw gold into a big fire and this calf rose up out of it." A note of accusation crept into his voice. "They made me lead them in worship since you weren't here."

"Bah!" The disbelief in the prophet's voice was plain.

∽∽∽∽∽∽∽∽∽∽∽∽∽∽∽∽

As the Levites spread out through the camp after fleeing idolaters, Caleb hurried to Perez's tent. He stopped at his own place to grab a large knife.

Inside his brother-in-law's residence, he told of Moses' return and the Levites' task. He looked at his wife the whole time. The woman shuddered and pulled close about her the cloak Perez's wife had loaned her.

A man's rough voice called from outside. "Where's the whore who danced before the idol? Bring her out and only she will die!"

Caleb stepped out to confront two large Levites with bloody swords in their hands. "This is Perez's tent. He does not give you permission to enter."

One of the Levites prodded Caleb's chest with the front edge of his weapon. "Bring out the whore who danced before the idol. You protect her at the risk of your own life."

"She is my wife; *I* will punish her." Caleb lifted the knife in his hand.

As the Levite raised his own sword to strike, the other one grabbed his arm. "This is the man who went among the dancers begging them to stop. He's on Yahweh's side."

The first Levite slowly lowered his sword to Caleb's chest. "I want to see the results of her punishment. Tomorrow!" He turned and strode away to look for more revelers.

Caleb collapsed to one knee and lowered his head onto his palm, his elbow on the other knee. "Oh, Yahweh! Thank you for Your mercy!"

He rose and entered the tent. To Perez he said, "Thank you for your protection."

The larger man shrugged. "She's my sister."

Caleb nodded and held out his hand to Sarah. "Come, wife. You and I have some business to do."

She moved behind her brother. "What will you do?"

Her husband drew himself straight and clenched his fist. "I will punish you far less than they would have." He tossed his head toward the doorway. "And far less than you deserve." Tears spilled down his face. "I love you and don't want to lose you." He held out his hand again.

Sarah bowed her head and stepped forward to grasp it. Before she could, he turned and led her out of the tent. With quick strides, Caleb stayed ahead of his wife and gestured her brusquely into their tent.

Inside, he sat on his cushion and stared up at her. When she removed the cloak, he averted his eyes. "Cover yourself, woman! Your nakedness is an affront to my eyes."

Sarah gasped and pulled the cloak back around herself. She didn't dare to sit.

Caleb's jaw muscle bunched as he stared at her.

"Your choice: do I beat you or not speak to you until you have sacrificed atonement before Yahweh?"

Sarah's mouth dropped open. "I-I don't know." She fell on her face before the angry man. "Caleb, please forgive me!"

"Why should I," he roared. "You almost got my wife killed! You chose to dance as you were forced to do in Egypt before you were freed from that bondage! You worshiped before a false image after all that Yahweh has done to free you and provide for you! And I would have died to keep those men from harming you!"

Tears flowed down the face of the woman as she lifted it to her husband. "Caleb, please! You said you love me! Please, forgive me!"

He drew in a deep breath and let it out. "I forgive you. I will never stop loving you."

As she began to smile, he scowled. "Which punishment do you choose?"

Sarah lowered her head to the carpet. In a low voice, she said, "Please, beat me. Don't ever not speak to me."

Caleb nodded and reached for the prod he used on the rumps and sides of their few sheep to keep them in the flock. Afterward, as the scarves lay in bloody rags across his wife's back, he said, "You will wear sackcloth against your skin and those rags over that until we have seen those Levites who sought you."

Sarah nodded and wept in pain and shame.

∽∽∽∽∽∽∽∽∽∽∽∽∽

Meanwhile, Moses pushed the idol into the fire then attacked it with a large mallet and reduced it to dust. With the help of Hoshea and others, he carried the dust to the stream and dumped it in. Then he forced the people to drink. "Here. Take your god into yourselves! Then go, all of you to your tents!"

Finally, the man of Yahweh took up his staff and strode to his own tent. Hoshea followed behind but did not enter with him. Instead, he sat, aghast at the turn of events.

Adah brought him food but he ignored it. From inside, the young man could hear the sobs of Moses as the prophet wept for the offense against Yahweh and for the people. Hoshea heard snatches of pleading.

"…Egyptians will say…will dishonor Your name…"

Finally, the voice within grew quiet.

Suzerainty Treaty with Yahweh

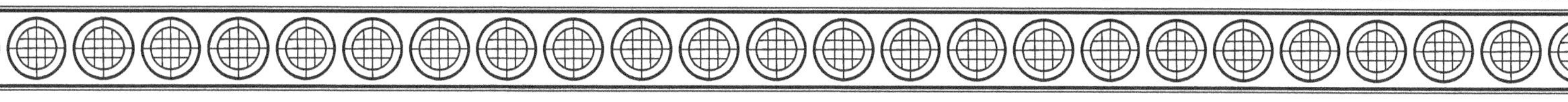

Moses cut two more hand-sized tablets as Yahweh commanded and returned up the mountain– this time without taking Hoshea. That young man continued drilling men in combat skills and waited with Aaron at the foot of the mountain.

Forty days later, they saw the prophet returning, the two tablets in his hands and a strange glow on his face. Aaron told Hoshea to run for the tribal leaders. Then he drew back, his hands, palm out, before his face.

Moses stopped and looked at his brother. "What is it?"
Aaron pointed. "Your face. It glows…brightly."
Moses grunted. "Gather the leaders at my tent."

As he strode off, he heard Aaron say, "I have sent Hoshea after them."

The next morning, Caleb heard the summons of the clan leader. "We are all to come before Moses' tent to hear the words of Yahweh."

The middle-aged man called to Sarah and led her with their neighbors to Judah's place of assembly. She leaned back against him with his arms about her waist as they waited for Moses to appear.

After a while, the prophet came out of his tent, followed by his brother. Aaron raised the two tablets above his head and called out, "People of Israel, hear the words of the treaty Yahweh has made with you, His people!"

The crowd grew quiet and Aaron continued.

I am Yahweh, your God, who brought you out of the land of Egypt, out of a life of slavery.

I do not want you to have any other gods; only Me. You must not make any carved gods of anything whatever, whether of things that fly or walk or swim. Do not bow down to them and do not serve them because I am Yahweh, your God. I am a jealous God, punishing the children for any sins their parents pass on to them to the third, even to the fourth generation of those who hate me. But I am unswervingly loyal to the thousands who love me and keep my commandments.

You must not use the name of Yahweh, your God, in oaths or silly banter.

You must observe the Sabbath day to keep it holy. Work six days and do everything you need to do. But the seventh day is a day of rest to Yahweh, your God. Do not do any work— not you, nor your son, nor your daughter, nor your servant, nor your maid, nor your animals, not even the foreign guest visiting in your town. For in six days God made Heaven, Earth, and Sea, and everything in them; He rested on the seventh day. Therefore Yahweh blessed the Sabbath day; He set it apart as a holy day.

You must honor your father and mother so that you will live a long time in the land that Yahweh, your God, is giving you.

Do not hate and bring death to another.

Do not be disloyal to your spouse or anyone else.

Do not take what is not yours.

Do not tell lies about your neighbor.

Do not lust after your neighbor's house or wife or servant or maid or ox or donkey. Don't set your heart on anything that is your neighbor's.

Aaron looked up from his reading of the stipulations. "These commands I have set before you are for your good. If you will follow them faithfully, Yahweh will bless you with prosperity and long life and will always be with you." He took up the large scroll to read the various laws meant to keep peace and justice among the individuals of the nation and to provide for the prosperity of all.

Along with the suzerainty covenant and various laws, Yahweh also gave to Moses instructions for the construction of the covenant container or ark; a tabernacle with a courtyard, holy space, and most holy place; an altar for the burning of sacrifices; and other furnishings. Despite his building of the golden calf, Yahweh chose Aaron as High Priest and the men of his clan as priests for Israel. Yahweh gave instructions for the sewing of priestly garments for these priests.

Then Moses said, "The time has come for the construction of the Tabernacle of Yahweh and of the covenant holder. Proclaim to your people that all who wish to give freely may contribute to these projects. We will need gold, silver and bronze; blue, purple and scarlet yarn and fine linen; goat hair; ram skins dyed red and another type of durable leather; acacia wood; olive oil for the light; spices for the anointing oil and for the fragrant incense; and onyx stones and other gems to be mounted on the ephod and breast piece. Yahweh has put His spirit on Bezalel son of Uri and Oholiab son of Ahisamak to plan and organize the work. Bring your offerings to them."

Over the next few days, as the Israelites gave freely of the gold, silver, and jewels they had taken from the Egyptians, Bezalel and Oholiab requisitioned the use of construction machines. They obtained looms, forges, and other manufacturing machines from the booty taken from the Egyptians. They organized those who offered time and skills to melt gold and prepare gems, to weave curtains and sew garments, to build frames and implements of worship. Hoshea's parents assembled their loom and brought out the threads and cloth they had brought out of Egypt.

Soon the carts set aside for the contributions overflowed. Bezalel and Oholiab sent word to Moses, saying, "Please, stop the people from giving. We can't deal with all of it."

When all was built and the priest's garments were sewn, Moses sacrificed a bull and two rams and splashed their blood over the Tabernacle, its furnishings and utensils, over Aaron and the priests, and over the people. He thus purified the whole nation of Israel before Yahweh and set them apart to live in Him.

Moses and Hoshea also reorganized the placement of the tribes within the camp. First, they had the military supplies removed to locations on the outside. This left the large middle area under the pillar of Yahweh open for the Tabernacle.

Next they established the Levite clans around the Tabernacle. The Kohathites were to care for the holy utensils to be used in making sacrifices. They were assigned the south side of the Tabernacle. The Gershonite clans were set to carry the curtains of the Tabernacle and were assigned to camp on its west side. The Merarites were to carry the frames of the Tabernacle, its crossbars, posts and bases, and other structural equipment. They camped north of the Tent.

Finally, Moses, Aaron, and Aaron's clan— that is, the high priest and the priests— camped east of the Tabernacle. Their work was to prepare the sacrifices brought by the Israelites and to offer them to Yahweh on behalf of the people.

The Israelite tribes surrounded the Levite clans at some distance from them. On the east, the tribes of Judah, Issachar, and Zebulun camped under the banner of Judah. To the south, Reuben, Simeon, and Gever camped under the banner of Reuben. Westward, Ephraim, Manasseh, and Benjamin camped under Ephraim's banner while Dan, Asher, and Naphtali camped under the banner of Dan to the north.

Whenever the pillar of Yahweh lifted from over the Tabernacle, the tribes packed up and set out in formation according to their placements. The divisions of Issachar, Judah, and Zebulun set out first, following the banner of Judah. With the Tabernacle taken down, the Gershonites and Merarites, who carried it, set out.

The tribes of Simeon, Reuben, and Gever went next under the standard of Reuben. Then the Kohathites set out, carrying the holy utensils.

The divisions of Manasseh, Ephraim, and Benjamin went next under the banner of Ephraim. Finally, as the rear guard for all the units, the tribes of Asher, Dan, Naphtali and set out under the standard of Dan.

At the place wherever the pillar stopped, the tribes resumed their placements around the Levites who surrounded the Tabernacle. This would be erected under the pillar of Yahweh.

∽∽∽∽∽∽∽∽∽∽∽∽∽∽

The new nation struggled to change the behaviors they had learned in Egypt to live by Yahweh's laws.

One Sabbath morning, a small crowd of men wearing the tribal colors of Issachar gathered in front of the tent of Moses and threw a bleeding man on the ground. The prophet looked out and turned to fetch his staff.

"What is the meaning of this?" He stooped to lift the man to his feet. The man's face was a mass of blood, two swollen eyes, and missing teeth.

Moses recognized the clan leader who stepped forward to speak. "This Sabbath-breaker was caught out of the camp, gathering wood. We have brought him to you for judgment."

The prophet studied the leader, who puffed up his chest with importance and grinned around at the crowd. "Did you have to beat him to get him here?"

"Uh, no." The clan leader looked abashed.

Moses turned to call to his wife. "Zipporah, would you bring water, please, to bathe this man's wounds?"

The crowd gasped in outrage. "This man should be stoned for working on the day of rest."

"Maybe so," Moses replied, "but you might treat him with kindness until then." He took in their tribal colors. "Issachar. Send for Nethanel son of Zuar." He raised his voice to the next tent. "Aaron!"

When the elder of Issachar arrived, he found his man being tended by the wife of Moses while the prophet and his brother sat nearby conferring. He knelt beside the seated man.

"What has happened? People tell me you were gathering wood."

"My lord," the man pleaded, his hands clasped before him, "I forgot to get wood yesterday. I needed only a few sticks to keep my fire going through the Sabbath."

The elder's face turned grave. "So you went out and gathered them."

The man raised his hands. "Please, forgive me, Nethanel. They were just a few."

Nethanel nodded. "We will hear what Moses says."

The man looked at the woman who gently bathed his wounds and grew hopeful.

The elder of Issachar stood, crossed over to the spiritual leaders of Israel, and sat before them. The other men sat in an arc further back.

The brothers looked up and Aaron rose to speak. "Yahweh has spoken. His holy day of rest was violated. Enough witnesses saw him. The man has confessed to his rebellion. Let him be taken outside the camp and stoned. All of Israel will gather to witness."

The man uttered a wail of despair. He lifted up his hands as Zipporah backed away. "Mercy!"

Aaron gave him a grave look and shook his head. "You broke a fundamental law of Yahweh. You will bear your guilt." He strode off toward the Tabernacle.

The crowd moved in to bind the man's hands and march him outside the camp.

In a flat, rocky space before a bare face of the mountain, the whole of Israel gathered. The man's feet were bound so that he lay against the rock face. Levites with swords and spears held the crowd back about ten paces while Moses and Aaron stood in the open space.

The high priest wore the tunic, robe, turban, and accessories of his office. He raised his hands to still the noisy people.

"Men of Israel, hear me!

"This man of Issachar went out on God's holy day of rest to gather wood. Yahweh has condemned him to be stoned."

The crowd's murmuring rose until he raised his hands again. "Let those who witnessed this rebellion come forward to cast the first stones. Let those of his family, his clan, then his tribe follow until his body is buried beneath a heap of rock."

The Levites parted to allow three men to step inside. These were followed by men wearing the colors of Issachar, Nethanel among them. They all stooped to pick up large stones.

The first three men looked at Aaron who nodded. One by one, they stepped to the bound man, lifted the stones above their heads, and smashed them down on the man's body. The others followed suit.

The man screamed and wailed until one man smashed his head with a large rock. In the silence that followed, men stepped forward to drop stones on the growing heap.

Finally Aaron called for them to stop. "Judgment is done. Return to your tents."

Some months later, a young man was caught coupling with his younger sister. When brought to Moses for judgment, he pleaded that many in Egypt even married their siblings.

Moses replied, "Those are the ways of people in bondage to false gods. It must not be so with God's people. He has forbidden it."

Both the man and his sister were taken to the wall of rock and stoned.

Another time, a muttering, scowling mob brought an angry youth to Moses. A man in Egyptian clothes and an Israelite woman followed behind, sobbing and supporting each other. The leader of the crowd pushed the boy, his hands bound behind his back, to the ground before the prophet.

He said, "This youth has become a trouble-maker since we passed through the waters of Yam Suph. This morning, he picked a fight with my brother, who was telling the story of our deliverance to some of the clan children. As they fought, this one cursed the name of Yahweh."

Onlookers standing around gasped at the blasphemy. Moses looked troubled as he knelt to help the youth to his feet.

"Why would you do such a thing before your God, who delivered you out of bondage in Egypt?"

The young man snorted. "Your murderous God killed my older brother. My father may have turned to follow Him for my mother's sake but my brother and I kept to Ra and Isis. When my father splashed lamb's blood on the doorway of our house, we refused to come inside. The next morning, Mahalalel was dead and we were being thrust out of our home."

The youth pressed his lips into an angry line. "I thought sure Pharaoh and the army would rescue me but your accursed Yahweh managed to drown them in the sea."

Moses slapped the youth for his continued blasphemy. "Yahweh is a good God, gracious to all who call on His name in faith. The night He passed over your father's house, the day He drowned Pharaoh and His army in the Sea of Reeds, He was bringing judgment against His enemies and the enemies of His people. You are wrong to blame Him for your brother's failure to seek the protection of the lamb's blood. You are wrong to curse His holy name."

Turning to the crowd, Moses said, "Stone him."

Part 4

Mission to Canaan

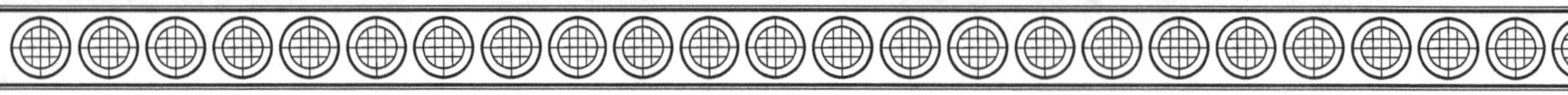

CHAPTER 16

Preparations for Departure

A year after the establishment of the covenant with Yahweh, Moses began the march toward the land of promise. As the new nation neared the Wilderness of Paran, Moses called together the elders of the twelve tribes. He said, "I am about to send spies into the land of promise. Select one man from each of your tribes for this mission. He must be a man of good reputation, a keen observer, and a leader in your tribe."

The elders returned to their tribal encampments and discussed Moses' instructions with their clan chieftains. The next day they returned to the tent of Moses, bringing with them the chosen twelve.

Hoshea ben Nun marched in beside Elishama, the elder of Ephraim. He looked around and recognized several of the others. One middle-aged man with graying red hair and beard sat with the elder of the tribe of Judah, quietly strumming a lyre.

Moses saw that Hoshea was included and nodded his approval.

He stood up before the seated men and welcomed them. "My brothers, we will be moving soon to conquer the land Yahweh promised to our ancestors.

You have been chosen by your elders to go throughout the land as spies. I want you to pair off and travel to six different areas of the country.

"Bring back samples of the produce. Get descriptions of the terrain. Learn what you can about fortifications. Talk to the people and hear what they say about Yahweh and His people."

Hoshea found himself paired with the red-haired man, Caleb ben Jephunneh of Judah. As they stood discussing the hill country they would be exploring, Moses joined them.

"My lord," the younger man saluted the prophet. "Why was I chosen for this mission? I had hoped to continue helping you with organizing the tribes and our movement into Canaan. Decisions need to be made about how to divide the land, where to set up the Tabernacle for Passover and other festivals, how the army is to be trained for combat."

Moses frowned at the young man. "I'm sure you have some good ideas for organizing things but those are decisions for the elders and Aaron's people. Your task right now is to bring us information about the hill country of the land."

"My lord," Hoshea protested, "I believe that, as my name declares, I'm destined to bring salvation to our people."

The prophet placed both hands on his staff and leaned his head against it. After a moment, he said, "Hoshea, your name says you are salvation. However, I now call you Joshua to remind you that Yahweh is the one who will save Israel."

The young man gaped at the prophet. "Now hold on! I like my name. I like the idea of being the salvation (Hoshea) of our people. I'm ready to fight to bring us into the land promised to us."

"I know," the prophet said. "I was the same way when I killed that Egyptian I told you about. It turns out *I* was not to be the deliverer of Israel. Yahweh worked through me to bring about their deliverance."

Moses watched the younger man relax the gritting of his teeth. He continued, "You may one day be a great leader in Israel but it will be Yahweh who saves (Jehoshua) them– even if through you."

The young man breathed deeply. "As you say, my lord." He stood erect and saluted again.

Moses turned to Caleb and shook his head. "I hope you can soften this pup's intensity."

The red-haired man grinned and nodded. He sobered. "I want to thank you for agreeing to our going to Hebron. It means a lot to me."

The prophet nodded his understanding. He led them to a small chest at the back of the tent. He opened it to reveal a hoard of gems and crafted jewelry.

Moses turned to the two spies. "I'm outfitting you two as jewel merchants. You'll want to take weapons for protection. As valuable as these gems are, they are only tools for your mission. I value your lives and your information more. Leave them behind if you must. Now, go and dress yourselves as Egyptians and may Yahweh give you success."

Caleb pawed through the jewelry with curiosity. He picked up a pair of earrings that side-by-side filled his flat hand. "These are interesting."

Each piece consisted of two concentric silver wire circles connected by crossed silver wire diameters. The inner circle sported two wires parallel to one diameter crossed by two wires parallel to the other, an altogether pleasing arrangement.

Back at their tent, Adah brightened when her husband told her to seek out Egyptian clothing for him. "We're going back?" She rubbed at her pregnant belly.

The young man sighed and shook his head. "Moses is sending me to spy out the land of promise. I'll be traveling for several weeks with a man from Judah." He paused. "And Moses has given me a new name. I am now Joshua."

"Hoshea, you can't! I may give birth before you return! Then what will I do? How am I supposed to live in the meantime?"

"Adah, calm down! You'll have people all around you to help out. I'll arrange for Mama and Abba to get manna and quail for you. If I'm not back before the baby is born, the midwives will help you. They'd do that best even if I were here.

"Now, go ask our neighbors for Egyptian clothes I can wear. They need to be good quality. I'm posing as a jewel merchant."

Adah jumped up with excitement. "Jewels? Oh, Hosea!" She wrapped her arms about her husband's neck.

The young woman murmured, "With jewels we can return to Egypt and set ourselves up in style."

Joshua seized her arms and pushed her away. "How dare you? Yahweh has said, 'You must not steal.' Besides, I'm never going back to that place! That would only mean a return to bondage."

Adah fled into the sleeping area of the tent and threw herself on their bed. Joshua strode in and found her sobbing and pounding the pillows. He smacked her once on the bottom and spoke sharply. "Stop this nonsense! Crying about it won't change anything and beating your fists is childish. Now, get up and bring me the clothes I asked for."

Adah spun to sit up. She glared at her husband. Through gritted teeth she declared, "You're mean."

"Yeah, well, just do what I tell you."

Adah huffed and stomped out of the tent.

That night, Caleb lay beside Sarah and talked about the mission. "I can't believe he gave me a sword! Like I know how to use it!" He shuddered and his wife clutched him tightly.

It still amazed her that Caleb no longer struggled to move his right arm and leg. Now, instead of merely strumming his lyre as they sang together, he was able to pluck the strings more creatively. He was even able to grasp the rope of a water bucket and fetch the heavy liquid.

She caressed that arm. "Caleb, you can swing a sword now. I'm sure you'll be able to learn how to use it properly."

He grunted noncommittally. He had noted Joshua's military manner. Maybe the Ephraimite would teach him.

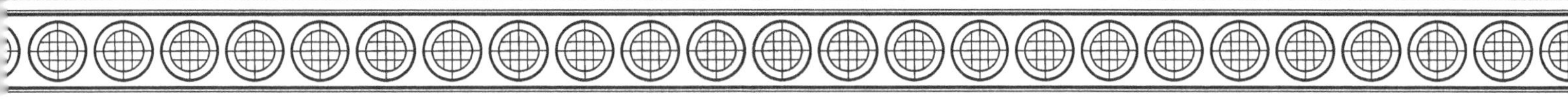

CHAPTER 17

Encounters in Beersheba

Midway through the day that they started out, Caleb was glad to stop for a meal. He sat on the ground, puffing and massaging sore legs, as he let Joshua set out the provisions.

The younger man looked at his companion and snorted. "You're not used to this, are you?"

Caleb shook his head. "I feel like an old man."

Joshua nodded and looked in the direction they were headed. "I've heard there's a caravansary a day and a half away. I wanted us to leave early today so we could get there before Sabbath. I thought we'd take it fast for today then more slowly tomorrow when we're weary."

"What's this 'we' stuff?" Caleb protested. "I'm weary already."

Joshua looked toward the donkey that carried the chest and their bags of provisions. "Didn't I see you pack a lyre?"

"Yes. So?"

"So, why don't you sing the song of Moses from the Sea of Reeds?"

"Hmm. Maybe I will," came the reply, "After we settle down for the night."

Caleb was surprised the next day to hear his companion humming the song as they traveled– and quite pleasantly at that. He nudged the young man. "I think you'd better not hum while people are around. You'll give yourself away."

Joshua grinned at him and raised his head to look about. Seeing no one, he raised a pleasant, tenor voice.

I will sing to the Lord for He is highly exalted
He has thrown the horse and its rider into the sea
The LORD is my strength and my song
He has become my salvation
This is my God, and I will praise Him
My father's God, and I will exalt Him.

The LORD is a warrior; Yahweh is His name
He threw Pharaoh's chariots and his army into the sea
The elite of his officers were drowned in the Sea of Reeds
The floods covered them; they sank to the depths like a stone.

"You seem to act like a soldier yourself," Caleb said. "What's your story?"

Joshua told him about the general of Pharaoh's troops who was his master. "At first, it distressed me to watch him endure much of the hard training he put his men through. I finally came to realize it made him tough enough to handle whatever happened in leading the troops."

The younger man eyed his companion. "So, what's your story? You told Moses how glad you were to take this trip."

Caleb laid his hand on the donkey's back and gazed toward their destination. After a moment he sighed. "Just as Joseph ben Jacob was unjustly sold into slavery by his brothers, my brother, Kenaz, and I suffered a similar fate. It's been twenty-three years since we were dragged away from our family home near Hebron."

"A-ah." Joshua suddenly understood. "That's why you asked that we be sent there."

Caleb tightened his jaw then his mouth relaxed into a grin.

"My father, Jephunneh the Kenizzite, was a coppersmith near Hebron. He did well, making household utensils; blades for farm implements; and, by adding tin, bronze weapons. My brothers and I worked with him, though I was much more interested in wandering the fields of the region and creating songs to El Shaddai.

He glanced at his companion. "You realize, I hope, that the descendants of Jacob are not the only ones to worship El Elyon."

Joshua nodded then shrugged his indifference.

Caleb caressed between the donkey's ears and grimaced. "My brothers, Esau and Kenaz, were good smiths but I never got the knack. Father would beat me for daydreaming, especially if I ruined the work because of it." He sighed. "Sometimes, I really hated sitting in the shop when I could be wandering the hills on such a clear day.

"One day, Anak entered the shop. He had with him several soldiers with drawn swords. He told Father he was accused of blaspheming the goddess, Qedesh. The shop was forfeit to the king and the family would be sold into slavery. Father protested and tried to fight so they killed him. My brothers and I were confined for a couple days until we were summoned before the king.

"Witnesses were produced to confirm the accusations and the king passed judgment. Esau, as the eldest son, would continue to work the shop. Anak had bought it on the promise to supply weapons for the king. Kenaz and I were to be sold into Egypt. Our mother and younger sister would join Anak's household as slaves.

"Kenaz and I were put to work in a supply depot, making weapons for the Egyptian army. He did well and was chosen to supervise and to do special projects. I was miserable and did poorly. I received many beatings.

"Once, when treated by the priests of the temple of Ra, one of them discovered my ability to sing and play instruments. He arranged my sale to the temple where I was put to work, playing for worship and festivals. I met Sarah, from the tribe of Judah, who danced and sang.

"The two of us were chosen along with others to tour the Egyptian countryside and provide entertainment for parties and festivals. We fell in love and got permission from the priests and from her brother Perez to marry. We were soon sold to the master of a troupe of entertainers.

"I was distressed to find she wasn't a virgin. She wouldn't tell me about her first lover. Then, during one party, we observed one young girl being pressured to go to bed with a guest. She pleaded to be left alone. She was at the point of being dragged away when Sarah offered herself in the girl's place.

"I was horrified. The master prevented me from stopping her so I went home. Sarah wouldn't explain when she got home but a few days later she said she was accustomed to being used while the girl was still a virgin. Therefore it was easier for her than it would have been for the girl."

The older man hung his head and sighed. "Not many days later, a gang of Egyptian young men invaded our home, looking for the Hebrew slut who gave her favors to any and all. I fought to defend Sarah but they struck me on the head. They raped her and left me for dead.

"She and our master nursed me back to life but I was crippled on my right side. My foot twisted so I became lame. My back hunched so I could no longer stand straight. My hand curled into a stiff claw and became nearly useless. Fortunately, I could still pluck at strings and sing.

"Then her brother Perez began to come around with food and such. He said I was no longer able to provide for his sister as a husband should so therefore he would. Then he took her to bed– and she went with him. I learned that Perez had raised Sarah after their parents' deaths and took payment. She had learned to accept the arrangement and felt obligated to resume after my injuries."

The middle-aged man sighed. "And so life continued until Moses came."

Joshua scowled. "I knew I didn't like that man. I would gladly give him his wish to fight the Egyptians or the Canaanites, unprepared as he is."

Caleb gaped at the younger man.

Joshua and Caleb approached Beersheba late in the afternoon as the sun neared the horizon. Joshua hurried the older man along lest they be caught on the Way to Shur after sunset and risk breaking the Sabbath.

They came at last to the caravansary south of town. Caleb stumbled to a halt and leaned against the donkey, breathing heavily. His companion, meanwhile, went to arrange a room.

In his Egyptian guise, the young man found the proprietor of the inn scurrying back and forth, seeing to the needs of various guests. Joshua stopped the man's headlong flight toward another group of customers and asked about a room.

The innkeeper looked him up and down and frowned then shrugged with indifference. "I have one small room at a distance from the Hittite guests." He named his price for overnight.

"That seems rather high for one night," Joshua protested. He named a much lower amount.

"You dress like a wealthy Egyptian and you must expect to pay. I could give you a room next to the Hittites but I don't think either of you would want that." He named a lower charge.

The spy pondered a moment. "You're right. I don't want us to be disturbed by such as those." He named a higher price he was willing to pay.

The innkeeper shook his head. "For two of you, eating all that food, and caring for what, one donkey?" Joshua nodded. "Then you must pay more." He gave a final price for one overnight stay.

Joshua beamed. "That is agreeable." He counted out double the price.

The innkeeper looked at the silver and frowned. "You mean to stay two nights?"

The young man nodded. "My companion is not hardened to this kind of travel and is very weary. We will take an extra day tomorrow to rest up."

The innkeeper scowled, feeling cheated by such a price for more than one night's stay. He put the silver away and turned to lead Joshua to the vacant room. He spoke as he walked.

"There is music and a couple of dancing girls every evening in the common room. If you wish one of them for overnight companionship, you talk with her about price."

"That will not be needed," the guest said stiffly. He looked into the room and wrinkled his nose. It smelled as though something had died and not been removed or that a chamber pot had spilled and not been cleaned up. He was sure the two narrow beds teemed with unpleasant creatures.

Joshua returned to tell Caleb and help unload the pack animal. They cleaned up the room as best they could then went down to the common room for supper.

They'd already decided to be cautious about eating what was served. They were delighted, however, in the fresh vegetables such as they hadn't seen in over a year and in mutton roasted on a spit over a fire.

As they ate, the two men listened to the conversations of other guests sitting around the large room. They heard stories of a young girl in Hebron who spoke the words of Qedesh to the people of that region.

"She's not so pretty," shared one man, dressed as a merchant. "Looks rather boyish. But the promises spoken are wondrous to hear and see fulfilled. She speaks of plentiful harvests and lucrative deals for oil and grain and wine. Qedesh requires only that one continue to worship her through the *kedeshah*, the temple prostitutes. That, of course, we are all glad to do," he concluded with a leer.

Caleb spoke up, "Does this not-pretty girl also act as a temple prostitute?"

"Oh, no. She's a bit young for that. Although," the man looked thoughtful, "she is nearing the age of womanhood. Maybe if Qedesh makes me very successful and I donate much to her temple, I will be chosen as her first worshiper through the girl." He rubbed his hands together at the prospect.

Joshua stood and reseated himself with his back to the merchant. The stiffness of his shoulders and the trembling of his hands showed his agitation.

A huge, Canaanite soldier in one corner guffawed. "I'm not surprised the Egyptian doesn't like your talk of deflowering young girls. The whole country has become a nation of effeminates. Look at how they let several tribes of slaves just walk away from them last year."

Joshua stood to face the soldier and laid his hand on the knife at his waist. Caleb jumped up and grabbed his companion's arm. "Easy, Bes. He doesn't know the whole story."

The older man turned to the listening assemblage. "You don't know how horrible it was in Egypt before the Israelite slaves left. Ten plagues were visited on the land because Pharaoh refused to heed the word of their god, Yahweh, to let His people go into the desert to make sacrifices. The blood, the frogs, the flies…" He shuddered dramatically.

The soldier asked the company, "Would you hear the story as I got it from my journey there?"

There was a chorus of assent so Caleb gave him a slight bow and pulled Joshua to an out-of-the-way seat.

"I am Ahiman, captain of the guards of the temple of Qedesh that you have been discussing…and yes, the oracle is a mere girl. Through her mouth, however, the goddess does speak as you have heard.

"Yes, the temple prostitutes are very beautiful. Many men come to worship through them and our city and the land around it are bountiful.

"My brother, Sheshai, who is high priest of the temple, is very powerful and knows many things. He is always seeking more knowledge of the gods and how to please them so they will continue their bounty.

"My brother had me go with him to the great temples of Ra and Osiris in Egypt to investigate the stories he heard of the god of the Israelites and how they abandoned Egypt and stole its wealth. He heard about the plagues of blood in the Nile and frogs and flies. There were stories of a great darkness and hail that burned. Locusts destroyed crops and boils sickened their cattle. But the worst was what the Israelites themselves did.

"Here was Egypt whose army had made a suzerainty treaty to be overlords of the Nubians. The so-called mightiest nation in the world allowed a bunch of Hebrew slaves to plunder their homes, kill their firstborn sons, and march away in triumph. When the Egyptian army set out to recapture the rabble, they got themselves caught in a flash flood and drowned."

The soldier chuckled. "I wasn't surprised. Just a few years ago, I was part of another diplomatic trip to the Pharaoh. I was not impressed by their army even then. When I sparred with one of their officers, I toyed with him for a bit. Then I showed him how real soldiers fight."

Joshua leapt to his feet. "I saw that fight! You humiliated him!" The young man advanced on the soldier and drew his knife, holding the blade downward. The soldier didn't even reach for his own weapon; he merely stood up and crossed his arms, looking bored.

Joshua lunged, stabbing down at the man's body. The soldier stepped aside, pushed Joshua's arm away, and shoved him into a man who had leapt up to get out of the way. The man pushed back, helping Joshua to whirl.

The Ephraimite slashed across his opponent's middle but the soldier stepped back and grabbed Joshua's wrist. He twisted it painfully then with his free hand stole the knife and pushed Joshua to the floor.

The young man rolled over but the soldier knelt to hold the knife to Joshua's throat. "So, now I've humiliated you, too. I could kill you without blame since you attacked me but I'd rather you lived with the humiliation. You can get your toy back from the innkeeper in the morning."

He stood, stuck the knife in his wide leather belt, and turned back to his corner.

Joshua took the hand Caleb offered him and climbed to his feet. "I have got to learn how to fight better."

His companion just shook his head. "That was foolish. Why did you risk everything in our trip?" He gathered up their eating gear and followed Joshua to their room.

"Was that the same way he handled your general?"

"Yes. I should have thought he would use the same tactic again." The young man grimaced, massaging his shoulder.

"Maybe that will teach you not to pick fights with armed soldiers. Why did you do it?"

"I was angry that he had humiliated my master with insults. I guess I wanted revenge."

"And you would have killed him if you could? That's murder! That breaks Yahweh's law!"

Joshua lowered his head. "Yes, you're right. I'll have to make sacrifice when I return."

They made their preparations and went to bed. The next morning, Caleb arranged for breakfast while Joshua headed for the outside privy.

Joshua noticed a lad about twelve years old sitting on the wall, observing travelers. He wore a knee-length, dirty-brown tunic, held at the waist by a length of twine. A filthy cloth covered a cap of stringy, brown hair and a narrow, girlish face. Dusty legs and feet ended in sandals.

As the man proceeded, the boy jumped to the ground.

"You're a Hebrew!"

Joshua finished and fixed his clothes then turned to him. "I'd rather you didn't tell anyone. Where can I wash my hands?"

The lad pointed toward a gate to the street beyond. "You'll find a well on the other side of that wall. Come on! I'll draw the water for you."

"Sure, why not?"

The boy ran ahead, the hem of his tunic flapping under the rope belt at his waist. He was hauling at the well rope when Joshua arrived.

As he rubbed his hands under the pouring water, the man asked, "So, what's your name?"

The kid got a look of apprehension on a face that was rather plain under a layer of dirt. He shrugged. "I'm Gever."

"Kid, eh? Mine's Joshua and my friend is Caleb. We're looking for someone who knows the area around Hebron."

The boy gasped and nearly dropped the water bucket. Joshua grabbed and set it squarely on the ledge of the well. "You know the area. Would you be willing to guide my partner and me?"

The boy clenched his fists and turned away slowly, a thoughtful scowl on his face.

He turned back. "Sure. But when you leave again, you take me with you. I'm looking for the people of El Shaddai."

Joshua held out his hand. "Agreed." After the boy shook it, he invited, "Come eat with us and tell us about the country we'll be visiting."

Inside the inn's main room, Joshua introduced the boy to Caleb. The older man blinked as his eyes swept over Gever then turned to Joshua. "I got us some breakfast." He gestured to a table that held cooked grains and fresh fruit.

Joshua sat and rubbed his hands together in anticipation then motioned Gever to sit beside him. He started a prayer of thanks to Yahweh when Caleb motioned him to stop.

"Remember, we're Egyptian."

The younger man closed his mouth and scowled. He relaxed when he remembered his former master's manner at meal times. Reaching for a slice of melon, he silently thanked the Lord for His provision.

All three of them dug into the meal, Gever watching the men as they obviously relished the food. These men acted as though they hadn't eaten such food for a while.

Halfway through the meal, Gever arose. "I need to use the midden." He scampered out the back.

Joshua explained his deal with the boy. "Then we're to take him back to camp with us."

Caleb glanced after the boy. "He looks like he'd be a good guide for the area."

Two soldiers walked in. One carried a large spear along with the *khopesh* in his belt. The other wore the clothes of a priest of Qedesh. They moved from table to table, obviously seeking information. Joshua watched their brusque manner in growing irritation.

"And who might you be?" The soldier jostled the young man's shoulder. Joshua leapt to his feet.

"Who do you think you are to speak to us like that?"

The soldier grabbed Joshua's shoulder and shoved him back onto his seat. "I'm one of the guards of the temple of Qedesh in Hebron. And I don't take trouble from Egyptians. Get it?"

"Bes," Caleb spoke in warning. He turned to the soldiers with a smile and spoke more soothingly. "Sir, we're simple merchants from Memphis, seeking a market for our wares in Canaan. Is Hebron a large town? It must be if it's home to a temple of the great goddess, Qedesh."

The soldier stepped back from the table. "Hebron boasts not only the temple but also the largest market in the hill country south of Jebu-salem."

Caleb clapped his hands once. "Wonderful! We'll have to stop there in our travels and try our luck."

The priest stepped forward. "Sar, the girl?"

"Hmm, yes." The guard turned back to the Israelites. "We're searching for a twelve-year-old slave girl who ran away from the temple seven days ago. Her master, the high priest of Qedesh, sent us to find her."

Joshua and Caleb looked at each other and shrugged. The older man said, "We have come by the road from Egypt so we haven't seen any run-away girl."

"So you say." The soldier moved a finger from Joshua to Caleb and back. "You will take any news you hear to the temple at Hebron. The high priest there values the slave girl highly and will pay well for her return."

Joshua crowed in delight, "Is that the way it is? She must be pretty."

"Not particularly," the soldier replied. "She's the mouthpiece of Qedesh during religious ceremonies."

He leaned into their faces. "Fail to help and you will do no trading in Hebron."

Joshua moved to stand again but Caleb's hand on his shoulder held him in place. The soldier merely stood, beckoned to his companion, and walked away.

"Of all the arrogant, self-satisfied, demanding…" Joshua spluttered.

Caleb looked at him. "Yes, I've observed that soldiers are like that."

The younger man scowled at him and began to clear their tableware. He turned to find Gever at his elbow. "Here, pack these away and meet us at the stable. We'll get the chest and other things. Then you can lead us through the hill country surrounding Hebron."

The boy nodded and hauled the sack of provisions toward the back door. The two men went up to their room.

CHAPTER 18

Training, Tricks, and Troublesome Dreams

On the Ridge Road north of Beersheba, Caleb brought out his harp and Joshua lifted his voice again to sing the triumph song of Moses.

> **Yahweh, Your right hand is glorious in power**
> **Yahweh, Your right hand shattered the enemy**
> **You overthrew Your adversaries**
> **by Your great majesty**
> **You unleashed Your burning wrath**
> **It consumed them like stubble**
> **The waters heaped up**
> **at the blast of Your nostrils**
> **The currents stood firm like a dam**
> **The watery depths congealed**
> **in the heart of the sea.**

The enemy said: "I will pursue
I will overtake, I will divide the spoil
My desire will be gratified at their expense
I will draw my sword; my hand will destroy them"
But You blew with Your breath
and the sea covered them
They sank like lead in the mighty waters.

Yahweh, who is like You among the gods?
Who is like You, glorious in holiness
revered with praises, performing wonders?
You stretched out Your right hand
and the Earth swallowed them.
You will lead the people You have redeemed
with Your faithful love
You will guide them to Your holy dwelling
with Your strength
When the peoples hear, they will shudder
Anguish will seize the inhabitants of Philistia
Then the chiefs of Edom will be terrified
Trembling will seize the leaders of Moab
The inhabitants of Canaan will panic
and terror and dread will fall on them
They will be as still as a stone
because of Your powerful arm
until Your people pass by, Yahweh
until the people whom You purchased pass by.

You will bring them in and plant them
on the mountain of Your possession, Yahweh
You have prepared the place for Your dwelling
Yahweh, Your hands have established the sanctuary
Yahweh will reign forever and ever!

Gever smiled at the younger man. "That was lovely. You must tell me the story of that crossing." He frowned. "But who is Yahweh? My mother told me stories of El Shaddai and His love for our people but never mentioned Yahweh."

Caleb patted the boy on the shoulder. "Since the days of Abraham, our forefathers have worshiped the Creator of the heavens and the earth by the name of El Shaddai or El Elyon. For four hundred years our people languished in Egypt until the God of our fathers sent Moses to deliver us. He said we were to call Him Yahweh, which means I Am."

The older man, younger man, and boy halted their donkey by the side of the Road to the East for rest and a meal. Joshua gaped at the richly decorated water skin Gever pulled out of his girdle.

He grabbed and shook it in the boy's face. "How did you come by this? I know I saw it in a merchant's belt last night!"

Caleb looked over at the glowering man and startled boy. He, too, recognized the water skin. "Gever?"

Gever glowered at Joshua and swiped at the object. "Gimme that!"

Joshua pulled it out of reach. "You stole it from that merchant, didn't you?"

"What of it? He had others and I didn't. Besides, this one's pretty."

"You little thief! Don't you know it's against Yahweh's law to steal?" Joshua rose to put the water skin away.

"So now, you're gonna steal it from me?" Gever stuck out a belligerent lip and stood with his fists on his hips.

"Joshua, may I?" Caleb gestured for possession of the water skin.

The younger man handed it to him, turned, and stalked away. Caleb motioned Gever to sit in front of him. He caressed the fine beadwork.

"When you lived in Hebron, did you take things that belonged to others?"

The boy nodded. "Mostly little things they wouldn't miss much. Pretty things."

The man nodded in understanding. "You must stop taking what doesn't belong to you. Yahweh has said, '**Do not take what is not yours**.' People have a right to keep what they make, earn, or buy for themselves."

"Even a rich merchant who has more than he needs when I need one for myself?"

"Even then. He likely bought it with money he earned. It belongs to him. You must not take it for yourself no matter how much you need it."

Gever pondered the ground between them and slowly shook his head. He looked up.

"You told me that when you left Egypt, you took the riches of the Egyptians."

Joshua stood up from where he'd been sitting. "Are you calling us thieves?"

Caleb gestured for the younger man to sit down and let him handle this. "First of all, Yahweh told us to ask the Egyptians. And they gave what they had. Secondly, they were paying us for the many years of slavery to them. We had earned those riches. Third, Joshua and I would have shared our water with you. There was no need to steal for yourself."

Gever looked at Joshua who nodded in confirmation. He looked back at Caleb and sighed.

"So, now what?"

Caleb looked at the water skin then handed it to the lad. "The merchant is long gone or I would have you return it to him. Since we have it, you might as well use it."

Joshua scowled at the boy's look of satisfaction.

The first night out from the caravansary, Caleb and Gever settled down in their bedrolls inside small tents that faced the small fire while Joshua stood the first watch. Nights were cold on the Road to the East. He studied the brilliant stars and quarter moon high overhead. Pacing around the perimeter of the fire, he noticed the boy shivered in a thin bedroll. The young man spread his own blanket over the lad and continued to pace.

As the moon approached the western horizon, Joshua was startled from watching the fire and missing Adah by a shrill scream. He hurried around to Gever who thrashed at his coverings as though struggling to get loose.

The boy yelled, "No! Let me go! Not the fire!"

Joshua shook his shoulder. "Gever! Wake up!"

The boy bolted upright and looked around with wide eyes. He collapsed against the young man and sobbed.

Concerned, Joshua looked at Caleb as he embraced the shuddering child. Caleb shrugged and reached for his harp. As Joshua rocked the child, the older man began to play and sing.

The one who lives under the protection of the Most High
dwells in the shadow of the Almighty.
I will say to Yahweh, "My refuge and my fortress
my God, in whom I trust."
He Himself will deliver you from the hunter's net
from the destructive plague.
He will cover you with His feathers
you will take refuge under His wings.
His faithfulness will be a protective shield.
You will not fear the terror of the night
the arrow that flies by day
the plague that stalks in darkness
or the pestilence that ravages at noon.
Though a thousand fall at your side

and ten thousand at your right hand
the pestilence will not reach you.
You will only see it with your eyes
and witness the punishment of the wicked.
Because you have made Yahweh your refuge
the Most High your dwelling place
no harm will come to you
no plague will come near your tent.
For He will give His angels orders concerning you
to protect you in all your ways.
They will support you with their hands
so that you will not strike your foot against a stone.
You will tread on the lion and the cobra.
You will trample the young lion and the serpent.
Because he is lovingly devoted to Me, I will deliver him
I will exalt him because he knows My name.
When he calls out to Me, I will answer him.
I will be with him in trouble.
I will rescue him and give him honor.
I will satisfy him with a long life and show him My salvation.

Gever calmed to whimpering and occasional shudders then lapsed again into sleep. Joshua lowered him back down into his sleeping roll and moved to sit beside his companion.

"What was that all about?"

Caleb shrugged and finished the song then set the harp aside. "Child's dream, maybe?"

"He seems kind of old to be having nightmares."

"I don't know. I was wakened from my own dream."

When Joshua raised his eyebrows, he went on.

"I saw myself on a high hill overlooking a flock of sheep being guarded by a ring of men around them. Moses sat on a prominent shepherd's perch. Among the sheep, I saw a young lion and lioness cub wrestling in mock battle.

"I held a harp, which I strummed as I sang a song of praise to Yahweh. I knew the music calmed the sheep. When the song ended, a deep voice behind me said, 'Thank you.'

"I turned to face a huge lion, lying in repose. The magnificent animal glanced at me while keeping an eye on the flock. It said, 'You are a faithful watchdog, My *kelev*. Keep up the good work.'

"Suddenly, the lion leapt up and looked out over the sheep. 'Jackals are coming! Protect my flock!'

"I turned and saw the beasts slinking toward the flock from all directions. I turned back to the lion. 'But Lord, I'm only a harpist and singer.'

"I raised my hands to show the instrument but in my hands I held a *khopesh*. The lion said again, 'Protect my flock!'

"I flew down the hill, yelling the alarm. I attacked the jackals in front of me. Then I awoke."

The musician chuckled. "Imagine! Me with a sword!"

Joshua looked at him sideways. "What do you think it means?"

The harpist stretched out his arms to show his ignorance. He picked up his harp. "I'm awake now. I can keep watch."

The young man nodded and yawned. He laid out his bedroll near Gever's so he could respond quickly if the boy cried out again. The young man pulled off his sandals, slid under his blanket beside the boy, and cuddled close for mutual warmth. He felt the same tenderness as toward his wife when she woke him with late-night whimpering. As he fell asleep, he wondered if that should bother him.

Some time later, Gever awoke and wondered at the unfamiliar weight across his chest and the lump against his lower back. He lifted the weight and saw

Joshua's limp hand and heard the man's snore. Gever jerked away until he felt the cold night air and slid back under the warm blanket, facing the man.

Joshua looked so at ease without his habitual frown when awake. He lay on his side, his ground arm extended out and the other hanging bent and limp across his stomach, the hand against the ground. Bent legs kept his torso from rolling onto his back or stomach.

Gever had never cuddled with his father, not knowing which of the Anakites the man was. Desire for a man's embrace motivated the youngster to slide his back against Joshua's chest and to pull his arm again across his belly. He smiled as he dropped off to sleep again.

Joshua awoke slowly, a small, warm body in his arms, the familiar smell of hair in his face. He slanted his head to kiss behind one small ear and pushed himself against the round buttocks.

"Hey!" Gever scrambled out of his arms and swiped at the spot behind his ear.

Joshua looked in horror at the boy then wiped his hands down his face and violently shook his head to clear the lingering confusion.

"I'm sorry. I thought you were Adah…my wife."

∞∞∞∞∞∞∞∞∞∞∞∞

Having left Yahweh's provision of manna and quail for the Israelites, Joshua felt the need to gather food whenever possible on their spy mission. Also knowing its military value, Joshua continued his practice with a sling as he had learned as a boy. On the Road to Hebron, he used it to bring down hares and other small animals to be eaten in the evening.

One evening, he returned to their camp. He cleaned and gutted two hares and spitted them on green sticks over the fire. Gever watched with fascination then pointed to the weapon in Joshua's belt.

"Show me how to use that thing."

Joshua lifted the straps. "This sling? Why?"

The boy gestured to the meat browning over the fire. "I saw lots of hares when I left Hebron but had no way to catch them."

Joshua nodded his understanding. He remembered the hunger in Gever's face when they first met and knew a boy of his age grew a lot in a few months.

"Sure." He beckoned to the boy. "Put your hand on my shoulder."

When he laid his arm along Gever's, Joshua's wrist rested on the boy's shoulder. "Your arm isn't too much shorter than mine. You'll be able to use my sling all right."

He reached to turn the spitted hares then looked at the boy. "Go find rocks from the size of your thumb to the size of your fist. I'll get you started after we eat."

Gever left and returned in a short time with his tunic above the rope bulging with rocks. They gave him an oddly feminine look.

By the time they had eaten, stars shown in the dark sky and the moon hung overhead. Joshua pawed through the pile of rocks and selected the largest. Stepping away from the fire and pulling out the sling, he beckoned to Gever to follow. "Bring a couple more of the larger stones."

"Stay outside the circle of the swing." He swung the empty sling around to demonstrate.

The man faced the boy. "There are basically two ways to use the sling. One is to lob it high and bring the stone down on the head of your target."

Joshua dropped the stone in the pocket of the weapon and swung it back and forth, testing its weight. He swung the stone up over his head, his elbow bent at his side. When it had nearly reached its height again, he released one strap and extended his arm. The stone gleamed in the firelight as it swooped high then plummeted at a considerable distance.

Facing the boy again, Joshua gathered the loose strap and held out his hand for another stone. Dropping it into the sling, he said, "The other way is to shoot straight at your target."

He swung the stone around above his head, let it fall to about shoulder height, swung again and cocked his hand near his ear, then extended his arm forward to release the stone. Gaining little height, the rock flew out a great distance as it fell to the ground.

Joshua turned to the boy whose mouth hung open, his eyes bright. The man grinned and handed over the sling.

"Here, you try it…without a stone first."

Gever whirled the sling and wrapped it around his head where the pocket smacked his nose. Joshua laughed and helped peel it off the boy's scowling face.

"I want you to lob stones first until your hand and wrist get the feel of the motion. Then you can shoot at targets. Like this." He took the empty sling and demonstrated again.

Before long, Gever succeeded in hurling larger and larger stones into the darkness. He turned to Joshua with a grin then grimaced at the ache in his hand and arm.

Joshua patted the other shoulder. "You did well. Come, let's go back to camp."

∞∞∞∞∞∞∞∞∞∞∞∞∞

Joshua sat up in the tent, following the mid-afternoon rest and pushed aside his cloak. After a stretch and a yawn, he slipped on his sandals and crawled out of the tent. He saw Gever seated with his back against a palm tree, his eyes closed. Caleb knelt near the stream, filling their water skins.

When Joshua stood and took a step, he felt a tug at the heel of his right sandal. He looked back and down and quickly whirled. A sinuous length with the markings of a desert viper jumped toward him. The young man drew his knife and slowly stepped back

When his right foot moved, the length slithered toward him. That proved to be too much. He turned and ran until something tripped him and threw him down.

Joshua turned his head cautiously and stared at the rope wrapped around his ankles. One end was knotted to look like a viper's head and markings were painted down its sinuous length. A long, slender thong led from the "head" to the heel of Joshua's sandal.

The sound of laughter reddened the young man's face. Caleb lay doubled over and holding his belly. Gever sat on the ground in much the same position.

Joshua cut the thong with his knife and gathered up the offending rope. He advanced on the boy as he coiled its length around his curled fingers.

The roar of his voice and the ire on his face caused Caleb to stop laughing and step in front of his partner. "Easy, Joshua. I know you're angry but no harm was done." He struggled to suppress a smirk. "You must admit it was pretty funny."

Joshua scowled at the older man then at the boy who cowered behind the man of Judah. "You little scamp! You better not let me catch you setting up another prank on me!"

Caleb turned the boy toward the tent. "Come on, kid. Let's put your energy to better use." He patted Gever's back and gestured for him to start packing up.

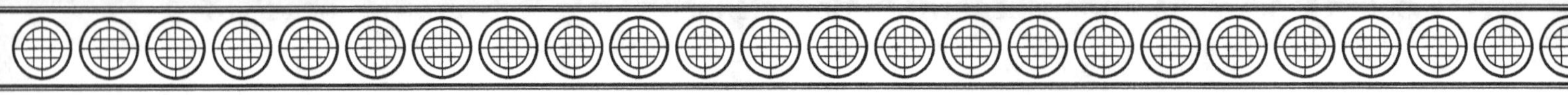

CHAPTER 19

Clashes of Will and Sword

As the two men plodded along beside the donkey, Joshua studied the terrain around them. He called ahead to Gever who trotted back to them.

The younger man waved his hand at their surroundings. "This is pretty flat country. How do soldiers fight around here?"

The kid shrugged. "I've seen soldiers practice in the hills around Hebron but not here."

"I hear they have chariots."

Gever frowned and looked away. "The Anakites drive chariots back and forth on the roads but they're no good in the fields and hills. Too many rocks and trees."

Joshua pressed him for more information but the boy shrugged and ran ahead.

Caleb looked at his companion. "You in a hurry to learn about Hebron?"

Joshua scowled after Gever then glanced at the older man. "We're on a spy mission. We need to gather information."

"We won't be in the area for a few days yet. Why don't you relax and enjoy the scenery." Caleb waved his own hands about. "The sun is shining. The birds are singing. Let's sing a song of God's Creation."

The younger man scowled. As Caleb began to play on the harp he'd pulled out of the bundle of his belongings, Joshua softened and began to hum along.

> **I love the Lord and all He has made.**
> **The land and sky, the lights in the heavens.**
> *Great is Yahweh and greatly to be praised!*
> **The forests and fields full of game**
> **The mountain streams full of fish**
> *Great is Yahweh and greatly to be praised!*
> **The orchards of fruit to fill root cellars**
> **The fields of grain to fill the barns**
> **The vines of grapes to overflow the wine vats**
> *Great is Yahweh and greatly to be praised!*
> **Oh, that people would praise the Lord**
> **for all His many bounties!**

Joshua sighed, "That was lovely."

Caleb smiled. "Yes, it was, wasn't it? Thank you."

They plodded on in silence with the donkey between them and Gever hopping around in front.

Caleb looked at his companion. "So, Joshua. What was it like for you in Egypt? I know your master commanded Pharaoh's troops."

Joshua stopped and looked at Caleb with compressed lips and clenched fists. He fought to push aside memories of indifferent parents and struggling to take care of himself. He had learned to ignore people and their irrelevant attitudes so he could get things done.

In a moment, he began to walk again.

The older man looked at him with concern. "Joshua? Are you all right?"

"I don't want to talk about Egypt. Things were too hard there."

"Yes, I know. We had it bad in the music troupe. The master was always pressing me to create songs for the festivals for their gods and for their parties. I wouldn't do it.

"My wife was a singer and dancer and very beautiful. I had to watch men take her off for private performances and there was nothing I could do about it."

He examined his right hand and slowly shook his head. "I was crippled trying to defend her against that gang of ruffians. I could still play the harp and lyre and sing but I couldn't do anything to defend her against abuse."

Caleb stopped talking and glanced at Joshua. The younger man had a pained look on his face.

"You didn't want to hear about that, did you."

Joshua shook his head. "It's bad enough remembering my own situation. What others went through…" He fell silent.

Caleb said, "I'm sorry. I didn't mean to upset you. I just wanted to make conversation to let us get to know each other."

Joshua waved a hand in abrupt dismissal. "Forget it. I don't want to talk about it."

Stung, Caleb paced along, his head down.

After a while, Joshua shook his head. "I'm sorry. I shouldn't stop you from sharing your story. It's just that I've had so much of my own grief."

Caleb sighed and looked at the road ahead. "The God of our fathers allowed his people to suffer so much before He delivered us. Makes me think of the story your family has about Joseph. I hear he had a harsh existence before El Shaddai raised him up to rule over Egypt."

Joshua nodded. "Yes. And that's what led to our living in Egypt in the first place." He shook his head in dismay.

Caleb said, "You don't see it, do you?"

Joshua looked at him astonished. "What?"

"After so many years of suffering, we too took control of the wealth of Egypt. We marched out in triumph as conquerors– not as runaway slaves. Because Yahweh is with us, we can hold our heads high and march into Canaan…and take over there."

Joshua inhaled sharply and lifted his head. He pulled out his *khopesh* and held it high. "Yes! By God, we will do it!" He danced forward, swinging the sword as if slicing through enemies…some of them high up.

He panted when he returned, his sword in his girdle again. "I can now see how my troubles have brought me to where I am now."

Caleb beamed at him. "Tell me."

As he walked, Joshua rested his hand on the donkey's neck and watched Gever pick up stones and sling them off to the side. The young man grimaced.

He gestured toward the youth. "I was rather younger than he is when my grandfather was killed. He had been the only person to pay attention to me, encourage my little games of sorting things and listening when I talked about better ways for people to do things."

He shook his head at the memories. "I usually had to yell at other people to get them to listen."

Joshua gave a little smile. "Grandfather didn't punish me when I fought the other boys to keep them from messing up my things.

"It was Grandfather who told me stories about our fathers and El Shaddai. I particularly liked the story of Abraham fighting the five kings who captured his nephew Lot." Joshua sighed. "It was Grandfather who said I would become a warrior for our people one day."

Caleb nodded his understanding. He saw his companion's face turn grim.

The young man continued, "The master's son– an older youth– joined the other boys one day in messing up my storage boxes. I fought them until the son started beating on me. I think he would have killed me except Grandfather struck him and got him off."

He sighed. "I recovered but Grandfather was beaten to death. I thought for years I was to blame for his death. Eventually, I realized the evil was in the Egyptians. Soon after I recovered, the general took me into his household and I eventually became his aide."

When they stopped near a spring for their midday food and rest, Joshua rummaged through the pack a couple times. Then he called out to Caleb.

"Where did you pack the cumin?"

Caleb looked up in surprise at the intensity in his companion's voice. "It should be there somewhere. I threw it into one of the sacks when I packed up this morning."

"You threw it in?" Joshua was plainly unhappy. "Why didn't you put it back where I had it on the left near the top? Then we could get at it more easily."

"You don't have to yell at me." Caleb beckoned. "Give me the pack; I'll look."

"I hope you find it in that mess you've made of the pack." Joshua stood and dropped it at his companion's feet then stalked off toward the spring. He knelt and splashed water onto his face.

Caleb watched him then looked at Gever. Tears trickled down the boy's face.

"Awk," the man said in irritation. "Come here, boy." He held out his arms.

Gever sprang into the comfort of his embrace and sobbed.

"There, there. This isn't something to cry over. We're just having a little disagreement. No one's really getting hurt."

Gever nodded and pulled away, wiping his eyes, his mouth set in disapproval. "Boys aren't supposed to cry."

"Who says," the man asked. "There are times I feel the need to cry out to El Shaddai over the difficulties of life. Your uncle used to cry a lot when he was your age."

"My uncle?" Gever's eyes widened in surprise.

"Yes. You are the very image of Kenaz ben Jephunneh the Kenizzite. I figure you are closely related."

The boy wiped his nose on the sleeve of his tunic. "My mother is Tivona bat Jephunneh." He lowered his eyes. "My father is one of the Anakites."

Caleb inhaled sharply. "So, they got to her, after all. I'm your uncle Caleb. Kenaz is back at the Israelite camp with our families. I'm glad to know you were looking for us."

Joshua strode up then and stood with his fists on his hips. "Did you find the cumin?"

"No. I was comforting Gever after you upset him with your yelling."

Joshua gritted his teeth. "That wasn't yelling. It wasn't nearly loud enough for that."

"It was certainly harsh enough to upset Gever."

Joshua just shook his head and reached for the pack. Caleb snatched it up and pawed through it a moment before producing the spice. He handed it to the younger man.

Joshua took it and made use of it but kept quiet through the meal. Afterward, he put away his stuff and turned to Caleb.

"I want to practice knife fighting before we start out. Why don't you get out your dagger and spar with me?"

"Oh, I don't know. I'm not much for fighting with any weapon."

Joshua gazed at his companion. "So, what if someone came along and decided to take our merchandise? Would you fight to protect it or our lives?"

Caleb scratched at his chin through his beard. "Moses did say the information we gather is more valuable than the contents of the chest."

"And if we're on the way back and get captured as spies?"

Caleb frowned. "I just don't like the idea of killing. The Law says not to kill."

"Moses also said to love your neighbor but hate your enemy. That law is about murder– not combat. You must be able– and willing– to protect yourself, your loved ones, your property."

The older man nodded and grimaced as he thought about the assault on his wife and himself so many years before. He drew his knife and looked at it then shrugged.

The two men took guard positions and Joshua flicked his blade toward the older man who jumped back. Joshua followed and soon had him backed against the donkey.

The younger man stepped back. "This is not about just avoiding injury. You must want to hurt the other guy– even kill him."

Gever returned from the field and saw the men sparring. He flew at them shrieking, "Stop it! Stop it!" He launched himself at Joshua, beating at him with his fists.

The younger spy stepped back and flung the boy off with his free hand. Caleb dropped his dagger and reached to help Gever. Joshua stopped him with the point of his knife against the older man's throat.

"Don't ever drop your weapon in the middle of battle. That's a sign of surrender and may get you killed. Now, pick it up."

As Caleb stooped to pick up the fallen knife, Joshua turned toward the figure sobbing on the ground. "What's the matter with you? Don't you know better than to come between two men with knives flashing?"

Gever jumped to his feet and raised his fists. *"You were trying to hurt Caleb."*

"So you just came at me to protect him." The warrior shook his head. "Your courage amazes me!"

The boy dropped his fists and grinned at the compliment. Joshua turned back to Caleb who stood at guard position.

"Alright," Joshua said, "that's enough for this morning. Think again about what happened here and draw lessons from it."

The next day, when Joshua backed the older man against the donkey's side, he slapped the harpist with his free hand. Caleb's eyes flared at the insult and he came at Joshua, his knife flashing with deadly intent. The young man parried the musician's slashes and thrusts then managed to topple him.

The warrior grinned as he offered his hand. "That's the attitude you need! You were ready to hurt me." He skipped back, laughing, as Caleb plunged his knife into the ground near Joshua's foot.

Another day, Joshua easily blocked the musician's *khopesh* slashes. "Your sword arm is weak. From now on, instead of strumming your harp, I want you to swing your sword all day."

Caleb gasped. "That's my weak arm! A year ago I couldn't carry anything with it." He watched with renewed awe as he fully opened and closed his once-stiff fingers.

"All the more reason to strengthen it." Joshua lifted his own sword and swung it through the full reach of his arm. He slashed mightily side to side, down one diagonal and up the other.

Caleb grimaced. "My arm hurts just thinking about it."

The warrior nodded. "It will really hurt tomorrow and the next day, but after that your arm will get stronger."

The musician embraced his lyre. "I don't want to do this."

Joshua huffed out a breath. "I know, but would you rather cower in a corner with your songs and watch your wife get raped or stand up and fight to protect her?"

Caleb gasped in outrage. "Did you have to say that, given my inability to protect Sarah in Egypt?"

Joshua nodded. "You have a choice. Either clutch your lyre and return to the way it was in Egypt or grab your *khopesh* and learn how to use it to protect your loved ones."

Caleb glared at the younger man, then turned to put away his harp.

CHAPTER 20

Canaanite Farms of Iniquity

One afternoon Gever managed to sling down a hare and bring it in for supper.

As they ate, Joshua asked Gever to tell them about the Anakites. The kid said that with the death of Anak, his sons were running things in the temple, at court, and in the army.

"Sheshai uses…um…the Mouthpiece of Qedesh to guide the people. Talmai is advisor to the king. Ahiman trains the men for combat and to police Hebron and its surroundings.

"Did I hear that one of these Anakites is your father?"

Gever lowered his head and attended to his food. Joshua almost asked again but Caleb motioned him still.

In a moment, the youth swallowed. "My mother says that some time after the family farm was taken away and the people enslaved, she was raped by all three triplets. By the time she was given to Sheshai as a house slave, she was pregnant and I was born the next year."

"My whole life, Eema has told me stories of the Hebrews and the God of Abraham, Isaac, and Jacob. She told me that one day El Shaddai would free His people from bondage to the Egyptians. We were excited to hear the same time Sheshai did that the god with a new name had plagued the Egyptians and brought His people out of bondage. Eema told me she wished we were with them.

"A few weeks ago, Sheshai decided to visit the temples in Egypt. Eema saw the chance to get me away from the high priest. She instructed me to run south along the Road to Shur and seek news of the Israelites. I have lived off the land and otherwise survived until I met Joshua."

Caleb raised his eyebrows at the boy. "And now, you intend to return to Hebron with us? What about your mother's instructions to find our encampment?"

Gever shrugged as he took another bite of rabbit. "I figured if I stick with you, I'll eat better and you'll take me back with you. Besides," he looked at Joshua, "I like you."

Caleb put a hand up to rub his mouth. "So, you were at the caravansary the same day that the temple guards were there?"

"Oh, sure. I recognized them from afar and got out of sight." He looked at Joshua again. "Did you really attack Ahiman with a knife?"

The young man sensed the boy thought he was incredibly foolish. He reddened. "Well, I tried to. He showed me how inept I am. And he let me live."

Gever shook his head. "Unbelievable! He doesn't often let attackers off so easily."

As they walked along, Caleb questioned Gever about his upbringing. "Was your mother the only Kenizzite around? Was there no man to teach you?"

The boy shook his head and continued practicing with the sling Joshua had made for him.

Caleb asked, "Have you been circumcised according to the traditions of Abraham?"

Gever looked up in alarm. "Er…no. Eema didn't think she should since there were no men around."

∽∽∽∽∽∽∽∽∽∽∽∽∽∽

The travelers soon approached farms west and south of the city. Near midday, they walked along a shoulder-high stone wall behind which they saw rows and rows of vines, sagging with huge clusters of grapes. Caleb stepped to the wall and peered in wonder at the size of the clusters.

"Joshua, we must take some of these back with us! They will show the people the bounty of the land Yahweh will be giving us!"

"Caleb, please! Someone might hear you! We don't want to get chased away before we half-complete our journey."

The younger man looked at Gever. "Do you know this vineyard?"

The boy shrugged. "Not to look at it. We haven't seen any people for me to recognize."

As they walked along, they began to hear the sounds of women wailing and men cursing. Past the end of the rows, they came upon a footpath up to a sturdy house, a vast wine press, and other buildings. A group of women huddled together, wringing their hands and wailing loudly. On the other side of the path, men in simple tunics stood about arguing loudly or muttering to silent, sullen companions. Other men in soldiers' leather breast protectors carried bundles out of the house and tossed them onto the ground.

Joshua and Caleb went up to a young man dressed in finer clothes than the others. He stood apart from the others with his fists clenched and rage on his face. He whirled at their greeting, his fists raised.

"Easy, fellow." Caleb raised his open hands to show he was weaponless. "We are merchants, passing through the land and passing by your home. We merely wish to know what's happening."

The young man lowered his fists but kept them clenched at his side. "I am Zomeir bir Menashya. Ordinarily we would welcome you to our home. However, the magistrate has judged that all this is not truly ours and we are being evicted. My father was killed earlier this year and could not defend us against false witnesses who said he never really purchased this vineyard. Ya'akov bir Rami will take over my land just before a bountiful harvest could pay off our debts. Now my mother…" He lifted a hand to wave toward an older woman in the midst of the maidservants. "…will have nowhere to go."

Caleb bowed his head and said, "We are grieved to hear of your troubles. We will not endeavor even to show you the trinkets we had hoped to display for your purchase. If there were some way we could help…"

Joshua tugged at his friend's arm before the older man could continue. Caleb said, "Please, excuse us."

The two men drew their donkey aside and stood beyond it to confer.

"Caleb, we mustn't get involved here. We're here to gather information quietly. If we help out, we will be remembered."

"But these poor people! If there's any way we can help them…"

"Then we mustn't!" his companion insisted. "We've heard only his side of the story. It may be this Ya'akov bir Rami has every right to the land. It may be this is just part of Yahweh's judgment on these people. In any case, we mustn't interfere."

Caleb nodded his submission and the two of them returned to the young man's side. "We can't offer you much help, I'm afraid. Shall we tell your story to other people?"

Zomeir only shook his head. "Sheshai, the high priest, has supported Ya'akov. No one will speak out against his will. My only course is to get my mother settled somewhere and to go join the marauders."

"Marauders?" Joshua spoke up for the first time.

Zomeir bowed his head and spoke grimly. "There's a gang of other men dispossessed by Ya'akov bir Rami and his ilk. They go about raiding homes and waylaying travelers. A friend of mine joined them just a few months ago. It's the only way they know to survive and get back at our enemies."

"Surely there are other options," Caleb protested.

Joshua grabbed his arm. "Bakari, please! Do not get involved."

The older man bowed his head and turned away. They passed beyond the pathway along another section of wall. At the corner, they came upon Gever, squatting on the ground and eating from a large bunch of grapes. The boy stood and held out the fruit toward them.

"Eat, masters. See, I have gotten us some food."

Joshua grabbed the boy's shoulder and shook it. "Where have you been? And where did you get those grapes?"

Gever blinked in surprise and pulled away. "Isn't that obvious?" He lifted an elbow in the direction of the vineyard as he wiped juice from his face.

"So, you stole grapes from a family who is being forced from their land. What makes you think you have the right?"

The boy's face held a pained look before he dropped his head. "I recognized these people once I saw them. The oracle spoke the words of Qedesh to Ya'akov bir Rami, encouraging his actions against the wife of Menashya." He huffed in frustration. "I decided to get us lunch at the expense of Ya'akov. He won't miss this small amount."

Joshua put his fists on his hips. "It's stealing! Yahweh forbids it! I would make you return what you stole except you've eaten half of it."

Fear sprang into Gever's eyes. "No! Please, Joshua! I mustn't go back!" He turned and ran toward the vineyard until Caleb shouted after him.

With a sideways glance at Joshua, the older man called, "We won't make you go back. We still need you for our guide."

The boy slowly turned back and walked at Caleb's side away from Joshua.

A couple days later, the spies and their guide came upon a farm surrounded by ripening fields of barley and oats. Men of various ages sat on benches along the side of the house, fixing or sharpening sickles or repairing grain flails. As the travelers approached, two men– one older and one younger– stood to meet them.

This time, Joshua spoke for them. "Greetings. We are merchants bringing various wares from the lower reaches of the Nile. We seek a small space on which to pitch our tents and an opportunity to show you what we have for sale."

"Greetings," the older man said with a smile. "You may pitch your tent against that wall there. It is warmed by our fire inside. We would be honored, as well, if you shared our food this evening."

Joshua replied, "We thank you for your hospitality but my companion must be careful of what foods he eats. It would please us to bring what we eat and share with you. Then we may choose from what is served."

"Good," was the reply. They exchanged names then the older man turned to his son. "Why don't you talk to your mother about a special meal in honor of our guests?"

The young man stiffened. "You forget your place. I have allowed you to greet our guests but I will not be ordered about by you."

The father lost his smile as he glared at the younger man. With a shake of his head, he strode away toward the house.

The young man spoke to the travelers. "Why don't you go ahead with setting up your tents then join us with samples of your wares?" Then he turned to go back and oversee the workers.

Joshua and Caleb glanced at each other. They moved to the indicated side of the house and erected the tents while Gever unloaded the donkey.

For supper, they cooked some mutton obtained the previous evening along with some fresh vegetables. They were delighted their hosts served a pilaf of mixed grains but they avoided chunks of pork that were with it.

The young man of the house brought out a jar of foamy beer and filled their cups. He waited expectantly for their approval, avoiding his father's disapproving frown.

"This is pretty good!" Joshua exclaimed. He held out his cup for another draught.

As he poured, the young man explained. "As I'm sure you saw, we grow barley and oats on our land. Until this year, we have always sold to the bakers in Hebron as well as individual homes. This year's harvest will go to the makers of this beer. Sheshai, the high priest, has told me this new arrangement will be highly profitable. He says our people will readily buy the beer and he plans to make use of it in future festivals honoring Qedesh."

The old man growled, "We never needed drunken orgies to worship the goddess when I was young. The temple prostitutes were pretty enough and we had what the bakers needed. Our grain is better used to make bread and cakes than this stuff." He set his cup aside.

The young man sighed. "Yes, father, we had a small but steady increase in wealth when we sold our grain to the bakers of Hebron and to neighboring farms. Now, however, we have a chance to make a lot of wealth quickly. We need to seize the opportunity."

"Awk," the old man waved his hand in disgust. "Ever since I let you take over running the farm…"

"But you did," the son interrupted. "Qedesh supported the decision and the goddess has blessed us with bountiful crops to sell. Now, I want to hear no more about it."

The old man lapsed into angry silence while the others turned to different talk. Afterward, in their tent, Caleb said, "These people dishonor their parents." Joshua shook his head in disgust.

The next morning the spies laid out some jewelry for the family to ogle. The women were delighted to see loops of silver, copper, and gold wire strung with beads of bone, pebbles, carnelian, lapis lazuli, feldspar, turquoise, colored glass, and alabaster. These were formed into bracelets, anklets, necklaces, pendants, and forehead ornaments.

While setting out the pieces, Caleb kept an eye out for the unbeaded silver wire earrings he had admired before. He frowned when he didn't see them.

The three companions traveled on a couple days then stopped near a field where a group of men were harvesting grain. The harvesters shuffled along, swinging their sickles back and forth just below the hands that held the heads of the grain.

A man of about thirty sat in the shade of a tree at the edge of the field with a couple sickles beside him. He used a stone to whet another sickle in his hand. At the threesome's approach, he set aside his tools and rose quickly. He spread his empty hands and strode up to them.

"Good day, strangers. I am Bachur. Welcome to our farm. What brings you in our direction?"

Joshua stepped forward with his own empty hands out. "We are merchants from Egypt, selling certain goods from farm to farm as we draw closer to Hebron. May we stay a while and show you what we have?"

Bachur turned and looked back at the men who had stopped working and were watching them. He called out, "Machir, we will have guests tonight. They have come to sell what they carry. Finish up this field while I take them to the house to meet Mother."

A younger man among the reapers dropped his hands from his hips and scowled. Bachur turned back to the three. "Come. Let's go up to the house."

He led them to a house solidly built of rocks from the fields. Several children played in front of the door as three women worked on weavers looms set up outside.

"Mother, Rakael, Makeda," the young man called as they approached the house. "Merchants from Egypt have stopped by on their way to Hebron. They want to show us what they have. Come. Let us make them welcome."

The youngest woman stood and moved toward the building. She was beautiful. All three men watched as she entered the house. The older women followed and all three returned with goblets of wine and plates of refreshments.

Bachur introduced them as the refreshments were served. Joshua and Caleb gave their Egyptian names.

When they turned to introduce Gever, they saw the boy over with the other children, kicking a stuffed leather ball. As they watched, a boy of about ten or twelve deliberately kicked the ball into the guest's stomach. Gever doubled over for a moment then straightened and leaped on him, scratching and hitting.

Bachur and Joshua raced over to separate the boys. The host cuffed his son as Joshua shook Gever.

The spy scolded, "What do you think you're doing? You're a guest here! Act like one!"

Gever protested, "He said I kick like a girl then he hit me with the ball! I couldn't let him get away with that!" He rubbed at his belly and tears sprang into his eyes. He wiped the back of a dirty hand across his face.

"Yes, you could have!" Joshua grabbed the boy's arm and pulled him toward the donkey. "Self-restraint is one mark of a good warrior."

As he was being dragged away, Gever turned to stick out his tongue at the other boy.

Bachur showed his guests where they could pitch their tents and chatted with Caleb as the spies and their guide worked to set up.

"The latest news around here is about the disappearance of the oracle from the temple in Hebron."

"Oracle?" Joshua looked up and asked, "We've heard of her."

"There was a young girl at the temple who spoke as the voice of Qedesh. Sheshai brought her out for festivals to predict how hard the winter would be or how plentiful the crops. She sometimes called for special sacrifices.

"Usually, one of the beauties of the region gets chosen for the part of Qedesh while Sheshai plays the part of Ba'al in harvest festivals. Makeda is often chosen. This year, I hear, the oracle herself is to be paired with the most successful farmer." Bachur rubbed his hands in anticipation.

"Anyway, Sheshai went off to Egypt after he heard tales of some new god who creates plagues and steals away slaves."

Joshua and Caleb straightened from their tasks and looked from each other to their host. He caught the look and grinned.

"I take it you know the stories. You'll have to tell us sometime while you're here. As I was saying, the priest of Qedesh went off to Egypt and the girl who was his oracle disappeared. Sheshai came back and erupted with fury.

"He sent his brother Ahiman out to search the countryside. He and his soldiers came by here twice and questioned everyone." Bachur shook his head at the effort made.

He turned at the sound of his sister's husband and the other men returning from the harvesting. "Ah, good, Machir."

Inside the tent, Caleb sat down and beckoned Gever to sit beside him.

"I understand how you feel about being compared to a girl. No boy your age wants to hear such a thing."

Gever nodded and scowled at his feet.

Caleb continued, "However, your fighting might have caused them to send us away. We would have lost the sale of some jewelry. More importantly, we would have lost the opportunity to gather information, which is our mission here."

He bent forward to peer at the boy. "You must learn to control your behavior when things happen that you don't like."

Gever scowled. "So I should just let him get away with it?"

"Maybe…if the situation requires it." Caleb scratched his scalp through his head cloth. "I told you why this time. You'll have to think about other situations."

He patted the boy's bare leg and Gever shied away to scramble up and pull out his sling.

"I'm ready for some practice."

After the evening meal, Joshua and Caleb set out their displays on the eating table. The family exclaimed at the beauty of the gems and settings in necklaces and bracelets. Machir and Makeda held hands as they examined a set of matching rings. Bachur eyed them narrowly.

He picked up a diamond necklace. "How much for this?"

Caleb had watched him and named an excessive price. Joshua jerked his head up and started to protest. Caleb motioned him to be still.

The householder crossed his arms and began to dicker. He settled for a high price and pulled out a fat purse.

Caleb looked at his companion and shook his head in resignation. Joshua shrugged, confused.

Bachur counted out the price agreed then held up the necklace to admire its brilliance in the firelight. Rakael gave a sigh of pleasure.

The householder turned to his sister. "Makeda, this is for you."

People gasped as he moved to fasten it around her neck. Machir moved between his wife and her brother.

"No! She's my wife; it's my place to give her such things." He clenched his fists.

Bachur sighed. "Machir, you don't have the means to give her such things. I do. Besides, at the up-coming festival, all will see her greater beauty and give great honor to the family."

Machir's eyes blazed. "No," he said softly. Abruptly, he turned and stalked out.

Disturbed to have made such a sale, Joshua and Caleb packed up their merchandise. They took their leave and went out to the tents.

Caleb said, "I saw Machir sitting by himself on the wall. I'm going over to talk to him."

Joshua protested. "I thought you agreed not to interfere."

"I feel a kinship with that young husband. I'm going to talk to him."

He seated himself on the wall next to the young farmer. "I think I know something of what you're going through. I have felt powerless against my wife's brother."

"Yes?" Skepticism marked the response.

"In Egypt, my wife's brother took advantage of my…inabilities…and slept with her."

Machir looked glum as he nodded his understanding. "His sister?"

Caleb continued. "Such is the custom in Egypt sometimes. I was unable to provide well for her and the family. Her brother had done so before our marriage… and exacted payment. He resumed the custom when I was incapacitated and I couldn't stop him."

He sighed. "How I wish I could have stood up to him! Even now, I fear I am unable to prevent his insistence."

Machir clenched his fists. "I have no power over Bachur in this. He's the head of the family. Since the death of his father, he has had the position of authority. I would kill him if I thought I could get away with it." He hung his head. "And if I thought I could run the farm as well as he."

Caleb inhaled sharply at the desire for murder, more information to give Moses. Yet, so he had felt himself. "Can't you get help from someone in authority?"

Machir shook his head. "I spoke to Sheshai once about it and about the use of my wife in festivals. He said I must accept the will of Qedesh. Ha! He's the only one who speaks for Qedesh. Who can say this isn't his will instead?"

"The use of your wife?"

The young man sighed. "Because of her great beauty, Makeda is used by Sheshai to play Qedesh in fertility rites. She is also called upon to "worship" Qedesh for the sake of the family and farm."

Caleb sighed and laid a comforting hand on the other man's arm. "I need to go to our tents. We will be rising early in the morning to depart."

Machir nodded. "Thank you for your understanding."

A couple days later, they heard the sounds of wailing coming from another farmhouse in the distance. They hurried their donkey along until they came upon the stench of fresh blood and a group of women and children huddled together. Several bodies in men's clothing littered the yard and a man with a drawn sword kept an eye on the group of women.

Seeing them, the man called sharply toward the house. Several men of various ages ran out, carrying swords and spears and bags of booty. They dropped the loot and ran to surround the travelers and their donkey.

Meanwhile, Joshua and Caleb managed to pull out their own swords and stand with the donkey and Gever between them.

"Zomeir," the boy exclaimed and the two spies saw that the widow's son had joined the gang.

One of the gang carried a wooden cudgel. He called out, "Zomeir, you are obviously known here. You, Achaziba'al, and Yassib stay here and dispose of these witnesses while the rest of us return to the hideout."

The rest of the marauders grabbed up the loot and ran while Zomeir and his two friends advanced on the Israelites. The widow's son attacked Caleb while the others went after Joshua. The older man parried a slash across his middle and countered with a flurry of slashes and lunges. He drove the youth back, cutting across an upper arm, then retreated to protect Joshua's back.

As the youth came forward again, a sinuous length flew through the air at his face followed by a small form. He flinched away and was bombarded by the flailing fists of Gever, screaming at him. The boy jumped on the youth and brought his mouth close to the youth's ear.

Zomeir pushed Gever away and rose. He advanced on Caleb, his sword raised. As he slashed downward, the older man stepped forward and sideways, blocking the stroke with his own weapon.

Caleb punched the youth in the gut. Doubled over, the back of Zomeir's head was exposed to the flat of Caleb's blade. He struck the youth unconscious.

Meanwhile, Joshua quickly slew his attackers and turned to assist his companion. He found the older man binding the youth's wrists behind his back as he began to stir.

Joshua turned to survey the group of women and children and the bodies strewn about. He spoke to Caleb as the older man stood up.

"I want to talk to your prisoner. How about if you do your soft-spoken act with those women and get them back into the house."

Caleb nodded and started toward the women. Joshua called after him, "If you hear screams, don't concern yourself."

His companion stopped dead for a moment then continued on his task. Joshua turned toward the youth and boy sitting on the ground. He heard the widow's son speak to Gever. "I did like you. I wouldn't have done that if Sheshai hadn't told me to."

Joshua drew his knife. "Gever, maybe you should go help Caleb."

The boy looked at Joshua then at the knife then at the prisoner. He sprang up and scurried after his uncle.

"Now," Joshua said, tapping the knife blade against his open palm, "tell me how you came to be with those murderers. Silence and lies will get you pain. Other crimes will be left for the people of the region to sort out."

Zomeir gritted his teeth. "I won't tell you where the hideout is."

"Did I ask that?"

The youth shook his head.

Joshua said, "Tell me this: Is it between here and Hebron?"

Another shake of the head.

"Your friends went that way." Joshua pointed with the knife. "Is that the right direction?"

Zomeir looked from Joshua to the knife. His head nodded.

"Good," Joshua was delighted. "We're going the other way. Now, tell me how you got into the gang."

Zomeir poured out his tale of learning his friend had joined the marauders after being cheated out of a season's wages. The friend learned of the youth's eviction from his farm and invited him to join as well.

"Every one of us was thrown off his land or cheated in business by an important friend of Sheshai's. That man over there…" he pointed to a well-dressed body. "…robbed another marauder of an inheritance.

"I got my mother settled with friends in Hebron then left to find my friend and his gang. Today we were taking back some of what that one owed. The one cheated also took his revenge."

"I see," replied Joshua. "And how is your mother now?"

Zomeir grimaced and looked away. "I can't go back to find out. I haven't seen her since I left."

Joshua tapped the knife some more, thinking about this story of theft to share with Moses. He put the knife away.

"I want you to forget my friends and I were ever here. I would advise you to return to your mother and find another way to win against the high priest and his friends."

He turned and walked to the house. Inside, he found Caleb and Gever listening as the women yammered about their men and how were they to bring in crops or deal with farm chores. He clapped his hands together loudly, which caused everyone to fall silent.

"Number one, I have left the prisoner tied up outside. I would suggest you make use of him for more than a target of your vengeance. Number two, my friends and I were never here. It was you women who captured the prisoner or maybe he snuck back to give himself up to your justice. Do you understand?"

A well-dressed woman of middle years stood and put her hands on her ample hips. "If you were never here, how can you tell us what we should do?"

"You do understand. Good. Bakari, Gever, let's get out of here."

Surprises in Hebron

The three spies traveled on from that farm. About midday, a large soldier in a chariot appeared ahead of them, coming over a rise in the road, accompanied by a squad of soldiers.

The man in the chariot said, "Hold up, there!"

Gever took one look at the soldiers, yelped, and ran for the grove of olive trees they were passing. The charioteer gestured and two soldiers sprinted after the boy.

Joshua and Caleb turned to their donkey and reached for their sickle-swords but were quickly surrounded by the points of spears held by the rest of the squad.

The man in the chariot dismounted and strode up. The spies saw it was the Canaanite soldier who had insulted the Egyptian army and so easily handled Joshua at the caravansary. The younger spy stiffened and clenched his fists at his sides.

Ahiman smiled unpleasantly. "Well, well. What are you two up to?"

Caleb laid a quelling hand on Joshua's arm and stepped forward, his head lowered and his hands clasped together.

"In case you don't remember, sir, we are two merchants from Egypt. We are traveling from farm to farm on our way to Hebron, selling our merchandise."

"And stealing back that merchandise from what I heard. You have been accused of the theft of a diamond necklace after selling it for a rather high price."

Caleb's head came up at that. He turned and blocked Joshua from advancing on the giant.

"Now hold on there," the younger man demanded. "Bachur agreed to the high price for which he bargained and we did not steal back the necklace."

Caleb said, "Easy, Bes. We know you're right but do we know Gever hasn't done so?"

At that moment, the scalawag was being carried, kicking and pounding on a captor's breastplate, out of the olive grove. "Let me go, you syphilitic son of a she-camel!"

As his companion laughed, the soldier freed a hand and swatted the boy on the behind. Gever yelped and began to sob.

"Now see here!" Joshua turned toward the trio as they approached the captain. Spear points prevented further objections.

The soldier set the boy on his feet in front of the officer and saluted. He held out the glittering necklace.

"When we got to him, he was trying to stuff this into a hollow space made by tree roots."

The giant held up the jewelry and eyed the boy. "Bachur and Makeda will be glad to see this again. And Sheshai is going to be glad to see you again.

"Bring her…and them," he ordered and stepped into the chariot. The soldier pushed Gever in and stepped in as well. He held the squirming youth as Ahiman snapped the reins.

"Joshua, save me!" Gever writhed and sobbed as the chariot disappeared over the rise.

"Gever!" Joshua ran after the chariot. He stretched an arm forward to grasp empty air.

The squad of soldiers surrounded the two spies, spears ready to strike. The young man turned back and leaned his head against the donkey's side and softly pounded its hide.

Caleb turned to the soldiers. "What will happen to the boy?"

One man looked at the others and shrugged. "He'll be taken back to the temple. You are to come with us."

Their swords and knives taken away, the spies trudged, unbound, with their donkey in the middle of the squad.

<div style="text-align:center">~~~~~~~~~~</div>

Caleb supported himself on the spine of the donkey as he stumbled wearily after Joshua. The younger man plodded resolutely toward the inn on the other side of Hebron where he planned to stay a few days until after Sabbath. Both of them worried over the disappearance of Gever. Around them, townspeople wandered from stall to stall as shopkeepers hawked their wares.

Joshua bargained with the innkeeper, who rubbed his hands together in anticipation.

The Israelite asked, "What has you excited?"

The innkeeper beamed. "You will not have heard nor would you appreciate what it means. The priests at the temple have announced that Lilith has returned from her absence. There will be a special service tonight to give thanks to Qedesh and to hear the latest from her mouthpiece."

The innkeeper rubbed his hands together again. "That means another worship time with a *kedeshah* afterward."

Joshua scowled and turned away.

Caleb stood upright from leaning against the donkey. "Why don't we get these things to our room?" He started to untie the donkey's load.

The younger man grunted. He turned again to the innkeeper. "Have you heard news of a boy brought in for the theft of a necklace? He is our guide around Hebron and we worry about him."

The Hebronite shook his head slowly. "No, I haven't heard about that. Your best course of action would be to go to the king's palace to inquire. You would have seen it opposite the temple of Qedesh in the marketplace."

Joshua nodded and picked up the jewel chest to take to their room. Settled in, the two spies sought out the palace and asked for news of Gever. They were summoned to meet with the king's chief advisor.

The two men sat in a room set aside for meetings with special visitors until a chubby version of Ahiman strode in. He wore a robe made of a single piece of cloth, dyed in a pattern of wide stripes that zigzagged across his ample frame. This was wrapped around his body and secured at one side with a toggle pin. A large carved bead dangled from the toggle pin like an official seal. A band of cloth with the same design circled his head.

The spies rose and bowed as Talmai eyed them with crossed arms. "What do you say for yourselves? I hear you are friends of a thief."

Joshua said, "My lord, we are merchants from Egypt with beautiful jewelry to sell at the surrounding farms. We wish only to sell our wares in the marketplace." He frowned. "We also desire the return of our guide who was picked up for the theft of a necklace sold to a landowner north of Hebron."

Talmai turned to take a seat on a nearby chair but not before Caleb saw an amused look on his face. It was gone when the advisor faced them again.

"You wish to take back your guide who has turned out to be a thief. And why should I do this for you?"

Caleb spoke up. "My lord, we have grown to admire the boy. His intelligence and enjoyment of life, his loyalty as our guide have captured our hearts. The necklace can be returned to the one who bought it. Then when we have finished our business with your great city, we would take him far away, teach him the ways of our god, and impress on him how evil it is to steal."

The advisor frowned at his words. He nodded thoughtfully, his chin in his hand, his fingers covering most of his mouth. He straightened.

"This is what you will do. You will come to the temple service tonight after sunset. She who is the mouthpiece of the goddess has recovered from a long illness and will again speak the words of Qedesh. You may even worship the goddess with her *kedeshah*. Then we will see what will happen with your guide."

The advisor rose and turned to leave without another word.

Joshua scowled at the delay but before he could reply, Caleb said, "Thank you, my lord. We will call on you again tomorrow."

∽∽∽∽∽∽∽∽∽∽∽∽

That evening, Joshua and Caleb followed the men who crowded toward the temple in the middle of the city. They passed between the bored eyes of guards stationed at the gate, the only opening in the stout walls that surrounded the building. Before they entered the worship room, the older man pointed to the frieze carved into the stone over the entrance. It depicted a nude woman standing on lions between symbols of Egypt and Syria, offering the two countries medicinal gifts of herbs and snakes.

"Qedesh," the older man muttered.

Joshua's lip curled at the blatant sexuality of the figure.

Inside the torch-lit room, they stepped aside to let their eyes adjust and to study the layout. Two columns of benches filled the floor space nearly to the altar, which stood at the far end of the room.

The outer end of each bench slanted closer to the front wall than the end at the wide middle aisle, making a split stack of chevrons pointed toward the entrance.

Three windows high along the left wall let air in to flutter the torches under them. Under these and down the length of the wall stood six comely young women. The windows, torches, and *kedeshah* were repeated for the wall on the right.

The shortness of the women's white tunics showed off their slender legs and bare feet. Decorated belts emphasized their narrow waists and rounded hips while decorative head bands held their long hair back from their pretty faces. The open collars of their tunics showed off slender necks and shoulders. One of the *kedeshah* standing near the front scowled, clearly unhappy about something.

At the far end of the room in the open area bounded by the first two benches, several musicians stood near a stone altar that held ashes from previous sacrifices, both of grains and of produce, the riches of the land. In a niche built into the far wall stood a stone figure, in size the length and breadth of a large man's hand. Its great age showed in the crude exaggeration of its feminine features.

Joshua grumbled as he took a seat on one of the many benches. "I don't like this breaking of Yahweh's law. I'd rather be out seeking for ways to get Gever released. As much as he angers me at times, I've grown to like him."

Caleb patted his shoulder as he sat beside his friend. "We were told to attend this speaking of Qedesh's oracle. I think we will find answers to our questions."

He quieted along with the other men in attendance as Talmai strode in with the king, who was richly dressed and crowned with a gold diadem. He marched down the middle aisle to take a choice seat at the front. Then various priests entered from one side. The finely dressed high priest looked the image of Ahiman and Talmai but was more slender than their muscular or flabby bulks. He stepped in front of the altar and raised his hands.

"Men of Hebron! The Mouthpiece of Qedesh has been returned to us from the valley of death! Her illness was grave but she has recovered. In a moment we will again hear her speak. First, I wish to announce her final dedication to the goddess.

"Next month, when the harvests are in and you have brought offerings to Qedesh, Lilith will begin her service as *kedeshah*. The man who brings in the most pleasing sacrifice will be the first to worship with her."

A murmur of appreciation rumbled through the male crowd. Joshua turned to his companion.

"What's he saying about this Lilith?"

Caleb curled his hands into fists. "She will become *kedeshah*…a temple prostitute." He swept his forefinger toward the young women along one wall. "They are honored among the people for their work in the temple."

Joshua blanched in horror. He turned back toward the high priest, who raised his hands to still the crowd.

"Listen now as Lilith speaks the words of our goddess."

He turned toward the side entrance and beckoned. Joshua gasped as a girl with short, light-brown hair and a tall, slender body stepped into the open area in front of the altar. She wore a thin linen tunic with a sash tied just under her small breasts. She also had the vacant look of the drugged on her face.

"Gever!" The young man sprang up and would have rushed to her if Caleb hadn't seized his arm and pulled him down.

"I thought you wanted to remain unnoticed."

Joshua looked around at the men watching him and subsided. He glanced at the king's advisor, who smirked with amusement.

Caleb continued, "She's not being hurt right now. Let's see what happens."

The younger man huffed then narrowed his eyes at his companion. "You knew!"

Caleb shrugged. "I suspected. I'll tell you later." He nodded toward the girl.

Sheshai gestured toward the musicians who began to play. Lilith turned toward the statue of Qedesh and bowed low. She lifted her hands in entreaty and shifted her weight from foot to foot, making her hips sway in time to the music.

The young dancer turned to her audience and spread her arms. Still swaying with her eyes closed, Lilith mumbled unintelligible words. She twirled, shooting her hands above her head, and pranced left then right. Her short hair snapped with the tossing of her head from side to side.

Panting from something other than exertion, Lilith shouted the meaningless babbling louder and louder. In a frenzy, she suddenly shrieked and froze. She held her arms out stiffly from her sides and stood rigidly. "Hear the words of Qedesh."

> **Prepare, my people, for the coming invasion.**
> **Gather provisions and arms against the siege to come.**
> **The people of Israel are at the threshold;**
> **They stand ready to enter the land.**
> **Rise up, O people, and declare the greatness of Qedesh.**
> **Flock to your goddess with many sacrifices.**

Lilith looked to the ceiling, her face ugly with rage. She raised her fists over her head.

> **As for the people of Israel, let them be cursed!**
> **Let them flee before the wrath of your goddess!**
> **Let them be mocked before all the nations!**
> **Let fire and sword devour them.**
> **May pestilence consume them.**
> **May they be destroyed before all the peoples!**

Lilith slowly lowered her fists and sank in a heap to the floor. As the girl collapsed, a middle-aged woman hurried in. Seeing her, Caleb jumped to his feet while the woman wrapped the girl in a blanket and carried her off. The *kedeshah* who had scowled scurried to help.

Caleb turned and hurried out the temple entrance with Joshua close on his heels. The young man noticed a smirk on the face of the advisor and a scowl on the face of the giant soldier, who stood near the entrance.

The spies ran to the back of the building then stood, uncertain where to go, until the scowling *kedeshah* emerged from a doorway. Caleb put out a hand to stop her.

"Is Gever in there?"

The young woman spread her arms across the doorway. "What are you doing here? Men aren't allowed in this part of the temple."

Caleb seized her shoulder. "She's my niece. I want to see that she's alright."

Frowning, the *kedeshah* studied his face then nodded slowly. "Yes, you have the likeness. But her name is Lilith." She moved away from the door and hurried toward the worship room.

The older spy knocked on the door. It opened and the middle-aged woman peered out, a look of concern on her face.

Caleb said, "Hello, Tivona."

The woman flinched at this stranger who knew her name. As she peered more closely, her eyes widened.

"Caleb!" She leaped into his outstretched arms and kissed him. The older man held her tightly and buried his face in her hair.

After a moment, she pushed him away and looked back to the room. Her anxiety turned to amazement. She pointed at her brother then into the room.

"She found you!"

Caleb nodded.

The woman's face darkened. "So why did she return?" She rounded on her brother. "I sent her away to save her from the life I saw for her here. Why did you bring her back?"

Caleb gripped her shoulders. "Tivona, she offered to be our guide. I did not know her story until it was too late to send her back."

He gestured at his companion. "My friend and I are on a mission. Gever has been invaluable in guiding us and helping us observe the people of this region."

Tivona inhaled deeply and looked about. "Come in."

She went in and stood watching the girl who slept fitfully on a simple bed. Joshua and Caleb looked and saw a transformed Gever.

This girl's face was clean and showed boyish features, surrounded by her short haircut. The bumps of immature breasts raised the thin blanket that covered her.

Joshua turned to his companion. "How long have you known?"

"Almost from the beginning," Caleb replied. "First, she looks so much like Kenaz at that age, I knew she was a relative. Then various mannerisms reminded me more of you, Tivona, than of our brother. She told us her story and I knew."

He laid a hand on his sister's shoulder. "I have looked forward to this reunion for a long time."

Tivona hugged her brother again.

Joshua sat on a nearby stool. "So you expected the announcement of her dedication to Qedesh?"

The mother sat on the bed and buried her face in her hands. After a moment, she straightened. "Yes. When Zomeir began to hang around and Lilith told me he'd been feeling her chest, I knew I didn't have much time.

"When Sheshai went to Egypt and took Ahiman with him, I seized the opportunity. I cut Lilith's hair, dressed her as a boy, and told her to flee into the Negev to find the people of Israel."

Tivona sighed and gave a small smile. "She's shown an ability over the years to handle herself. I thought it better to risk her to starvation or marauders than the certainty of bondage here."

Joshua nodded. "Then we'll just have to take her with us when we leave."

Tivona went quickly to the door and looked out. Relief showed on her face when she turned back.

"Where are you staying? You'd better get out of here. I'll try to visit so we can talk about getting Lilith out of here."

Caleb took her shoulders. "You have to come, too."

His sister pushed him toward door. "We'll talk when I can get away. For now, you go. I don't want Sheshai or Ahiman or one of the guards to find you here."

The two spies left and hurried to the inn. In the quiet of their room, Joshua raised his hands and eyes to the ceiling. "Thanks be to Yahweh!"

Caleb responded, "Yes! Thanks be to God Most High I have found my sister and her daughter!"

Joshua clasped his companion's arm. "You don't understand. I've been troubled by a growing desire to take Gever to my bed. Now that I know she's a girl, I feel better about it!"

Caleb smirked at him. "So wanting to commit adultery is better than wanting to commit perversion?"

Joshua looked startled. "What? No, no! I don't want to be unfaithful to my wife but I'm glad I'm not being tempted by a boy."

He turned and sat on the bed with his back against the wall. "Now, about rescuing Lilith, is it?"

Caleb nodded.

"How are we going to get Lilith away without notice for long enough to make it to Beer-Sheba?"

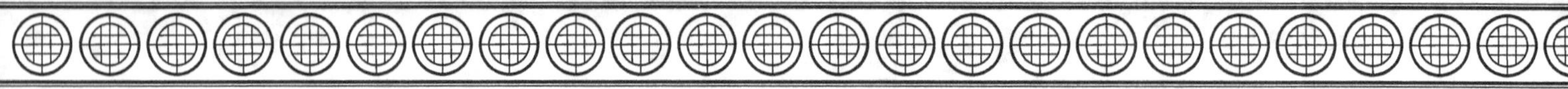

CHAPTER 22

Fight and Flight

The next morning, Caleb was out back of the inn when Joshua heard a light tap on the door to their room. He opened it to see the scowling *kedeshah*, now dressed in a plain robe, wool belt, and sandals. A woman's plain headband circled her long, dark hair. She peered furtively down the hall then tried to push her way into the room.

"Whoa!" Joshua held his hands against her shoulders. "Where do you think you're going?"

"Please, let me in," she whispered urgently. "People might get suspicious if I'm seen standing here in the hall."

Joshua crossed his arms and stepped closer to bar her way. "There's no way I'm going to let the likes of you into our room."

The young woman's mouth dropped open then snapped shut in another scowl. "I am no *zonah*, seeking payment for my services. I am *kedeshah*! I have been set apart solely for the worship of Qedesh!"

She wilted. "Please! I don't want to be challenged by any soldiers."

Caleb, coming along the hall, called out, "Bes, let her in! She's from my sister."

The younger man stood back to let them both enter then closed the door and leaned against it, his arms again crossed. Caleb motioned the young woman to sit at the head of the bed against the wall while he sat at its foot.

She smoothed her robe and straightened her headdress then sat regally to face the men. "My name is Renana and I am Lilith's closest friend. Tivona could not leave Lilith and sent me to tell you what's happening and to plan our escape."

Joshua scowled at her. "What can the likes of you do for us?"

Caleb waved his hand sharply to quell his companion while Renana glared at the younger man.

At Caleb's prompting, she continued, "My family owns a farm west of Hebron and on that farm is a small cave only the family knows about. We can hide there for a few days while the soldiers hunt for us."

Caleb inhaled sharply. "That was my family's farm! I used to play in that cave!"

The *kedeshah* looked at him a moment then shrugged. "It is now ours."

Joshua stood away from the door. "You speak as though we're sure to get Gever away from the temple."

Renana looked at him. "I thought I'd talk about the easy part first. If you wish, I'll tell you how Lilith is doing and what Tivona wants to do." She waited for a response.

Joshua snorted and leaned against the door. "Go ahead."

The *kedeshah* looked at Caleb. "I understand you're Tivona's brother."

The older man nodded.

"Tivona said we need to get Lilith away tonight."

"Why?"

"Sheshai has put Lilith into bondage to Qedesh."

"How's that?" Caleb sat up straight to stare at her.

Renana set her mouth in a grim line. "Before she ran away, Sheshai could easily put Lilith into a trance to bring forth the words of Qedesh. Since she was brought back, she has been having trouble sleeping. She shows signs of gods within, fighting over her. Sheshai heavily drugged Lilith for this latest prophecy. She was just waking up when I left for here." The young woman looked worried. "Tivona fears for her mind if she is separated from Qedesh."

Caleb and Joshua exchanged grim looks.

Renana frowned and looked at her hands clasped in her lap. "You're to pack up and come to the temple tonight. By then, Tivona will have arranged to get Lilith free. Then you– and I– will take her to the cave to hide out before you leave the Hebron area. Tivona says, 'You just get her away from here safely.'"

Caleb clenched his fist in his lap. "Oh, we have every intention of getting Lilith out of here. Tivona, too." He looked at the young woman. "You could come with us."

Renana shook her head as Joshua gave a grunt of protest. "I will go north to Jezreel. Sheshai is not going to like losing his chief *kedeshah* as well as Lilith. He'll send troops after me, as well, which will make your escape easier."

Caleb nodded and looked at his companion. Joshua sighed and lowered his arms in surrender. The *kedeshah* stood, nodded regally to each of them, and left. The men hurriedly packed up their belongings and quietly left to buy more supplies before loading the donkey.

∞∞∞∞∞∞∞∞∞∞

Late that night, Joshua and Caleb pulled their swords from their waistbands and the younger man stepped forward to tap on the door of the temple compound. It swung inward and Tivona held a lamp up so it lit all three of them. She smiled with relief and stepped back to give them entrance.

Joshua asked, "How come the door wasn't guarded?"

"It was." The woman moved her lamp to show a guard lying in a heap a few feet away.

Caleb bent to examine him. He found the handle of a dagger protruding from the man's lower back and shuddered. He pulled it out and looked at his sister.

"Didn't he cry out?" Joshua looked grim as he faced Gever's mother.

She shook her head. "Not much." Her face wore a look that said no one had better get in her way. She moved the lamp to indicate the direction to take.

Joshua went on in a low voice, "How many other guards are there?"

"Two. They walk all around the temple and rest where they can see other doors."

A guard stepped away from the shadow of the wall and grabbed Tivona's arm. "And here's one now. What do you think you're doing?"

Caleb reacted on instinct. He stepped forward and plunged the knife into the guard's side. He stared in horror as the man sank to the ground, pulling the knife from the musician's slack grip.

Caleb stared at the smear of blood on his hand. "What have I done? I've killed him! Oh, God Most High, forgive me!"

Joshua grabbed his arm and shook it. "Quiet! You don't want to bring the other guard!"

Caleb hissed, "But I've killed him!"

"You had to. If you hadn't gotten to him first, I would have killed him. This is a combat situation. You did not hate in bringing death to another. He was interfering with our rescue of Gever."

The musician frantically wiped at the blood on his hand. "I didn't agree to go around killing people."

Joshua stepped close and glared up at him. "You must! You must be able and willing to defend yourself, your loved ones, and your mission from Yahweh. Now, pull yourself together and let's get Gever."

He turned to the mother. "Where is she? And where's the *kedeshah*?"

"She is locking the others into their rooms." Tivona led them toward the rooms in the back of the temple.

Tivona stopped at one door and pushed it open. She screamed in outrage at the sight of Ahamin's naked body hiding the girl lying naked on a bed.

"How dare you!" She flew across the room and grabbed a fistful of hair. "She's your niece– maybe even your daughter!"

The man lunged upward with a roar and brandished the iron knife he'd been holding to the frightened girl's throat. "You think I care? I've wanted to bed her for the past year. There's no way I was going to let some jerkwater farmer take her first. I claim that right."

Tivona drew back her lamp but the captain blocked her throw and thrust his knife upward into her belly.

"Mother!" Lilith scrambled up to reach for her mother's sagging body.

By this time, Joshua and Caleb had pushed in and Ahiman grabbed his *khopesh*. The officer faced the Israelites.

Joshua rushed forward, swinging his weapon. Ahiman parried and used his knife hand to push his attacker's shoulder.

Joshua stumbled further and banged his head against the stone wall. As he slumped to the floor, Lilith threw her naked body at the giant. She beat at him with her fist, shrieking.

Ahiman tossed her off and turned toward Joshua. He raised his sword but Lilith scrambled to cover the crumpled form.

The giant turned his stroke and barely missed the girl. He spun away to put a wall at his naked back.

Caleb stood frozen as he stared with frightened eyes at his sister and friend crumpled on the floor. He eyed the giant who stood with his back to the wall and waved his sword back and forth.

The musician wanted to plead with the man, adopt a friendly attitude and seek some non-violent end to this. However, he saw the look of frustrated lust, the hatred in the man's face. Ahiman would kill them all just to have his niece.

Joshua was down, an injury to his head. Tivona was mortally wounded. Both of them had not hesitated to attack the monster who assaulted Lilith. They shamed Caleb with their determination to protect the girl.

He gripped the handle of his *khopesh*. He must not let his inhibitions dictate what he did now.

He spoke with passion. "El Shaddai, Almighty God, you have brought me to this place where I must either kill or be killed. I'm all that's left between this man and these loved ones. If I don't stop him, he'll kill Joshua and finish his assault on Lilith. Yahweh, You must give me the will and strength to stop this evil man and rescue Your people."

During the moments of this prayer, Caleb glided toward the soldier, both hands warily holding the length of his *khopesh*. He felt a sudden rush of anger. This man had been assaulting his niece just as the Egyptians had assaulted his Sarah after crippling him. Once again, he had to protect a young woman he cared about. This evil man had to be stopped.

The man of Judah stepped in to attack. He wielded his sword in a flurry of slashes at the vital parts the giant's body. The soldier struggled to block Caleb's blows and stepped close to get inside his reach. The tall musician lifted his elbow high to smash Ahiman in the nose. The giant stumbled back and Caleb reached down to hook his *khopesh* behind the Canaanite's ankle.

As he fell, Ahiman banged his head against a wall and slumped in a daze. Caleb raised his sword again, hesitated a moment, and slashed the blade at the wrist of the giant's sword arm, removing the hand.

With a rumbling scream, Ahiman grabbed at the bloody stump and fainted. Caleb set his sword aside and tied off the end of the soldier's arm with a leather thong. As he worked, he muttered to the unconscious man, "I probably should have killed you but I couldn't bring myself to do that. This way I have merely made you unable to fight anymore. That's good enough."

The musician wrapped one end of Lilith's blanket around the stump to soak up blood and turned to his sister. The older woman lay beside the bed, bleeding freely from the stab to her belly. She feebly reached up to caress her daughter's cheek.

"I'm glad…" She coughed blood. "…brought back uncle."

Tivona winced and clenched her fist. "Go with him…Israel's camp." She coughed again. "Don't come back…Hebron."

The dying woman looked at the brother kneeling at her side. "Take care… little girl."

Caleb bit hard on his lower lip and nodded. Tivona closed her eyes and the blood flow around the iron knife slowed and stopped.

Lilith shrieked, "No-o!" She clung to her mother's bloody robe until Caleb lifted her sobbing into his embrace.

"I know you're grieving. This is a blow to both of us. But we need to get you and Joshua out of here before the other guard comes. Can you collect your things and get ready to leave? I'll help Joshua."

With a cry, the girl broke from her uncle's arms and rushed to Joshua. Caleb joined her in examining the back of the younger man's head. The wound bled freely and showed signs of swelling. The older man used his knife to cut a strip from the other end of Lilith's blanket. He tied this around Joshua's head, leaving the knot to one side.

Rising, he pulled Lilith up. "We must get you dressed and out of here. If we're caught, none of us will live long."

Lilith nodded and moved to gather her clothing while Caleb helped his friend to stand.

"How are you feeling? Can you function?"

The younger man nodded and reached up to feel the seeping lump on his head. "I'll do."

Renana chose that moment to appear at the door. She shrieked at the sight of the blood and Tivona unmoving on the floor.

Caleb moved quickly to cover her mouth. "Shh!"

The *kedeshah* nodded, wide-eyed, and Caleb removed his hand.

He said, "We need to get going. But first, we must take the idol with us."

Renana gasped while Joshua's face moved from surprise to a scowl.

Caleb continued, "As Renana said, Lilith is somehow bound to Qedesh. We'll never get her away successfully without the idol." He shrugged. "Maybe Moses will be able to free her."

As Lilith and Renana struggled to get Joshua to the donkey at the front gate, Caleb made his way to the front of the temple. Inside the worship room, Caleb's hand trembled as he reached for the stone figure. As if an evil power resisted his desire to touch it, he stopped and drew back.

"Yahweh, help me," he murmured. "It's only a piece of stone, cut to look like a woman. Its power is only in men's minds and hearts. My mind and heart belong to You."

He drew a deep breath and grasped the idol. Nothing happened.

He let go of the breath and lifted the figure out of its niche and carried it out to the chest. He quickly scooped gems and gold over to conceal it and gave the chest a shake to level the contents.

Good. Nothing of the idol showed. He closed and secured the lid.

The four of them left the temple of Qedesh and hurried the loaded donkey through the darkened streets of Hebron. At the western outskirts, they paused to breathe deeply.

Joshua stumbled against the donkey and clutched at his head. Caleb hurried to support his other side while Lilith scrambled to unplug the water skin. Joshua waved the girl away. "Thanks, Gever."

She gave him a wounded look and turned slowly to put away the water.

Caleb examined him. "You need a couple days to heal."

"I know," the younger man winced at the effort of speaking. "Tomorrow is Sabbath and I, at least, can get a day's rest."

Caleb turned to his companion. "Can you go another hour or so until we can find the cave?"

Joshua stood up straight and took a deep breath. "I'll have to."

<hr>

Renana led her friend and the two men behind a copse of trees to a rock outcropping that hid the opening of the small cave from casual view. Inside, she held her torch to the wick of an oil lamp then another and soon the space was lit enough to see.

The sides of the cave were as round as a bubble– about three paces across and just as high. A stone block had been set against the back and a crude stone figurine of the goddess perched at the back of the block. The ashes of fruits and produce littered the space before the idol.

Joshua eyed the figure with distaste then sagged with his back against the wall near the entrance. He laid his head back but lurched forward with a groan when the back of his head touched the smooth rock.

Lilith stood in the middle of the dirt-covered floor, staring blankly at the altar. At the young man's groan, she turned toward him slowly and knelt to examine his wound. The girl got a small jar of light salve to put on the bump.

Joshua took in the dazed look on her face and frowned then winced as she probed the injury with her fingers. He caught her hand and pulled her to sit beside him.

"You all right?"

The girl looked at him, a bit dazed, and shook her head. The young man pulled her against him and held her as she trembled.

"Things will turn out all right. Yahweh is with us. I know you grieve for your mother. I grieve with you."

Lilith gave a sob and turned to cling to him.

Caleb ducked in from settling the donkey and took in the scene. He looked at Renana and rubbed his arms briskly.

"Can we build a fire in here without risk of discovery?"

The *kedeshah* nodded. "Sure. I'll show you where we keep small pieces of wood for sacrificial fires."

The four of them soon sat on bedrolls laid out around a small fire that warmed the cave. Joshua swept a finger back and forth between Caleb and himself. "I want one of us to keep watch at all times. I need to sleep first but wake me up to check my condition. I hope to be able to relieve you toward morning."

"What about me?" Lilith sat with her hands on her lap and her head down.

Joshua looked at her. "You and I have had it rough today. We both need to sleep."

"Besides," he said as he lowered himself onto his bedroll, "I think you'll do better keeping watch during the day."

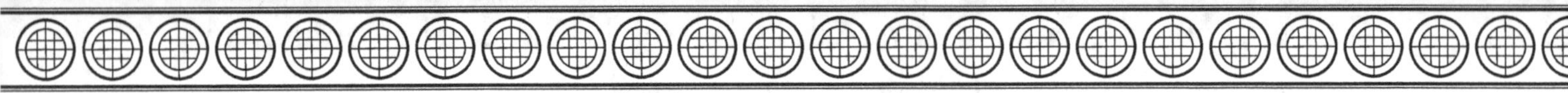

In the Cave

Joshua felt well enough after a few hours to relieve Caleb and climbed to a convenient perch halfway up the hill over the cave. He was relieved to see only a faint glow of firelight on the protective outcropping and to realize no light showed beyond it.

Then Lilith woke up screaming. Caleb sat up but she held out her arms to his companion as he scrambled in to wrap her in a comforting embrace.

"Easy," Joshua murmured, "I'm here and so is Caleb."

The girl shuddered. "He was on me again and I couldn't get him off. Mother lay dying on the floor and I couldn't go to her. Oh, Joshua!" She wept bitterly.

The young man settled her on his lap and rocked her, humming a soothing tune from his childhood. After a bit, Caleb settled nearby with his harp and quietly took up the song.

Heavens, raise the roof!
Earth, wake the dead!
Mountains, send up cheers!

God has comforted his people.
He has tenderly nursed those He loves.
Can a mother forget the infant at her breast,
Walk away from the baby she bore?
But even if mothers forget
I will never forget you.

Lilith turned to wrap her arms around Joshua's neck and laid her cheek against his shoulder. The young man felt the bumps of her unbound breasts and the warmth of her body relaxing into slumber and grew increasingly uncomfortable.

He leaned forward to lay the girl back on her bedroll. She whimpered and tightened her clasp on his neck but he crooned softly and she allowed him to tuck her blanket snugly around her. Joshua motioned for Caleb to bring his blanket to put over the two of them. Then he spooned himself around Lilith and laid his arm over her slender waist. She curled her fingers around his fist and tucked them under her chin. As Caleb backed away after covering them, he frowned at the smile on his niece's face.

The following day, while Joshua and Caleb took turns at guard duty, the girl kept her head down, miserably plodding around the inside of the cave. She thought about the fight inside her room, the death of her mother, Joshua being knocked unconscious, and the assault on herself. She decided she needed to learn self-defense and combat skills. She had always liked to watch Ahiman train the troops and practice his own skills.

That night, settled down on her bedroll next to Joshua, her blanket close around her, she again woke screaming. "Take me back to Hebron! The goddess promises death and destruction if I do not return but life and peace if I become fully hers!"

"Impossible," Joshua snorted in disgust. "Only Yahweh can give real life and peace."

She whimpered throughout Joshua's watch but quieted and slept soundly after the young man curled himself around her again.

That night Joshua dreamed. He saw a young lion lying among a flock of sheep that was ringed by guards. Moses sat on a prominent shepherd's perch and a huge lion watched from the top of a nearby hill. Caleb played a harp and sang a song of praise to Yahweh.

The young lion wished some of the sheep would come close and lie down with him but they were afraid. He went up the hill to speak to the huge lion, which pounced on him and licked his face with affection. The lion stood over him and said, "Love my sheep."

The young lion returned to his place among the sheep and a lioness cub attacked in mock battle. At first, he spurned her but soon relented and wrestled with her.

Suddenly an eagle's scream alerted him to an attack by jackals. He told the lioness to stay put then ran off to repel the invaders.

∞∞∞∞∞∞∞∞∞∞

Joshua awoke about mid-day and looked around. The donkey stood nearby, contentedly chewing on hay while Caleb played on his harp and quietly sang a song of praise to El Shaddai.

Joshua asked, "Where's Gever?"

Caleb looked straight up. "On lookout. I told Lilith to not be seen but to watch for any sign of someone approaching and come tell us."

The young man glanced at the *kedeshah* who knelt before the cave's stone idol. He went out to have a look around and it took him a moment to find Lilith's hiding place. He stood beside her and found he could see several approaches to the cave.

"Good spot." He knelt beside the girl. She had dressed again as a boy in a short tunic, rope girdle, and dirty headdress. Tear tracks streaked her face. "I wish I had known your mother longer. She seemed a remarkable woman."

Lilith gave a small sob and turned her face away, wiping a hand along her eyes. After a moment, Joshua rose to find some breakfast. Inside the cave, Caleb pawed through the chest of jewels. He turned to his companion with a perplexed frown.

"Joshua, have you seen that pair of earrings I showed you?"

The younger man looked up. "The ones made of silver wire? Circles held together by straight wires?"

"Yes, those."

Joshua shook his head and shrugged. Both men looked in the direction of Lilith on lookout.

Caleb said, "No. I've talked to her about stealing. We have to trust that she hasn't."

"And yet, she didn't stop," his companion muttered. He shrugged again. "Does it matter?"

The musician shook his head. "No. I just like to look at them. I'd like to see Sarah wearing them."

That night, Lilith disturbed their sleep again. "No! No! Leave me alone! I won't go back! I won't!"

The two men stared as she arched her back. "Easy, Lilith." Caleb spoke in a soothing tone. "It's just a dream."

She bolted upright. "Joshua! Help me!"

He clasped her in his arms and rocked as she shuddered. Caleb pulled out his lyre and began to sing.

> **The Lord is my rock, my fortress, and my savior**
> my God is my rock, in whom I find protection
> **He is my shield, the power that saves me**
> and my place of safety
> **He is my refuge, my savior**

the one who saves me from violence
I called on the Lord, who is worthy of praise
and he saved me from my enemies

Renana sneered and rolled in her cloak, her back to them.

Later, while Caleb kept watch outside, the young man submitted as Lilith examined his head wound. She spread more salve on the bump and said it looked smaller than before.

When she settled back on her haunches, Hoshea shook his head slowly. "I wish my wife was as caring as you. She wouldn't know how to treat my head so gently."

Lilith frowned at him. "Doesn't she love you?"

Joshua shrugged. "She does in her way, I guess." He sighed. "She just needs to grow up and think about others, not how hardships bother her."

Thin lips and a heavy scowl showed the girl's disgust. "She doesn't deserve you. When we get to camp, I'm going to kill her."

Joshua grabbed her shoulders and shook her. "Don't you dare! Don't even think it! I love my wife. And murder is against Yahweh's law, punished by stoning. I'd have to be the first to cast a stone at you and I wouldn't want to do that." He rose and stalked out, refusing to speak to her for the rest of the day.

⌇⌇⌇⌇⌇⌇⌇⌇⌇⌇⌇⌇⌇⌇

Joshua came in from watch and sent Caleb out to take his place. Then he lay down next to Lilith but at an arm's length from her. Examining her face, his frown eased when she smiled in her sleep.

Hours later, he startled awake when he felt her arm around his waist and her warmth pressed to his back. He scooted around to face her.

"What are you doing?"

She raised her arm to his neck. In a soft whisper she said, "I'm lying with you for warmth…like we did before." She pulled herself against him.

He pushed away. "No. I didn't know you were a girl, then. I'm married and must not sleep like this with another woman."

She lowered her head to look at him through her eyelashes. "Please, Joshua. I want you. I don't want the memory of…that man…lying on me to ruin my desire for love."

She lowered her eyes and shuddered. "Ahiman was ready to be brutal in order to have me but I know you would be gentle."

She looked at him. "Even if you were brutal with me, I wouldn't mind."

Joshua sat up and clenched his fists in front of his eyes. "I don't want to want you. I love my wife."

"But she's going to die!"

He lowered his fists and glared. "What! How can you say such a thing?"

The girl drew a breath at his anger. "I…I saw it in my dreams. They all are."

"What are you talking about?"

She blinked at his harsh tone of voice.

"In m-my dream I saw the b-bodies of all the people strewn around the desert. Only the l-little ones were left."

Joshua stared at her, breathing hard. He closed his eyes and shook his head. "No! Yahweh would never do such a thing! I reject that dream!"

He lay down again, his back to her. Lilith studied him for a bit then lay down by herself.

⌬⌬⌬⌬⌬⌬⌬⌬⌬⌬⌬

Joshua went out to relieve Caleb for the next watch. After he got settled, he noticed the older man still had not risen. "Hadn't you better get some rest?"

Caleb frowned at the clasped hands in his lap. "I'm concerned about you and Lilith sleeping together. I'm sure you haven't done anything you shouldn't but the opportunities are too many. You are at risk of committing adultery. Certainly, you are open to being accused."

Joshua sat upright in outrage. "I may have slept with Lilith for mutual warmth and to comfort her but I haven't done anything beyond that! How can you accuse me of adultery?"

"You may not have taken her as a woman when she offered herself to you but I want you to admit you wanted to…even though you're married."

The younger man tightened his grip on the handle of his sword and grumbled into the silence. Finally, he growled, "Alright, I admit it. I wanted to take her. In my heart I was disloyal to Adah." He turned to face his accuser. "But I didn't go through with it!"

Caleb reached out a hand in sympathy. "No, you did not follow through with the desire to bed Lilith. That is what Yahweh expects of you. But don't forget the desire is there. Seek His help to continue to overcome it and be merciful to people who have the same struggle."

Later, when Lilith went out to watch, Caleb asked, "How can we avoid being captured after we leave the cave tomorrow?"

His companion shrugged. "We can't outrun their chariots. Neither can we take other routes they wouldn't check."

"Lilith escaped their notice disguised as Gever."

"True." Joshua drew this out with skepticism. "But what about us?"

"You really aren't a bad singer. Suppose we went from town to town as musicians dressed in gaudy clothes…sort of hide in plain sight."

"Hmmm, yes." Joshua conceded. "You'll have to be the leader of our little troupe now."

He looked sharply toward the roof of the cave. "I don't think Gever should perform. He should stay out of people's notice. They won't see a mere donkey driver."

Caleb nodded, looking thoughtful. He scooped together a fistful of dust and reached it toward the younger man. "I agree but I think you should tell her…him."

Joshua gave his companion a wry look and climbed to his feet. He looked carefully beyond the outcropping then up to the perch. He climbed up to sit in front of Lilith so that he actually had to look up at her.

He repeated Caleb's gesture of offering dust. "You were smart to travel before, dressed as a boy. It made an excellent disguise." Then he outlined the plan.

The girl grimaced in distaste. "I didn't really enjoy it but it was as you say. Only someone who really knew me could recognize me."

She looked around at the distant scenery then back to search Joshua's face. "Is that why you haven't called me 'Lilith'?"

The man lowered his eyes and growled out, "No. This idea just came up. But as long as I think of you as a boy, I won't be tempted to treat you like a girl… or a woman."

Lilith frowned, remembering his rejection the night before. She reached down to pick up the dust and smear it on her face.

〜〜〜〜〜〜〜〜〜〜

When Lilith lay down that night, she dreamed again.

She saw a young lioness lying among a flock of sheep being watched by Moses and a ring of men on guard. On a hill behind Moses a huge lion watched over everything.

The lioness saw a young lion also among the sheep, as alert as the watchers. She rose to saunter in a direction behind the young male. She crouched when he looked away then pounced in mock attack. He swatted her away at first and she scurried away unhappy. Then he pounced on her in return and they wrestled and mock-bit.

Suddenly an eagle flew down from the hill, screaming in alarm. The pair leapt up to see jackals attacking the flock from all sides. The young lion told her to stay put and ran off to help the guards. A few jackals got through and attacked the sheep. The lion on the hill called, "Lavi'el, protect the flock!" The lioness attacked and killed some of the jackals.

The next morning, she hardly spoke, sobered by her dreams and the coming separation from Renana.

∞∞∞∞∞∞∞∞∞∞∞∞

After breaking fast, Joshua and Caleb repacked their bags, placing their gaudiest clothing near the top. When they came to villages and caravansaries along their route, they wanted to be able to clothe themselves as traveling musicians.

Finally, with the donkey packed and everything cleaned up, Caleb pulled Joshua out of the cave. "Let's give them some time to say Farewell."

Joshua glared at the *kedeshah* then looked at Lilith. "Don't be long."

The girl nodded and turned to her friend. They embraced, sobbing, until Lilith pulled away. "I wish you were coming with us."

The *kedeshah* shook her head. "Your God cannot be my God and your people would not tolerate my ways."

As her friend nodded, Renana continued, "I'm going to miss you while I'm living in Jezreel."

Lilith wiped her eyes. "And I, you. But this is not forever." She reached inside her boy's tunic and drew out two leather thongs– one dyed red, the other blue– and lifted them off her neck. Hanging from each was one of the pair of large silver wire earrings she had taken from the jewelry chest. On separate thongs, they became small pendants.

"El Shaddai also gave me a dream after Caleb soothed me with his music. I saw you old and gray, exchanging these with a large, weathered hand."

Lilith looked at her smooth, child's hand. "Not mine, I think, but sent by me."

She grasped the *kedeshah's* hands. "Not Jezreel, Renana, but Jericho."

The young woman frowned. "Jericho has such a large temple. I would be just another *kedeshah* there. In Jezreel, I can become a priestess."

"I know but my dream was of Jericho."

Renana shook her head. "I'm sorry but I do not follow your god."

Lilith nodded and handed her friend the pendant on the blue thong. "Until we meet again." She dropped the red thong over her own neck and reached to embrace Renana again. "Fare well, my friend."

At Joshua's call, she let go and trotted out of the cave.

After some time, Renana also left the cave and approached the farm house. Concocting a story about visiting Jezreel, she said farewell to her family. Stopping along the way to relieve herself in a patch of woods, she heard, then saw, soldiers and a temple priest march by in the same direction.

My family must have told them. Maybe I should go to Jericho instead.

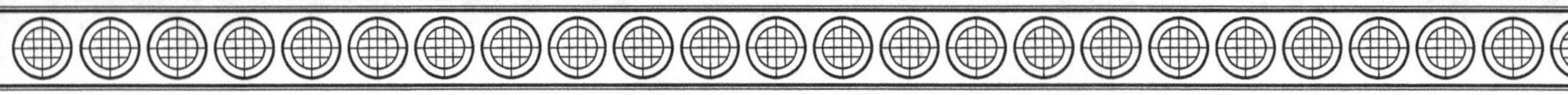

CHAPTER 24

On the Run

The three companions– now musicians– followed the Ridge Road north to Bethlehem. There they planned to entertain people and earn their keep before turning west for Azekah and the road south to Beer-Sheba and the Desert of Paran.

Their donkey carried provisions and the chest. This was half full of gems and held other items common to the Canaanite culture. The figure of Qedesh lay buried in a bottom corner.

With the resilience of youth, the comfort of Caleb's songs, and Joshua's rigorous training with the sling, Lilith– as Gever– seemed less and less morose. He practiced hard with his weapon of choice.

At night, though, while on watch, both men heard Lilith weeping and moaning for her mother. In the morning, Joshua found himself wrapped around the warm body. As much as he wanted to thrust away the temptation, he didn't want to hurt Lilith by depriving the girl of comfort.

They arrived in Bethlehem well before dark. This gave Caleb time to make a deal with the keeper of the caravansary.

"Tell you what," the innkeeper said, "You keep my customers happy tonight and I'll let you stay in my smallest room at half price. One bed and free supper and breakfast." He led them to the back for a look.

"Only one bed?" Caleb looked at Gever then Joshua. "What do you think?"

Gever lifted his chin. "I'll sleep with the donkey. That will keep me out of… uh…the way while you two sing."

"Are you sure?" Joshua looked skeptical.

Gezer worried about dreaming that night without Joshua for comfort but neither did he want to share the room with both Joshua and Caleb.

"I'm sure."

They went out to settle the donkey and make a place for Gever. He shrieked at the sight of several lamb skins being stretched on wooden frames. The companions looked to the innkeeper for explanation.

"Oh, sure," he said. "The men of Bethlehem have been selling lamb skins for generations. People from all around use them to swaddle their infants."

Gever just set his mouth in a thin line and shook his head.

Later, he joined the two men to eat and prepare for the evening entertainment. Caleb reminded him, "I want you to stay out of sight in case soldiers come looking for you."

His mouth full of mutton, the youth nodded. After a swallow, he said, "I can listen from the window and keep watch for suspicious people."

He did just that, enjoying the songs the two men performed for the guests at the caravansary. He ducked back to the animal shelter when two soldiers from Hebron strode in. Gever didn't see them question the musicians who barely mentioned their donkey driver.

As the youth settled down next to the donkey, he felt at peace. The shelter, with its various animals and a manger full of hay, seemed to radiate peace and warmth.

Rather than dreaming of the demands of Qedesh to return to Hebron, Gever heard the animals talking. In her dream, Lilith sat up to listen and watch.

"It's here that He'll be born," a goat bleated.

"In this manger He'll be laid," a cow mooed.

The donkey stood and brayed, "One of mine will carry His mother."

A sheep baaed, "They will swaddle him with one of mine."

Lilith asked, "Who is this that you're talking about?"

The animals chorused, "The Anointed One. The Holy One of Israel." As one, they bowed their heads and bent to one knee.

"But to kill the lambs just to…"

She stopped when she caught sight of a strange-looking altar. Bronze completely covered it, even to the horns that projected from its four corners.

On the altar lay a lamb, its throat cut and its blood covering everything. The lamb rose up and faced the girl.

"Be at peace, my child, the sacrifice is necessary."

Lilith awoke to her name being called.

"Did you sleep well?" Joshua asked.

The youth shrugged. "Well enough." She didn't want to share her perplexing dream just yet.

On the road west of Bethlehem, Gever strode beside the head of the donkey, head down and frowning. He occasionally looked at the animal with awe and slowly shook his head.

Meanwhile, Joshua and Caleb practiced various songs openly– though not praises to Yahweh when people were near. During their rest period and midday meal, Caleb turned to his friend.

"I'm troubled by the idea of dispossessing the Canaanites from this land."

Joshua scowled at him. "What's the problem? Don't you want your family's farm back?"

Caleb frowned and shook his head. "Certainly, I want to return to my family's farm and take back what was stolen from us. But after all these years of it being in the hands of a Canaanite family, what right do I have to dispossess them? What right do we have to drive out the Canaanites and take over their land?"

His companion huffed, exasperated. "Caleb, God Almighty promised this land to Abraham and his descendants. We are his descendants.

"Yahweh promised the land to us while we were slaves in Egypt. He promised to bring us out of slavery and He did. He promised to drive out the Canaanites and He will. Time and again, He said, 'When you enter the land I am giving you, you are to do such and such.' That means He *will* bring us into the land.

"I don't know what Yahweh has against the Canaanites that He would treat them so." The young man stopped and shook his head. "I take that back. When El Shaddai promised the land to Abraham for his seed, He said, 'In the fourth generation your descendants will come back here, for the sin of the Amorites has not yet reached its full measure.' He expected the Amorites to fill up their measure of sin.

"When Moses wrote in the Law about sexual sins with one's relatives, he put down,

> **Don't pollute yourself in any of these ways. This is how the nations became polluted, the ones that I am going to drive out of the land before you. Even the land itself became polluted and I punished it for its iniquities—the land vomited up its inhabitants.**

"You see, it's not merely that Yahweh is giving us the land; He's punishing the Canaanites for their sins. You saw how the inhabitants of the various farms behaved. Judicial robbery, theft, murder, incest, dishonoring of parents…" Joshua waved his hand as if he could go on.

"And notice that Yahweh keeps saying *He* will drive out the inhabitants. He may use our swords and spears but He will be the one driving the people out."

Caleb sighed in reluctant acceptance.

∽∽∽∽∽∽∽∽∽∽∽∽∽∽∽

On the coastal road, they turned south. As fast as they traveled to flee Canaan, within a couple days the companions caught up with a group of four men leading a couple donkeys. Two of the men carried on their shoulders a pole pushed through a single cluster of huge grapes held together by a cloth wrapping. As the companions approached, they saw that the donkeys were loaded down with baskets full of large grains and fruits of the country.

Joshua called out in recognition. Hurrying up to them, he clasped other spies by their arms. "It's good to see all of you!

He turned to his companions. "Caleb, Gever! Come, meet these men of Israel!"

Pointing to each, he said, "These are Shammua from the tribe of Reuben, Igal from the tribe of Issachar, Ammiel of Dan, and Nahbi from Naphtali."

Greetings done, they turned to the burdened donkeys.

What bountiful produce! Caleb told the others about the marvelous crops they had seen around Hebron. "It's a good land Yahweh will bring us into!"

Smiles dimmed on the other spies' faces. They looked away. Some even shuddered. Igal of Issachar finally spoke. "Those who live in the land are as much bigger than other peoples than these grapes are bigger than those of other countries." He swept a hand toward the huge cluster then widened his eyes at Caleb and Joshua. "Were there no giants in Hebron?"

"There were; three of them." Caleb plucked several discordant notes on the harp he'd been quietly strumming. He returned to strumming a song about Yahweh's mighty power.

"However, we have a story of defeating them that's for the ears of Moses and few others." He watched his fingers rather than seeking out Gever, who was talking to the donkey and cradling its head for comfort.

Caleb looked around at the other men. "You do believe Yahweh will bring us into this land as He promised, don't you? He said He will drive out the Canaanites before us even their mighty giants."

Some of the men straightened and sought the confidence in the musician's eyes. Others muttered and shook their heads.

Joshua jumped to his feet, fists clenched at his sides. "You're fools if you don't follow Yahweh's orders to go up into this land and take what He promised to our forefathers and to us!" He stalked off to seek out Gever who had disappeared into the surrounding darkness.

Hours later as Joshua stood watch, Caleb stepped in front of him, his face grave. "It was unwise of you to call those men fools."

Joshua replied with some heat. "I spoke the truth!"

"Maybe, but they won't love you for telling them so."

"I don't need their love. I have Yahweh's and that's enough."

Caleb shook his head at the young man's arrogance. "That may also be true but, if you don't learn how to win friends, you'll never be able to influence people."

Joshua gave a derisive snort and turned away. Caleb grabbed his arm and swung him back. The young man threw a punch but the musician blocked it and planted his fist into Joshua's belly.

Caleb blinked at the young man who sat on the ground, gasping and holding his belly. He looked at his fist then shook his head to clear away the irrelevancy.

"Listen, you arrogant son of a donkey. You have it in you to lead Yahweh's people in conquering the people here but not if you keep trying to bully them. Some of the men were beginning to listen to me as I reminded them of Yahweh's promises. You turned them away when you called them fools."

Joshua dragged in a deep breath and lowered his eyes. "I'm…I'm sorry."

"Don't tell me." Caleb jerked his head toward the men sleeping on the ground. "If you still consider me in charge, tell them." The musician held out his hand.

Joshua grasped it and climbed to his feet. "Thank you." He rubbed his belly again.

Caleb looked at his fist and grinned. "My pleasure."

<hr>

From Eshcol, they turned west toward the Road to Shur then south for Beer-Sheba. One evening past the border town, Joshua stood beyond the light of the fire, staring toward the south. When Gever brought him a plate of food the lad asked, "What's that glow on the horizon?"

The man accepted the plate and began to eat. Looking up, he said, "That's been growing the last two nights. It must be the camp."

He took a sip from his water pouch. "I expect we'll be there before tomorrow evening. I can't wait to see Adah."

Gever scowled and turned away to search the ground for stones.

Part 5

The Return

Arrival and Celebration

Travel-weary and dusty, the band plodded into camp. The spies from Issachar and Naphtali again took upon their shoulders the pole with the bundled cluster of grapes and marched toward the Tabernacle in the middle of the camp. Excited murmurs from the throng followed in their wake.

The men from Issachar and Naphtali laid the huge cluster before Moses and Aaron who stood outside the Tabernacle. Joshua and Caleb bent to untie the wrappings. Naphtali said, "My lords, see here only a sample of the bountiful fruits in the land of Canaan. It is indeed a land flowing with milk and honey, for we saw many cattle and many places of wild flowers and fruit trees."

Before he could speak further, Joshua said, "We, too, saw wondrous things around Hebron. But we have things to say to you in private. We should report to all the elders of Israel privately."

Moses raised his eyebrows but at Joshua and Caleb's look toward their young companion, he nodded.

The older spy turned to Joshua. "Gever and I will take the chest to my tent. We will report to Moses and the elders later."

Joshua nodded. "I am eager to get to my tent and see Adah."

Caleb turned the donkey with its burden toward the tents of Judah and Gever followed after him.

As they neared his clan area, shouts and cheers announced Caleb's return. Kenaz ran forward to throw his arms around him.

"Welcome back, brother! It is good to see your safe return!"

Seraiah, Caleb's nephew, pranced about, shouting while his mother stood beaming in front of their tent.

Caleb looked further to see Sarah who was standing in front of their own dwelling. He dropped the donkey's lead rope and hurried to embrace her.

"Princess, I am so glad to return and see you waiting for me!"

She smiled. "And I am happy to see your return."

She released him and turned to his companion. "And who is this?"

Caleb waved to his brother. "Kenaz, come and meet your niece!"

The younger man's mouth hung open. "My niece?"

Caleb placed both hands on his brother's shoulders and spoke quietly. "I met Tivona in Hebron. I'm sorry to tell you that she died there."

Sadness replaced the joy on Kenaz's face. Caleb pulled Sarah toward him and turned to the gathering crowd.

"People of my clan and of Judah, please welcome Lilith, daughter of Tivona. She was a great help in our journey. Lilith, this is your mother's and my brother, Kenaz ben Jephunneh, and my wife, Sarah." He gestured to the crowd. "And these are now your people."

The girl's eyes glistened as she removed the boy's headdress from her short hair and bowed all around. She turned anguished eyes toward her younger uncle and saw his sad welcome. He squeezed her hands and bowed his head. She turned to Sarah, who saw her sorrow and embraced her.

After a moment, Caleb clapped his hands together. "Now, we must get this chest into the tent." He started to unpack the donkey.

His brother stepped to help him. "Caleb, we must hold a feast in honor of your return."

The musician paused in untying the rope holding the chest. "Yes, I'd like that. I can share the tale of our adventure and how we found Lilith. However, I'd like to wait until tomorrow for that." He looked at Sarah. "Tonight I want to get reacquainted with my wife."

He finished untying and lowered the chest to the ground. "Here, help me get this into the tent. Sarah, we need a safe place for this."

"I see." The desert-roughened woman put her hands on her hips. "And do you expect me to dance for you while you play your harp?"

Caleb gave her a hopeful look. "Oh, would you?"

When she scowled, he said, "Hey, I was kidding!"

Sarah just shook her head and showed Lilith into the tent. "We'll have to find you some girl's clothing and arrange a place for you to sleep."

Later, after a wash to cleanse off the travel dust, Caleb sat on his usual cushion and pulled Sarah to sit next to him. He smiled beseechingly. "What's wrong, dearest?"

Sarah looked away. "You go away for nearly a month then not only do you return with a stranger– a young woman– but then you want to invite people for a party." She put her arms around his neck and looked up at him. "I've missed you."

Caleb closed his eyes and put his forehead against hers. "I am so sorry. I was so caught up in getting my niece safely here and returning with news of our trip, I didn't think. Shall I call off the celebration?"

"No," she said, giving him a peck on the lips, "just postpone it until tomorrow so I can take out my frustration on your body."

Clasping his hands together, Caleb said with a quaver in his voice, "Have mercy on me. I'm an old man."

"Old man, indeed," she snorted, swatting him playfully. "Moses is twice your age and I have heard he's still quite up to the job."

"Ahem."

Sarah turned and Caleb looked behind her at Lilith. She stood dressed in an older girl's long, white tunic and a brown robe. A woman's headdress covered her cropped hair.

"I'm sorry to interrupt but what's happening about the party?"

"I've decided to present you to your family and the rest of the clan tomorrow. We will tell your story and ask them to accept you as part of my family."

Lilith grimaced and sat facing her uncle and aunt. "I have been worried how people will react to me. I'm no longer the protected oracle of Qedesh."

Caleb grasped her hand. "Don't worry. I will raise you as a daughter– teach you Yahweh's Law- and Sarah will teach you what you need to know to be an Israelite woman. I will see you married well and glory in your children."

The girl looked down. "There's only one man I wish to marry."

Caleb compressed his lips. "We will see whom Yahweh brings to you."

◇◇◇◇◇◇◇◇◇◇◇◇◇

Joshua hurried on to Ephraim's camping area. He passed people hurrying toward the Tabernacle to see the return of the spies. The young man met his parents and stopped their progress.

His father grasped his arms. "So, you've returned. How was your journey?"

"It was an adventure. We have a lot to report to Moses." Joshua looked toward their tents. "Where is Adah? Is she well?"

Nun and Simichek looked at each other, frowning. "She's well, though she keeps saying otherwise. She said she's too uncomfortable to leave the tent to meet you." Joshua's father shook his head.

Joshua's stomach clenched then relaxed. "I just want to see her again." He hurried on toward their place.

In the tent, the young man found his very pregnant wife languishing on soft pillows. At the sight of him, Adah struggled to her feet and lumbered into his arms.

"Hoshea, you've come back! I've been so miserable with you gone!"

"Adah, I'm so glad to see you!" Joshua hugged her close then held her away to examine her. "You've gotten so big!"

She glared at him. "So now you think I'm fat!" She turned to lie down on their bed pallet. "It's your fault. I can't wait to get rid of this child."

Joshua gaped at her words. Surely she didn't mean she didn't want it. And she had enjoyed making the baby with him. He shook his head to get rid of the thoughts.

"Adah, I'm back now. I'm here for you. I want you to be happy."

"Well, good! I have not been happy. I've been miserable with all this heat." She turned her face away. "I wish I could lie in the cool water of the Nile."

"Adah, that would expose you to crocodiles and other dangers!"

She waved a hand in dismissal of the notion. "At least I would be cooler and less burdened."

Joshua shook his head at her childishness.

⚬⚬⚬⚬⚬⚬⚬⚬⚬⚬⚬

The next morning, Lilith woke early and dressed as Gever to seek the way across camp to Joshua's tent. She found him grimly flinging the flap to close the front of his tent, his *khopesh* stuck into his girdle. He turned and saw her.

"Gever!" His face lit up. "What brings you here?"

"I came to see you and to meet your wife."

He looked back at the tent and grimaced. "Adah isn't ready for visitors right now. Come, walk with me. I'm going to inspect the sentries."

They strode around the perimeter of the camp, chatting with the morning guards, inquiring what had happened during his absence. The Israelites had held in place, waiting for the spies to return and report to Moses and Aaron.

"We set up exercise areas beyond," one of the sentries pointed. "Quite a number of us practice with our weapons. Swords, spears," he hefted his lance. "Even slings." He nodded at the pouch in Gever's belt.

His face lit up at that. Joshua grunted with satisfaction.

Back at his tent, Adah had put together a simple breakfast. She glared when Joshua introduced Lilith and the girl took off her headdress. Lilith did not look directly at his wife. She gave her attention to Joshua and his desire to see how the men were doing as fighting units.

"Before I forget," Lilith held out a hand when he paused. "There's a feast tonight for the celebration of Caleb's return. I want you to come. He plans to formally adopt me into his family."

"We'll certainly be there," Joshua replied. "Adah, did you hear? We're going to a party tonight."

The pregnant woman objected. "All the way across to Judah's area? I don't think so." She rubbed her huge belly.

That evening, Adah again objected to going to Caleb's party. "I can't walk all the way around the Tabernacle like this."

Joshua pleaded, "Come on, Adah. The exercise will do you good. And I want you to meet Caleb. He's turned out to be a good man in a fight. And you can hear how Gever…Lilith…helped us."

He turned toward the tents of Judah but Adah stayed still. "Hoshea! Not her! I don't like the hussy with her short hair and her boy's clothes."

Joshua turned back toward his wife. "Adah, she's not a hussy. She cut her hair and put on the clothes to disguise herself when she ran away. Lilith was a valuable part of our trip, guiding us and telling us important things about the region we were in."

The pregnant woman narrowed her eyes at him. "And I suppose you slept with her."

Joshua held out his arms in protest. "Only when I thought her a boy and only for warmth." Before he finished, Adah turned her back and waddled toward their tent as fast as she could. He sighed and strode toward the Tabernacle.

Caleb wandered away from his family and friends to an open space among the clan tents, goblet in hand. He looked up to see Joshua come into the firelight alone. The musician hurried over to clap him on the back.

"Joshua! Thank you for coming! Come! Get some food!" He dragged the younger man to where Sarah watched various women slice meat off an ox suspended over a cooking fire or heap spoonfuls of vegetables or grains into the people's bowls.

Other musicians sat at the clan leader's fire, playing lyres and reed instruments while a boy beat on a drum, almost in time with the rhythm.

Holding a heaping bowl, Joshua looked around then asked, "Where's Lilith?

Caleb studied him a moment then gestured toward a group of giggling older girls. Lilith stood nearby with a long-suffering look on her face.

He said, "I sent her over to make friends after I saw her admiring Perez and his spear." He frowned in the direction of the big man.

Joshua recognized the man standing and eating meat from a bone while his spear rested against his shoulder. The big man avidly watched the group of girls. Joshua said, "That one has given me trouble before."

His companion turned back to him. "And where is your wife?"

Joshua didn't miss the slight emphasis on the last word. He looked away with a frown.

"Adah used the excuse of her pregnancy to not walk all the way across from Ephraim's encampment. Actually, she didn't want to see Lilith with me again." He shook his head and reached into his bowl for a slice of meat.

Caleb said, "Now that you're here, we can introduce Lilith and explain her presence."

Beckoning to Lilith, he headed in Sarah's direction. He caught up a bronze serving spoon and banged it a few times against the spit that held the ox roasting over the fire. As the music ceased and the chattering crowd grew silent, he lifted his hands.

"Family and friends, please attend to my words!"

He gestured toward Joshua, who eyed him while taking another bite of meat. "Joshua ben Nun of the tribe of Ephraim and I were sent as spies into the area around Hebron. While there, we visited the farm where Kenaz and I were born…which was stolen from my family. Kenaz and I were sold into slavery in Egypt while our sister, Tivona, was enslaved to the temple of Qedesh in Hebron.

"A youth from Hebron, who called himself Gever, guided us through the countryside around the city until soldiers carried him off. Joshua and I hurried to Hebron to rescue him only to find that *he* was Lilith, Tivona's daughter."

The musician paused and gripped the spoon with passion. "During the effort to rescue Lilith, my sister was killed. We, therefore, brought Lilith back with us to live among the people of Israel. I intend to ask before the elders to adopt her into my family."

Caleb held out a hand toward his niece. "People, please welcome Lilith bet Tivona, late of Hebron."

People cheered and clapped while the boy at the drum beat a rapid tattoo. Lilith beamed and dropped a curtsy then made the rounds of hugs from welcoming people.

When she came to Joshua, he couldn't help teasing her. "One of our ancient tales is about Lilith, the woman Adam loved before Eve was made. She was said to have been a demon woman, filled with evil spirits."

The girl gaped at him, tears flooding her eyes.

"Hey!" The squat man held out a hand. "I was joking! I didn't mean it!"

She clenched her fists at her sides. "Given my situation, you shouldn't have said it."

Joshua hung his head. "You're right. I didn't think." He peeked at her. "Forgive me?"

She wiped the back of her hand across her eyes then her moist nose. Her eyes gleaming, she said, "Sure." Then she stepped into his embrace and wiped her hand on his back.

∾∾∾∾∾∾∾∾∾∾∾

Later that night, Joshua reached toward Adah to feel the bulge of her belly. She moaned in protest and rolled away. "Leave me alone, Hoshea. It's been uncomfortable enough this past month. I don't need you bothering me."

"Adah," he protested, "I only wanted to feel the child moving."

"Well, it's not and I don't want you disturbing it. I've been getting little enough sleep as it is. And they say I'll get even less when it's born."

"So Caleb tells me. That's why I wanted to bring Lilith here to help you."

The pregnant woman struggled to sit up and succeeded only when her husband pushed on her back. "Oh, no! I won't have that hussy anywhere near me or my baby…or you, for that matter!"

"Adah! You have no reason to be jealous! I have already refused to sleep with her. You're my wife and I love you."

"So, she's already offered herself to you! That's what I mean; she's a hussy!"

Joshua sat up to protest angrily. "She's not a hussy! She's a young woman who thinks I'm the man for her. She needs to grow up and see that you and I have a happy marriage."

"Ha!" Adah lowered herself carefully to the pallet and turned her back to him. He watched her in the dim light of the pillar of fire filtering through the tent wall. He lay down as well.

After some time of not finding sleep, Joshua arose and put on his clothes and sword. As he stepped into his sandals, he heard Adah's voice, pleading.

"Hoshea, don't go to her. Please!"

He swung around and planted his fists on his hips. Coldly, he replied, "If you weren't about to give birth, I would beat you for saying that to me." Then he swept the curtain aside and stomped out to check on the sentries.

The next morning, Joshua took breakfast with Caleb and the two women in his tent. Lilith was delighted to see him again and served him gladly.

The two men talked seriously about the words of the other spies and the people's likely reaction. Caleb said, "We must consider carefully how we tell the story of our time in Hebron. We'll want to emphasize the overcoming of Sheshai's power and the seizing of the idol."

Joshua replied, "Then you should be the one to tell the story. After all, you overcame your reluctance to fight. That's the message we need to put forward."

The older man nodded and looked at Lilith. "How much do we say about her part?"

"A lot, I would think. She showed strength and mettle by taking a boy's disguise then returning to Hebron to be our guide. It shows a basic trust in El Shaddai our women could imitate."

"If only she would quit taking things," Caleb agreed with a wry grin.

Lilith looked up and stuck out her tongue at him.

<hr>

Later that day, Caleb stopped Lilith before she could leave the tent. "I want you to stay and help Sarah this afternoon."

"I asked to take Perez his midday meal."

"I'll take it to him. I want to talk to him about something, anyway." Caleb looked at his wife who glanced at the girl.

Lilith looked back, surprise on her face. Her chin rose and thrust out slightly.

The bundle of Perez's meal in his hands, Caleb stood at the side of the practice field and watched his wife's brother train a group of young men. The large man held a heavy spear in a two-handed grip, his left hand at mid-shaft, his right a quarter of the way back from that.

Perez sliced the gleaming bronze spearhead in quick arcs back and forth, up and down, in front of a practice dummy stuffed with wool. Occasionally, he stepped forward to thrust high toward the throat, low toward the crotch, forward at the torso. Twice he whipped the spear around to smack its butt against the dummy's side.

Perez stepped back and turned to the men sitting on the ground. "Once your enemy's down, leave him. Don't waste effort on killing a man who's harmless. Go on to the next enemy."

The men on the ground nodded. Perez motioned them up and they paired off against each other with headless spear shafts.

Caleb beckoned Perez over, lifting the bundle. When the big man took the meal, Caleb said, "I have heard rumors that you visited my tent and my wife while I was in Canaan."

Perez raised his eyebrows. "She's my sister. I was looking out for her while you were gone– seeing if she needed anything."

The slender man nodded. "Yes, she's your sister. You should have never gone in to her, used her for sex, even before I knew her. It's against Yahweh's Law."

Perez set his jaw. "We didn't have the Law in Egypt. I was caring for her as a husband would. I took a husband's payment. After you married her, you became unable to care of her. I again took payment."

Caleb stepped closer to the bigger man. "I am no longer crippled and the Law now forbids you going in to your sister…and my wife. You will stay away from her. And you will stay away from our tent. You are no longer welcome there."

Perez drew himself up and looked at the man who stood close to his height. "Why should I stop visiting my sister? How do you plan to stop me?"

Caleb drew his *khopesh*. He watched the curved blade as he swung it about, always turning the edge in the direction of the swing. He stopped and pointed the sword at the other man.

"I took the hand off a giant in Hebron. I will do worse to you."

Perez looked at him a moment, shook his head, then turned and walked away.

Caleb called to him. "And stay away from Lilith, too. She's not for you."

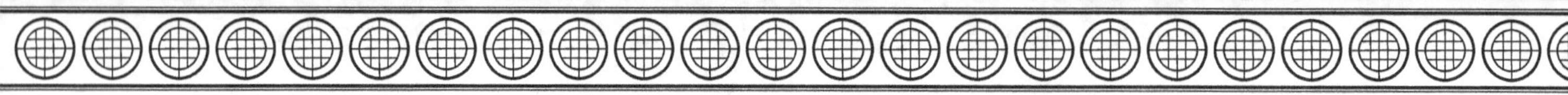

The Spies Report

The morning after the last of the spies returned, Elishama son of Ammihud, the leader of Ephraim, called out at the young man's tent. "Joshua, the time has come. Ah…you won't need your *khopesh*."

The spy stuck his head outside the curtain that closed off the tent's sleeping space and waved to the elder. He turned back to Adah, who lay panting in the heat, her huge belly rolling under her thin tunic.

"Be at peace, beloved. I may be gone all day so don't worry about making me supper." He kissed her forehead and laid a hand on the quivering mound. "If you need anything, or if anything happens, call out to Mother. She'll be listening for you."

"Hoshea, I'm scared."

The young man huffed at her use of his old name. "There's no reason to be afraid. Mother will be here at your call. Trust in Yahweh. He'll get you through."

Joshua watched her turn her head away, discontent on her face. He turned with an angry swirl of his robe and joined the leader of his tribe.

Entering Moses's tent, he looked around and touched Elishama's arm, drawing his attention to Caleb and Gever sitting with the elder of Judah. It made sense to Joshua that he and the spy from Judah should sit together. He moved in that direction and sat beside his friend. After a moment, Elishama took his fists off his hips and shook his head. He sat beside them. The four men and the boy exchanged greetings. Joshua caught the eye of Moses and gave a salute to the prophet, who sat talking with Aaron.

The tent gradually filled with the other spies and their elders. Even some clan leaders came in and sat near the entrance.

Finally, Aaron rose. "Brothers, all the spies have returned from the land promised to our forefathers and to us. Let us hear what they have to say about the people and their fortified cities." He turned to the left and held out a hand. "We wish to hear first about the huge cluster of grapes."

The spies who traveled to the valley of Eshcol rose and bowed to the assembly. "Brothers and leaders of Israel, hear our tale. We traveled up one side of the valley of Eshcol and down the other. We saw several vineyards with clusters of grapes much like the one we brought back with us. We also saw fields with huge heads of grain. We saw many fat cattle grazing in fields not planted with grain."

The two spies grimaced and held up their hands as the seated men grinned and murmured to each other. "Make no mistake. We also saw the large size of the people." The taller spy leveled a hand higher than his head. "A few of them were even bigger." He stretched his hand straight up then spread both hands apart at head level to indicate wide shoulders.

"They seemed to sneer down at us as though at insects and made us feel like such. We were happy to bring away that huge bunch of grapes. We were happier to escape with our lives."

They sat down amid cries of dismay and angry mutterings. Joshua scowled at the looks of alarm on the faces about him. *Didn't they trust Yahweh to help them overcome these enemies no matter how big they were?*

He moved his feet in order to leap up but Caleb grabbed his arm. "Our story will be much more effective if they hear all the bad news first."

Joshua took a deep breath then sighed and nodded. He looked at Gever, who shrugged and grinned at him.

Other spies gave their own versions of fruitful orchards and vineyards, herds of fat farm animals, signs of plentiful game in the forests. They also spoke of cities with thick, impenetrable walls, huge soldiers with massive shields and heavy weapons, chariots racing across wide fields. With every telling, the cries of dismay grew louder, the mutterings angrier.

When the time came for their turn to report to Moses, Joshua and Caleb rose with Gever and placed the chest in front of the leadership of Israel. Several men murmured at the presence of a boy. "Didn't he bring back a niece?"

Caleb heard and said, "My lords, please allow the presence of this youth whose story is such a big part of our own."

Caleb began, "I was glad when you asked me to go up into Canaan and I asked to be sent to Hebron. You see, I grew up there."

He summarized his family's life on the farm and their destruction. His father killed and older brother enslaved. Caleb and Kenaz sold into Egypt like Joseph, the son of Jacob. Their sister, Tivona, raped by the sons of Anak and taken into bondage to the temple of Qedesh.

"These many years later, Joshua and I were sent to Hebron and along the way, we met up with Gever here." He told the men about meeting the youth at the caravansary in Beersheba.

"He had run away from Hebron and sought the tribes of Israel he'd heard were in the Wilderness. Learning we were from here, he agreed to guide us around the area of Hebron if we would bring him back here with us." He laid an affectionate hand on the youth's shoulder.

"At the caravansary, we also learned the temple of Qedesh lost a valuable oracle, a girl who spoke the words of the goddess to the people."

Caleb related how the three of them had circled around Hebron, visiting various farms. "After the last farm, it became clear that Gever was the mouthpiece of Qedesh sought by the Anakites of Hebron."

He grinned and gestured to the girl, who removed her headdress to reveal hair falling around her boyish face. Caleb pulled the back of her tunic, making her feminine bulges obvious.

"My lords, please welcome into the people of Israel Lilith, the daughter of Tivona."

The men seated around gave a cry while Moses sat quietly and studied Caleb with amusement. The prophet said, "So you *had* brought your *niece* back with you."

Caleb sobered. "We rescued Lilith from the temple and hid out on what used to be my family's farm. It was obvious Lilith had been drugged by the high priest of Qedesh and enchanted by him so often that the goddess has a strong hold on her mind. Bound to her, she spoke Qedesh's curse on our nation if we come into their land."

As the men seated around muttered in angry dismay, Caleb opened the chest before him and scooped out jewelry and coins onto the lid until the idol lay exposed before them. Joshua and Aaron leaned away while Moses glared at the stone figure. Lilith's hand trembled as she slowly reached out, looks of desire and revulsion on her face.

Caleb quickly pulled her hand away. He looked up to Moses and Aaron. "We have brought Lilith and the idol to you so that you might break the hold the goddess has on her."

Moses shoved his hands into the sleeves of his robe and lowered his eyes. The others waited while he pondered. Finally, he lifted his head. "Yahweh will, of course, want to break the evil hold on her mind."

At that moment, a large man strode up, followed by two giants. "My lord, Moses. I have been sent to request an audience for two men of Canaan. They say that their statue and oracle of Qedesh have been stolen."

Sheshai and Talmai, priest and king's advisor, loomed behind the messenger, ducking their heads to get under the canvas. The priest pointed to Lilith.

"She is the oracle of Qedesh, the goddess of Hebron."

He spread two fingers to take in the men on both sides of her. "These two came into our temple, killed the guards, nearly killed our bigger brother, and made off with our goddess and her mouthpiece."

The Israelites seated before Moses gasped at the words, "bigger brother". Murmurs of "Anakites" and "giants" were heard.

Talmai laid a hand on the hilt of his sword. Leaning over the men, he growled, "We demand the return of Qedesh and her mouthpiece. In restitution for the theft, we demand that chest of jewels and coins in which the goddess lay during her journey here."

Several of the seated men voiced angry protests. Joshua reached toward his own girdle then remembered he'd left his sword in his tent. He pointed a finger up at the giant.

"What gives you the right to come in here and make demands?"

He turned to Israel's prophet and high priest. "My lords, you must not let them take her back! They will mistreat her and use her for their evil purposes."

Moses merely looked at the towering men. He turned to speak quietly to his brother. After a moment, the other nodded and rose.

"I am Aaron, high priest of Yahweh. Yahweh has spoken. What belongs to Qedesh, she may try to keep. What belongs to Yahweh, He *will* keep."

Before Talmai could respond, Sheshai laid a hand on his arm to silence him. The priest pulled a handful of black dust from a pouch and blew it across the fire at Lilith. It flashed into ash and smoke enveloped the girl's face.

The priest waved fingers toward her and spoke a few guttural words. As the men around her coughed and sputtered, Lilith pulled off her head covering and loosened her girdle. Belt, pouch, and sling hit the ground beside the sandals she dropped from her feet.

She raised her arms, crossed at the wrists, and moved her hips seductively back and forth. The girl stepped toward the fire then turned and bowed to the idol on the chest. She bowed to Sheshai then twirled and danced slowly, her face blank, around the fire.

Stopping to lean over Moses and Aaron, a look of disdain crossed her face. Dancing around to face the tribal leaders, she smiled.

In a low, soft voice, she said, "Men of Israel, hear the words of Qedesh."

Come to me in Hebron.
Bring your families, your flocks,
the tools of your trades.
I will make you prosper when you worship me.
Lie with my *kedeshah*.
Enjoy the fat of my land
As did my people for hundreds of years
while your fathers slaved in Egypt.

Lilith's face turned ugly with anger.

Those who follow the Destroyer of Egypt,
come not to my land.
Three great men rule by my power.
One holds the fire.
One holds the purse.
One holds the sword.
Poverty haunts those who follow the Destroyer.
Fire and sword await those who call on him.

Lilith slowly collapsed onto the ground, shivering. Joshua and Caleb rushed to her, the younger man calling for a blanket. They wrapped her in its warmth.

Sheshai gestured toward Caleb. "This man has told you of the curse put on your people by the goddess. Listen to her words. Take heed to the words just spoken. Return the goddess and her oracle and let us depart in peace. Otherwise, we shall return with our brother's army."

Shouts of dismay and anger erupted from the Israelites. Someone called out, "We can't attack those people; they are stronger than we are!"

Caleb rose and waved his hands. "Be still, my brothers, and hear me! Yahweh helped us overcome those giants! He helped *me* fight and win against one of them. He will help *us* beat them all! We should go up and take possession of the land, for we can certainly do it."

Amid a squabble of argument, Moses motioned Caleb to sit. He held up his hands until the men before him quieted.

Aaron stood to speak, "We will place this idol in the Tabernacle overnight. If in the morning, it remains intact, you may take it with you. If the oracle herself chooses, you may take her back as well."

Joshua and Caleb protested, "Never! We won't allow it!"

Lilith struggled to sit up. She spoke weakly, "Please, don't make me go back with them."

Israel's high priest turned to Lilith and gently said, "Daughter, the choice will be yours. If you wish to stay with us, prepare for the evening sacrifice a male lamb without blemish. Bring it to the entrance of the Tabernacle. Wear only a clean tunic, undergarments, and head covering. Er…and leave the sling behind."

The girl went out, supported by her two companions. Caleb looked at the sun, which shown low near the horizon.

"How are we going to get her and the lamb ready before the sacrifice starts?"

Joshua said, "Do you want to get a lamb for her?"

Caleb shook his head. "I'll help Lilith get ready."

The man of Ephraim nodded. "I'll get the lamb and make sure it's cleaned up." He turned and hurried toward Ephraim's encampment.

In his tent, he found Adah, languishing in a hot, uncomfortable position given her great pregnancy. Joshua scowled at her and started pawing through a hiding place.

"I need a coin for a sacrificial lamb."

The young woman narrowed her eyes at him. "What did you do?"

He halted in surprise then shook his head. "What? Oh, no. Not for me. It's for Gever…er…Lilith. She needs a lamb for the evening sacrifice. If she's not accepted by Yahweh, they'll take her back to a miserable life in Canaan."

"Let them!" Adah clenched her fists at her sides.

Joshua raised his fist to strike her then shook his head and continued after the coin.

CHAPTER 27

Sacrifice for Freedom

Lilith took the lamb in her arms and walked to the Tabernacle gate. After a Levite let her in, she looked around in shock at the animals lying on bloody tables in front of the smoking Altar of Sacrifice. Men in robes of the various tribes held sheep, goats, and doves on the tables while priests in white linen cut the animals' throats.

A priest reached for her lamb but Lilith shrieked and turned away. "Never! In Hebron, we sacrificed grain and produce– not harmless animals!"

The priest grabbed for the lamb. "That would never do here. Give me your sacrifice."

As they struggled over the animal, Eleazar, the son of Aaron, approached the pair. "May I help here?"

The priest pointed his knife at Lilith. "This girl brought a lamb to be sacrificed and now won't give it up."

She said, "I don't want it killed!"

Eleazar looked at her. "Aren't you the one claimed by the priest of Qedesh?"

Lilith nodded, her arms clutching the animal.

Aaron's son nodded to the other priest. "Thank you, brother. I'll take care of this."

The priest bowed slightly and moved off to another table.

Eleazar turned back to the girl. "Lilith, is it?"

At her nod, he continued, "I have heard of the dreams that disturb your sleep. They are from Qedesh?"

Lilith nodded again and lowered her head.

"Do you want to be free of Qedesh or go back with those men?"

The girl's head snapped up. "Don't make me go back with them! Please! I'll do anything to stay here."

The priest nodded. "To stay here– free of Qedesh, you will need to be acceptable to Yahweh. Only He can deliver you from bondage to her."

He pointed to the lamb in her arms. "To be acceptable to Yahweh, we must kill the lamb as a substitute for your life and sprinkle his blood on you and the altar."

Lilith protested, "This animal didn't do anything! It doesn't deserve to die!"

Eleazar nodded. "That's true. But you did. Were you to approach Yahweh and ask to be free, you would die. He has ordained that this lamb must die in your place. The sacrifice is necessary."

The girl looked at him, startled. The same words as in her dream. She wiped tears from her face on the animal's back. With a sigh, she placed it on the table between them.

The priest said, "Place your hands on the lamb's head and lean your weight on it. Do you accept this lamb as a substitute before Yahweh for your life? Do you trust this lamb to make you acceptable to Yahweh?"

Her weight focused on the wooly head, Lilith said, "Yes," to both questions.

Eleazar reached for a knife, raised the animal's snout, and quickly drew the knife hard across its throat. Blood sprayed over Lilith, who stepped back with a squeal. The priest grabbed a basin to catch the flood of red.

He looked up. "Since you're already covered with the blood, you may go. I will finish the offering for you."

Lilith turned and ran sobbing all the way to Caleb's tent where she fell into Sarah's arms. Her aunt held her close until she stopped shuddering and relaxed.

The older woman held her away and looked at her. "You've had a hard day. Why don't you turn in?"

Lilith nodded and went behind the curtain to her sleeping area. As she undressed and washed off the lamb's blood, she heard Caleb begin to strum his harp and sing.

> **The sacrifice lamb has been slain.**
> **Its blood on the altar, a stain**
> **To wipe away guilt and pain**
> **And bring hope eternal.**

(Words from <u>Sacrifice Lamb</u> by Joel Chernoff of Lamb)

The words of the song lingered in her mind as Lilith lay down and slipped into sleep. Immediately, Qedesh came to her with enticing promises.

In her dream, mounds of food stood before her, fresh vegetables, cooked grains, even roasted meats of cattle and sheep. Fine goblets overflowed with beer and wine.

The goddess purred.

> **Return me to my chosen people.**
> **Many good things I give**
> **to those who do my bidding.**
> **Come, speak for me anew.**

Many beautiful children flocked around Lilith's knees. Their faces shone with health and happiness such as she had never seen in Hebron.

Many children could be yours.
All would take pleasure in knowing you.
Return me to the City of the Goddess's Friends
where you will be honored and loved.

Handsome young men– Zomeir prominent among them– strode by, tall, muscular, naked, and erect.

Many will be your lovers.
Many will find pleasure in you.
Simply take your place among my dedicated women.

After her weeks of hunger, Lilith was tempted by the mounds of food. Her natural maternal instincts yearned for flocks of happy children. However, the large, naked men were more like Ahiman than short, stocky Joshua. He was the one she wanted.

Behold what will happen to him and his people.

As she dreamed, Lilith saw the Israelites marching through the wilderness and dropping one by one. She watched Joshua then Caleb grow gaunt with hunger and drop along the way.

"No!" She cried out in horror. "Yahweh would not let them die!"

Fear and loathing swept through her.

Speak not that name!
Death and destruction follow that one!

An angry rumble shook her from behind. She spun to face the snarl of a huge, crouching lion. Its eyes burned with intensity and light flowed from its mane.

The snarl softened as it spoke, "I am the God of Joshua, Caleb, and Tivona. Lavi'el, will you love me as much as they?"

Before Qedesh could well up within and stop her, Lilith said, "Yes, lord. Help me to follow you."

"Trust me," the lion said as the intensity of its eyes grew and burned within her. Bands of heat swirled around her, rising to her throat and head.

Lilith panted from the pain and let out a scream. From far away she heard the plucking of a lyre and voices raised in song.

Around her the piles of food decayed into puddles of sludge and mounds of rotting meat. The children's faces grew gaunt and full of sores. The naked men shriveled and fell limp.

At last, only three children– two boys and a girl, holding sword, spear, and sling– and one short, stocky man stood before her. Lilith smiled as she recognized the circumcision that had told her Joshua was a Hebrew.

The heat at her throat grew, threatening her breathing. Lilith struggled to inhale but an anguished wail blocked her. It grew into a scream, joined from afar by the anguished voice of Sheshai.

Abruptly the heat exploded and blasted through her mouth. The Canaanite priest's voice fell to a whimper while Lilith drew in a cool breath. She slept and continued to dream.

∞∞∞∞∞∞∞∞∞∞∞∞

She opened her eyes when she felt her blanket being removed. A putrid stench filled her nose and she looked down at a sticky, black sludge that slimed the covering and her tunic.

"E-ew!"

Sarah stopped at her grunt of disgust and smiled.

"You seem to have had quite a night of it. How do you feel?"

Lilith blinked in surprise. "I feel wonderful! Light and…happy!" She grimaced as she peeled off her tunic.

Sarah made a face, too. "You writhed and screamed in your sleep. Caleb, Joshua, and I sang over you until you vomited this mess and slept quietly. I finally chased them out so I could change you."

She gathered up the soiled clothes. "So, what happened to you?"

Lilith paused in pulling on a fresh tunic. "A lot! I want the others to hear about it."

Disobedience and Judgment

Joshua sat with Caleb at the fire in front of the tent, waiting for Sarah to finish with Lilith. They stood when the girl stepped out of her sleeping area.

Lilith pranced up and twirled Joshua by his hands. She said, "Joshua, I have been freed from the grip of Qedesh."

The young man gripped her hands. "That's wonderful! Praise be to Yahweh for showing His mighty power!"

Lilith sobered and clutched his arms. "There's more. Yahweh spoke to me in dreams and gave me messages." She stood straight and closed her eyes.

Hear the words of Yahweh to Joshua, son of Nun
Deep disappointment will bow your head.
Two tragedies will break your heart.
Turn to Me and I will comfort you.
Embrace my love and I will gladden you again.

The girl turned to Caleb and spoke to him, her face a frown of concern.

Hear the words of Yahweh

to Caleb, son of Jephunneh
A wayward ewe kicks to leave your arms
while a wolf crouches at the door.
As it is with My people,
the ewe must die but the lamb will live.

The girl looked from one perplexed face to the other. "There is more. I had another vision, this one about Israel itself."

Before she could continue, Caleb stopped her. "You should speak that before Moses and the elders."

They took some breakfast then went to the tent of Moses where he, Aaron, and the elders of Israel sat talking. At their approach, the prophet beckoned to Joshua who went to speak into his ear.

Moses nodded and smiled. He motioned his aide to sit and stood to get everyone's attention.

"Yesterday, the king of Hebron and priest of Qedesh came to reclaim their stolen idol and the oracle of their goddess. This morning, the idol was found shattered into pieces and the priest bereft of his senses. They left early this morning."

The men exclaimed in wonder.

Moses continued, "Yahweh has spoken further by her who was that oracle. Let us hear His words." He motioned to Lilith, who stood and looked around.

She closed her eyes, tilted her face up, and spoke.

"I stood in a mist. The billowing vapors around me shimmered from a light so bright it nearly blinded me.

"The mist pulled back to reveal the seat of a great golden throne. Hands emerged from the sleeves of a bright, purple robe and rested on the ends of the armrests. The lower length of a scepter or staff held the skirts of the robe between the knees of the One who sat on the throne.

"High above, a great eagle circled on outstretched wings. Occasionally, it would swoop down then spiral back to the heights. Beside the throne lay a strange creature. In the brightness, it sometimes looked like a large lamb, curly of hair and dazzling white. Though its eyes were lively as it observed me, I could see that its throat had been cut. At other times, the curly hair seemed to surround the large head of a lion that lay with forepaws outstretched, the great claws visible.

"People of every nation were arrayed before Him. Before the knees of the King stood two women. One was older and dressed in the sheer covering of a slave woman of Egypt. She trembled with fear.

"The younger was dressed in the unfamiliar armor of a new nation. Over a white, flowing tunic and girdle, she wore a new breastplate. Sandals covered her bare feet. From beneath a helmet her hair flowed like the mane of a lion. One hand held a *khopesh*; the other a shield. A bow was slung across her chest with a quiver of arrows at her back, while a sling and pouch for stones hung from her girdle. The warrior woman stood as still and confident as a soldier in the presence of a king he loves.

"Sorrow lined Yahweh's face as he gazed at the slave woman. He lifted His head to speak:

> **Weep with Me, O people;**
> **Mourn before Me for My beloved is dying.**
> **Disease and death have come over the one I love;**
> **Fear and unbelief have overtaken her.**
> **She has given her heart to disobedience.**
> **My beloved is plagued, therefore,**
> **with an incurable plague.**
> **She will die because she refuses to let Me heal her.**

"Yahweh gave a great sigh and the slave woman shrank to the floor and lay still.

"The Mighty One of Israel held out His hand to the warrior woman and He spoke again:

Look, you nations upon My new beloved.

Feast your eyes on the beauty of one who loves Me.

See her stand confident before My throne.

Her will I send to fulfill My purposes.

She will speak My words to you.

She will practice My laws before you.

Listen to her and be healed.

Hearken to her and be forgiven.

Then I will not send destruction upon your children.

The men seated about murmured together. "Who is this girl to say such things?" "She's a Canaanite witch." "Why should we listen to her? She wants us to go against the Canaanite giants…her own kin!"

Joshua leapt to his feet. "You fools! Cowards! Did any of you fight those giants you're scared of? Caleb and I did! Yes, I took a blow to the head." He put a hand to the mostly-healed wound. "The giant we fought would have killed me but for my partner. He is a *harpist*– hardly a soldier– but he fought the giant– their military leader– and took off his hand!"

Joshua grasped his left wrist and shook his fist at them. "If Yahweh can help this babe of a soldier– this *harpist*!– to disarm such a monster, who are you to not trust Him to help us take the land He promised us? What are you worried about? Isn't Yahweh in control?"

The young man held out his hands, beseeching them. "Yahweh is with us. He will overpower the gods of the Canaanites. He bids us go up and take the land. We must obey Him or He will drive us back into the desert and destroy us!"

Stung by his recriminations, the other ten spies and many of the elders and clan leaders leapt to their feet. They shook fists and screamed insults at Joshua.

"How dare you accuse us of cowardice? We are wise enough to know something can't be done! We can't fight the giants in the land! We can't breech the walls of their fortified cities! We can't win against their heavy weapons and chariots! We just can't!

"And you!" They turned on Moses. "You're the one who led us out into this desert! You brought us to this place of no food, no water, no shade but the tents over our heads!

"Now, these Canaanites will be coming down upon us to slay our children! Our future will be strewn along the road back to Egypt. We have decided! That is where we will now go!"

Moses looked wide-eyed at the panting men. He squeezed his eyes shut and rapidly shook his head as if to dislodge a terrible vision. Old as he was, he leapt to his feet and grabbed Aaron's arm.

"Quickly! To the Tabernacle! Before Yahweh destroys the whole nation!" The sons of Amram fled the tent and hurried to the entrance to the Holy Place.

Stunned by the prophet's words and the urgency of his departure with the high priest, the leaders slunk away to their tents.

That evening, both men stumbled out of the Tabernacle and called for all the leaders of Israel: the elders, the clan leaders, the judges, and commanders. Downcast, the prophet and High Priest sat and waved off offerings of food as they waited. When all were present before them, Moses stood. "Yahweh has spoken." He closed his eyes and continued, "He has said,

As surely as I live, I will do to you the very thing I heard you say: In this wilderness your bodies will fall—every one of you twenty years old or more who was counted in the census and who has grumbled against me. Not one of you will enter the land I swore with uplifted hand to make your home, except Caleb son of Jephunneh and Joshua son of Nun.

As for your children that you said would be slain, I will bring them in to enjoy the land you have rejected. But as for you, your bodies will fall in this wilderness.

Your children will be shepherds here for forty years, suffering for your unfaithfulness, until the last of your bodies lies in the wilderness. For forty

years—one year for each of the forty days you explored the land—you will suffer for your sins and know what it is like to have Me against you.

I, the LORD, have spoken, and I will surely do these things to this whole wicked community, which has banded together against Me. They will meet their end in this wilderness; here they will die.

That night, the ten spies who brought back woeful reports of the land of Canaan died of a plague. The whole camp went into mourning at the news of forty more years of wandering in the Wilderness until the youngest twenty-year-old had died.

Perez strode throughout the camp, holding high his spear and calling, "To me, all you fighting men! We will go up as Yahweh has commanded and take the land He has promised!"

A number of men followed after Perez to attack the hill country of Canaan though Moses warned them not to go. They did not take the ark of Yahweh's covenant.

In the tent of Caleb and Sarah, Joshua tore his tunic and clutched at the hair on his head. "Aa-gh! Look what these people have done to me! I'm ready to go up to possess the land but now I have to wait another forty years! Yahweh says not until all of them have died in the Wilderness! Well, I'm ready to kill them all right now!"

Sarah, Lilith, and others nearby stood aghast at the violence of the young man's tirade. Caleb sat in numb silence as Joshua continued to stomp around and rant against Israel's fearful disobedience. Finally, the musician set his mouth into a grim line and shook his head.

"Joshua, you know that would never work. Yahweh would not allow the murder of His people. Besides, all who would be left are little children and youths who could not feed themselves, let alone take on the Canaanites."

He pointed a finger at his young friend. "You're taking onto yourself Yahweh's anger and disappointment when they're not yours to bear. He will bring His judgment on these disobedient people in His time. This whole generation is going to die in the desert. After many years of toiling from here to there and never entering into the wonderful land Yahweh promised, they're all going to die!"

Tears filled his eyes. "My own brother is doomed as well. He will never return to the beautiful farm we lost so long ago.

"Meanwhile, we need to teach the next generation about Yahweh's love and care for them, about the need to obey Him and His commands. Only then will we two be able to lead them into the land of promise."

Joshua snorted. "I'll never be able to lead these people into the land."

Caleb gritted his teeth. "Don't ever say that! You told me Yahweh chose you to lead these people in. Don't give up!"

He raised his hands in his own frustration. "As it is, Moses now says don't go up. This expedition of Perez's is doomed to fail. Then where will we be? The only thing we can do is turn back to the desert and keep following the cloud."

At that moment, a child who tented next to Joshua and Adah ran up. "Joshua, come quick! Adah has begun to labor and Eema is worried!"

Joshua and the child ran along the fire-lit lanes to the tents of the tribe of Ephraim, followed at a slower pace by Caleb, Sarah, and Lilith. The young husband dashed behind the curtain of their tent to find Adah on the bed, writhing and screaming from birth pangs. The neighbor's wife, Ahuviah, and a midwife sat beside her, clutching the young mother's hands.

As the contraction eased, Adah looked wildly about. "Hoshea! Where's my husband?"

He lifted Ahuviah out of the way and took his wife's groping hand. "I'm here, dearest."

"Hoshea! You must help me! I don't want to die!"

"Now, Adah, you're not going to die. You need to relax and trust Yahweh to pull you through this."

"That's easy for you to say! You're not the one giving birth!" She thrust his hands aside. "Go away! You got me into this in the first place. If you hadn't taken me to wife, I wouldn't be in this mess!" She screamed as another spasm gripped her.

Joshua stood, outraged at her rejection of him. He had loved her and he was certain she had delighted in their nights together.

He felt like striding from the inner area of the tent but got a grip on his emotions. He sat again and took his wife's hand firmly in his own.

He looked at the midwife who frowned and shrugged her shoulders.

"If she would relax and let it just happen But she's scared and tense from the pain. That only increases the pain and makes it harder for the baby to come out."

Adah wailed again as another contraction seized her. She writhed on the bed and sweat stood out on her face. She clenched the hands of her husband and the midwife.

At the next time of relaxation, the midwife moved to check the progress of the delivery and pulled away a thick cloth, bright with blood. She stuffed another into position then spoke to Joshua.

"Time for you to go out. We have women's work to do here."

The young man nodded at her and pressed Adah's hand. "Dearest, I have to go. Trust in Yahweh and relax. Things will go well."

Adah merely moved her head back and forth. She was lost in the extremity of her ordeal.

Joshua went out and collapsed on a seat next to his friend who laid a hand on his arm. The young man said, "I'm worried, Caleb. She was bleeding when the midwife bade me leave."

The older man frowned and looked at Sarah who nodded and slipped behind the curtain. Lilith followed but quickly emerged behind screams of "Get out! I don't want you near me!"

Adah's wails continued through the night, growing weaker and weaker. When Joshua no longer heard them, he started to rise but stopped at Caleb's grip on his shoulder. The older man shook his head; there was nothing Joshua could do but accept the results.

Lilith busied herself with heating water and brewing tea from a container of herbs she sought out. Conflicting emotions warred in her heart. She was horrified at the screams of childbirth that grew weaker and weaker. She was elated at the opportunity they implied. She also winced at the fear and sorrow on Joshua's face. She wished she could comfort him.

Caleb thanked her for the cup of tea she handed him but rolled his eyes to indicate she should stay on the other side of the small fire.

Finally, Sarah came out and knelt beside the young husband. When he looked at her, she shook her head and opened her arms.

Joshua uttered a cry and collapsed on her bosom. Caleb shifted forward to circle his arms around the two of them. Lilith bowed her head and wept for the dead woman who had not only utterly rejected her but also tried to keep her away from Joshua.

As she stared into the fire, a familiar stirring alarmed her. Lilith tried to ignore the picture and words forming in her mind. The sorrow of the man she loved, weeping between Sarah and Caleb, pushed her to speak.

I see El Alyon sitting enthroned in judgment with Joshua at His side. Both wear wedding garments. Before them stand two women, dressed in filthy rags and trembling in terror.

The Lord God lifts His finger to point at the women. 'Because they refused My commands and did not trust in My love, they shall die in the Wilderness. Great will be our grief but together we will carry on.'

El Alyon gestures to two younger women dressed as queens, standing on the other side and clumsily holding swords. The Lord God says, 'See our new brides, young and in need of training. Teach them the ways of faith and warfare. Teach them the ways of faith and prosperity. Teach them the ways of faith and love.'

Lilith blinked her eyes and saw the three mourners staring at her. Her face reddened at the realization of her place in the vision. She lowered her eyes away from Joshua's.

The sound of fingernails on the curtain drew their attention. Ahuviah stared fearfully at the girl. She shook herself and addressed the others.

"Joshua, if you wish to see your wife and child…" She beckoned him behind the curtain. He rose and stumbled through the opening. The midwife finished pushing a blanket around the still form of Adah and the baby at her side. The mother's pallor was gray; the baby's face had a bluish tinge below long, dark hair.

The midwife gathered a bundle of bloody cloths inside a clean one and turned to lay a hand on the young man's arm. "I am sorry. There was nothing could be done." She lifted the bundle and carried it out.

Joshua knelt beside the pallet and caressed the baby's face. She was a beautiful girl and he would never get to see her grow up. He smoothed his other hand along Adah's cheek. It was still warm and held hints of the pain and fear she had endured.

He dropped his head to her bosom. Lifting his fists, he thumped them repeatedly on her still body.

Why? Why! Why?!

Why did you refuse to trust in Yahweh? Why did you constantly complain instead of accepting that life could be hard for a time? Why did you let discomfort, fear, even jealousy stand in the way of my love for you– of Yahweh's love for you?

After a time, Joshua stood and wiped his eyes on the sleeve of his tunic as he stared at his dead wife and child. He shook his head.

Never again. Never again will I give my love to an ungrateful, unfaithful wife.

Outside the curtain, Lilith stopped him. "Things will turn out all right. Yahweh is with us. I know you grieve for your wife. I grieve with you."

Joshua just looked at her then spoke to Caleb. "We will need to set up some means of dealing with all the bodies we will be leaving in the desert. I must speak to Moses about it."

The older man nodded. "Later, my friend, when the sun is up. The prophet will not appreciate dealing with it now.

"Meanwhile, you must come to our tent for the remainder of the night. Sarah has gone ahead to prepare sleeping mats for us. I will stay up with you this night then help you deal with their bodies in the morning."

Joshua nodded and bent to collect a few things to take with him. The two men trudged along the fire-lit lanes to Judah's encampment. At the tent, they found hot drinks beside sleeping mats with various pillows. A low fire lit the public area of the tent. From behind the curtain came low murmurs spoken with intensity.

Sarah's voice rose slightly. "First, you're too young. Second, you're too new to life among our people. Third, it's much too soon. You must wait, learn the ways of Yahweh and His people, and grow up a little. Then we'll see."

Caleb shook his head and glanced at his friend. Joshua seemed too wrapped up in his grief to have heard. He pushed the younger man down onto a mat and placed a warm drink into his hand. He sensed he would get no sleep this night and hoped the pillar of cloud would not rise up in the morning to move camp.

Meanwhile, cries of alarm rose up from the edge of the camp. Perez had returned, wounded, with a few survivors of the attack on Canaan. The Canaanites and the Amalekites had beaten them soundly.

Sarah hurried to her brother's tent to help nurse his wounds. She returned late and cried herself to sleep.

When Caleb awoke the next morning, he found that Sarah clutched to her breast a bracelet of gold filigree woven into a unique pattern. Gritting his teeth, he carefully slipped it out of her hand and hid it in a pocket of his robe.

Caleb went to the tent of his clan leader and showed him the ornament. "I accuse Perez ben Yoseph of adultery and incest but I have no other proof. What can I do?"

The clan leader frowned and shook his head. "Perez has been a problem." He examined the bracelet. "I'm not surprised at this."

He looked at Caleb. "The best thing you can do is to ask around if anyone witnessed anything. 'Two or three witnesses' as Moses said. Meanwhile," he held up the ornament, "I'll keep this in a safe place."

Caleb bowed his assent and left.

The musician returned later with a middle-aged man and a young woman as witnesses. The leader called his older son to fetch Alon and Selig, two large, capable men. He sent his younger son for the tribal elder.

When Alon and Selig arrived, the clan leader said, "Good. Perez ben Yoseph lies wounded in his tent. Bring him here to me. If he resists, compel him."

Selig stiffened. "Perez is a good soldier. What has he done?"

The leader looked at him. "Do you consider him your leader?"

Selig nodded. "In many things, yes."

The clan leader said, "He is accused of a serious crime. I call you to follow *me* and bring him here."

Selig sighed and nodded. "As you wish." He gestured to Alon and the two of them left.

Some time later, they returned, bearing Perez on a stretcher. The large man's hands were bound in front of him. Nahshon son of Amminadab had arrived and heard the charge. He called all to sit.

Perez was set down in front of the elder but his eyes blazed at Caleb. "What have you said about me, you dog of a liar?"

Before the musician could reply, Nahshon spoke. "Perez ben Yoseph, attend to *me*. You have been accused of adultery and incest with your sister, the wife of Caleb ben Jephunneh the Kenizzite. Do you confess to this?"

The spearman glared at Caleb. He faced the leaders. "What proof is there? Where are your witnesses?"

The tribal leader withdrew the bracelet from his robe and held it up. "Do you deny this is yours?"

Perez blanched. "Where did you get that? Of course, it's mine."

The leader returned it to his robe. "It was taken out of your sleeping sister's hand." He gestured to a man sitting by. "Please tell us what you saw."

The man stood, looking flustered. "I…uh…I was returning late one night from the latrines. I…uh…saw this man go into Caleb's tent. I thought it strange with Caleb being gone. I heard a gasp and what sounded like mutual enjoyment." He shrugged, "But then, I thought it was none of my business."

The elder nodded. "Thank you." He turned to a young woman who stood behind the seated men, holding a baby. "What did you see?"

The woman scowled at Perez. "I saw that man come out of Caleb's tent late one night, a look of satisfaction on his face. I would have gone to check on Sarah but my child was fussing."

The men surrounding Caleb murmured in disapproval. Nahshon looked at Perez then faced the men.

"You have heard two witnesses and seen the bracelet. Does anyone doubt the guilt of this man?"

The men murmured and shook their heads. Caleb sat and watched his wife's brother with anger.

The elder turned to Perez. "Do you have anything to say in your defense?"

The spearman winced as he turned on the stretcher. He glared at everyone in turn. "All of you are a bunch of dung beetles. I led men against our enemies, came back wounded, and you want to stone me for what is common practice in Egypt?"

He glared at Caleb. "And you! Who are you to complain? I took care of my sister for *years* before you came along and for years after you let her get raped. You deserved the injuries you got! I've always been a better husband to her than you ever were!"

The musician couldn't speak. He merely gaped at his wife's brother in shock.

The elder cleared his throat. "Perez, do you deny going in to your sister in Caleb's tent while he was away on his mission?"

The spearman sneered. "No! I don't deny it! Just like all the other times in Egypt, she welcomed me!"

Over the disapproving cries of the men, Caleb shouted, "You lie!"

"Do I?" Perez grinned at the musician. "Ask her yourself."

Nahshon's voice cut through the uproar this caused. "Perez ben Yoseph!"

In the quiet, the elder continued, "You have confessed to adultery and incest with your sister, the wife of Caleb ben Jephunneh the Kenizzite. We are no longer in Egypt where such activities are tolerated. We have lived under Yahweh's law for more than a year now and it says, 'Do not be disloyal to your spouse,' and ' "Do not have sex with your sister, whether she's your father's daughter or your mother's.'

"Because you have violated these commands, you will be taken outside the camp and stoned to remove the pollution from among us."

The elder looked up from the man on the stretcher. "As the most offended party, Caleb will cast the first stone, followed by the men of his family, then his clan, then the men of Judah until your body is buried under a heap of stones."

Perez roared and struggled to rise. The two guards fought to restrain him until Selig punched him on the forehead. This stunned the large man enough for them to bind his feet as well as his hands. They carried him out of the tent and the seated men leapt to their feet to follow, leaving Caleb before the elder who looked at his anguished face.

"Caleb, I understand that you, of all people, do not wish to cast any stones. However, you *must* cast the first stone. The woman with whom Perez committed adultery was *your* wife."

The musician nodded and crawled to his feet with the help of the elder's outstretched hand. His spine stiffened against the elder's encouraging pat on the back. Instead of heading out of the camp, he turned toward his tent…and his wife.

Outside the tent, Sarah stood rigidly with Lilith and other women. Her husband walked up to her, his arms out, pleading. "What have I done? Sarah, I must cast the first stone!"

His wife gasped. "No." She drew breath. "No!" Sarah shrieked, "NO-O! Caleb, he's my brother!"

"My queen, I'm sorry! I only wanted to make him stop." He dropped to his knees before her.

Her hands above her head, Sarah screamed at him, "*You* did this! This is *your* fault!" She began to beat at him with her fists.

Caleb merely covered his face with his hands and didn't resist. It took a couple men nearby to restrain her.

Lilith looked at her aunt who dropped, sobbing, on the ground and shook her head. The girl placed comforting arms around Caleb, who knelt beside his wife.

Nahshon stepped forward and clapped his hands for attention. "Men of Judah, give ear! For the sins of adultery and incest, Perez ben Yoseph has been condemned to be stoned! All of Israel is called outside the camp to witness judgment. Caleb ben Jephunneh will cast the first stone, followed by the men of his family."

The tribal elder looked at Kenaz who nodded grimly. Nahshon continued.

"Then the men of his clan and the rest of Judah. You know how this works."

The men standing about nodded and the elder went to the musician and Lilith. "Come, Caleb. We must go."

He lifted the stricken man to his feet. Behind Caleb's back, the elder motioned to the men about. The sobbing woman was to be brought soon after the two of them left. The men nodded again.

<hr>

In a rock-strewn open space, backed by a wall of stone, the crowd of men was joined by excited women and children. Perez's bound form lay against the bare rock face.

After Caleb and Nahshon pushed through the mob, a man scurried up and thrust a large rock into the musician's hands. Caleb looked at the glee in the man's face and dropped the stone at his feet. With a yelp, the man scurried away.

Nahshon gazed at Caleb then bent and picked up the rock. He held it out to the husband. "You must."

The Kenizzite squeezed his eyes and fists shut. He breathed deeply, opened his eyes, and reached for the missile. He stepped forward and saw the hatred in Perez's eyes.

Caleb thought of all the times he was forced to allow arrogant men like this one take *his wife* to bed. He remembered his disappointment that Sarah had not been a virgin when they married, and why. Anger grew within him as he thought of Perez entering *his tent* to bed *his wife*.

"Damn you, Perez! You should not have done that!" He raised the rock above his head and slammed it down on the man's chest. Rocks from the men around him pelted Perez's arms, shoulders, hips, and legs. Caleb hurried away from the blood, the gleeful shouts, and the thud of rocks on flesh. He got to the edge of the crowd and threw up on the ground.

Sarah was brought to the stoning. She walked regally between her escorts, her face grimly set. The escorts pushed through the crowd to get to the front. She took one look at her brother's bloodied face and broken limbs and she screamed.

Sarah wrenched free of her escorts' grasp, flew past the startled Levites and men with stones, and crouched defensively over his form.

"Stop this! You men are just as guilty of wanting other women as he was!"

The men holding rocks hesitated. Someone said, "She's the sister! The adulteress! Stone her, too!"

Everyone turned to look at Moses and Aaron. The two leaders scowled and nodded their heads. As one, the men turned and threw their rocks at the woman.

Caleb had been bent over, vomiting on the ground. At the sound of his wife's voice, he straightened. "No! Not her!" He moved to interfere but the armed Levites, more alert now, held him fast.

Stones flew, hitting an arm, the chest, her stomach. A large rock smashed into her leg, sending her crashing to the ground beside her brother. Before long, a heap of rocks buried both their bodies.

The next day, the Israelites turned back toward the desert.

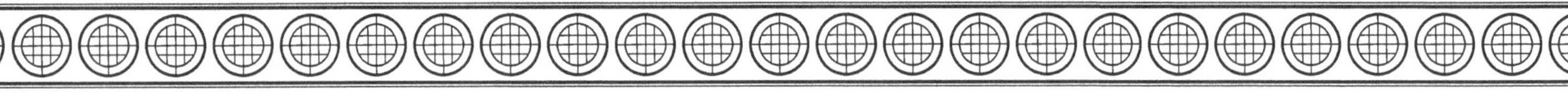

Despair and Hope

She stood before the elders of Israel assembled in the tent of Moses.

"My name was Lilith of Hebron, once the mouthpiece of Qedesh.

"My father was an Anakite, one of three brothers who run things in Hebron. Sheshai is the high priest of Qedesh who bound me to her to speak her words. Ahiman leads the temple guards who also act as the city's soldiers. Talmai advises the king and holds control over if not ownership of much of the countryside.

"My mother was a Midianite who worshiped Lord Most High and taught me to seek after Him. Before she died, she sent me away to find the people of Israel who had escaped the clutches of Egypt."

She drew in a deep breath and looked at Caleb, who sat behind the elder of Judah. Her uncle nodded encouragement.

"Yahweh freed me from bondage to Qedesh. I renounce all that she made me say and do. I renounce all relationship to the Anakites and all allegiance to the people of Hebron. I will follow the laws of Yahweh, accepting Him as my king.

"I have taken a lamb to the priests as a sacrifice for my sins. I wish to be adopted into the tribe of Judah, into the family of Caleb the son of Jephunneh, my uncle.

"When I was in Canaan, fleeing with Joshua and Caleb, Yahweh gave me a dream." She told of fighting off attacking jackals.

"Also, Yahweh spoke to me the night of my deliverance from Qedesh. He said:

> **You are a lioness of the tribe of Judah.**
> **The lioness hunts with the help of others.**
> **The lioness protects her cubs and those of the pride.**
> **The lioness reigns beside the king of beasts.**

The girl straightened and spoke in a loud voice. "Henceforth, I wish to be called Lavi'el according to the word spoken to me by God Most High."

She walked over to Caleb and sat behind him. Aaron climbed to his feet and stood before the assembly.

"What say you, people of Israel? Shall we accept the words of this young woman who wishes to join our people?"

The elders muttered to each other then the elder of Judah rose to his feet.

"We have learned that you, Moses, are the mouthpiece of Yahweh. You are the one who tells us when we are to go and where we are to stop. It is for you to say whether this young woman will be one of us."

The others muttered their agreement as the elder sat again. Moses leaned his head against his staff and closed his eyes.

When he looked up again, he said, "Hear what Yahweh says,

> **Just as I delivered Israel out of bondage to Pharaoh so that he may serve me in the land of promise, so have I delivered Lavi'el out of bondage to Qedesh so that she, too, may serve me in the land of promise.**

"Let her be adopted."

Caleb turned and held out his arms to his niece. Lavi'el threw herself into his arms and hugged him fiercely. "Come," he said, rising, "let's go tell your family."

Outside the tent of Moses, they saw Joshua trudging with a squad of men toward the practice fields. Even from a distance, Caleb could see the stiffness in his companion's gait. Before he could turn to stop his niece, she called out.

"Joshua, wait! I've got wonderful news!"

Caleb hurried after the young lioness. He came up in time to see Lavi'el clasp the young man's hands.

"Joshua, I've been accepted by Yahweh and the elders of Israel!"

As she spoke, Caleb studied Joshua. Sorrow and fatigue lined the man's face. He was overworking to keep from thinking about Adah and Israel's journey back into the desert.

He needs another wife to look after him, Caleb thought. He glanced at his niece and shook his head. *Too young. She isn't ready yet.*

Joshua patted the hands that held his arm. "I'm happy for you, Lilith."

He turned to go but the young woman still clutched his arm. "No, no! I'm Lavi'el now! Yahweh Himself called me that."

He chuckled and shook his head. "Kid. Demon woman. Lioness of God. What will you have us call you next?"

He turned to leave, waving his men onward, and didn't see the tears that trickled down Lavi'el's cheeks. Nor did he hear her murmur, "I want you to call me Beloved."

Caleb took the girl's arm and steered her toward their tent. "Joshua has suffered two blows to his happiness. His wife died and his desire for Yahweh's land of promise was thwarted by Israel's disobedience. All he has is Yahweh's word that he– and I– will survive to enter in eventually. There's nothing you can do but leave him to God Almighty."

The middle-aged man waved his right arm around and watched its smooth movement. "It's been only a year or so since I've been able to move about freely. What will I be like in forty years?"

He shrugged. "I'll just have to trust God Almighty to see me through. I don't even know how long I'll be able to enjoy the land afterward."

He sighed. "At least I'll be able to leave it to my nephew."

EPILOGUE

The tribes of Israel turned back toward the Sea of Reeds. For forty years they wandered from place to place though the cloud no longer led them.

Finally, the last of that rebellious generation died and Israel turned toward the country east of the Jordan River. Because he struck again the water-gushing rock instead of just speaking to it as instructed, Moses saw from a high mountain the land of Canaan but was not allowed to enter it. He died, at age one-hundred-twenty, and Joshua became the military leader of Israel.

The younger man, now in his sixties, led the still-younger men of the nation across the river and against the fortress of Jericho. From there this younger generation took possession of the land and divided it among the tribes and clans and families. Only the tribe of Levi took no possession in the land; their portion was to serve Yahweh as priests and workers in the Tabernacle.

Joshua 14:6-14

Now the people of Judah approached Joshua at Gilgal, and Caleb son of Jephunneh the Kenizzite said to him, "You know what the Lord said to Moses the man of God at Kadesh Barnea about you and me. I was forty years old when Moses the servant of the Lord sent me from Kadesh Barnea to explore the land. And I brought him back a report according to my convictions, but my fellow Israelites who went up with me made the hearts of the people melt in fear. I, however, followed the Lord my God wholeheartedly. So on that day Moses swore to me, 'The land on which

your feet have walked will be your inheritance and that of your children forever, because you have followed the Lord my God wholeheartedly.'

"Now then, just as the Lord promised, he has kept me alive for forty-five years since the time he said this to Moses, while Israel moved about in the Wilderness. So here I am today, eighty-five years old! I am still as strong today as the day Moses sent me out; I'm just as vigorous to go out to battle now as I was then. Now give me this hill country that the Lord promised me that day. You yourself heard then that the Anakites were there and their cities were large and fortified, but, the Lord helping me, I will drive them out just as he said."

Then Joshua blessed Caleb son of Jephunneh and gave him Hebron as his inheritance. So Hebron has belonged to Caleb son of Jephunneh the Kenizzite ever since, because he followed the Lord, the God of Israel, wholeheartedly.

Joshua 24:32

And Joseph's bones, which the Israelites had brought up from Egypt, were buried at Shechem in the tract of land that Jacob bought for a hundred pieces of silver from the sons of Hamor, the father of Shechem. This became the inheritance of Joseph's descendants.

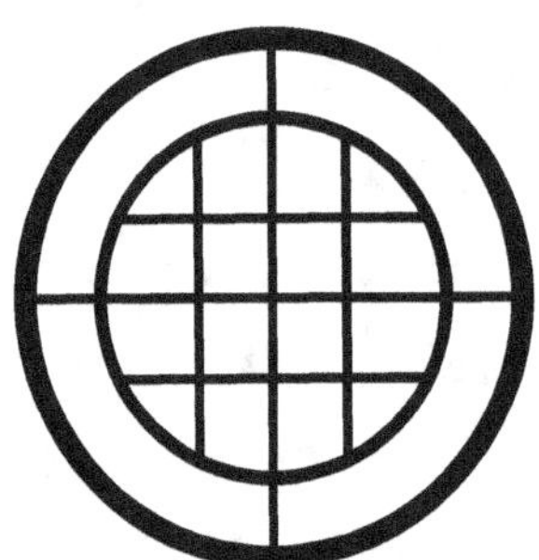

www.ingramcontent.com/pod-product-compliance
Lightning Source LLC
Chambersburg PA
CBHW080423010826
48976CB00020B/2671